Halflings

Halflings

BOOK ONE

Heather Burch

ZONDERVAN®

ZONDERVAN.com/
AUTHORTRACKER
follow your favorite authors

ZONDERVAN

Halflings
Copyright © 2012 by Heather Burch

This title is also available as a Zondervan ebook.
Visit www.zondervan.com/ebooks.

Requests for information should be addressed to:

Zondervan, *Grand Rapids, Michigan* 49530

ISBN: 978-0-310-72818-4

Cover design: Cindy Davis
Cover photography: Dan Davis Photography
Interior design and composition: Greg Johnson/Textbook Perfect

Printed in the United States of America

12 13 14 15 16 /DCI/ 22 21 20 19 18 17 16 15 14 13 12 11 10 9 8 7 6 5 4 3 2 1

For the men in my life:

My sons Jake and Isaac;
you guys are the music in my universe.

My brother Skyler;
your commitment to our mom humbles me.
When I grow up I want to be like you.

My father-in-law, Pops;
thanks for being my toughest critic ...
but also my biggest fan.

And most of all, my husband, John;
thank you for making the world small
so I could conquer it.

The sons of God saw that the daughters
of humans were beautiful, and they married
any of them they chose.

Genesis 6:2

Chapter
1

Fangs sank into Nikki Youngblood's leg, setting her skin on fire. A scream gurgled in her throat, but she willed herself past trees smeared by her jarred vision. Her jacket snagged on a branch. No, no, no … She jerked free, casting a glimpse backward at the gnarled faces behind her. The lead beast stumbled over paws caked with mud. She seized the moment to widen the distance.

Run. Her lungs burned. *Just keep running.*

Her feet, now numb, thumped against the dense carpet of the forest floor. Once a place of security, a quiet sanctuary of solitude and escape, her woods had morphed into a house of terror complete with four grotesque dog-wolves tracking her every step.

Despite her years of martial arts, of seeing herself as tough and in control, Nikki was completely helpless. But that didn't mean she had to die. Karate had taught her to stay calm in all manner of attack. *Though I don't think this is what you had in mind, Sensei.*

One minute she's perched against a rock, drawing. The next, she's running from ... from ...

She started to glance back, but stopped herself. *Concentrate on escape. Don't concentrate on your enemy.*

Besides, she didn't even know what those dog-things were. But one thing was certain: they were out for blood and Nikki was an easy mark for the vicious beasts.

Exhaustion squeezed each muscle, depriving them of strength. Likewise, it pushed at her consciousness, promising failure. When she thought her lungs might literally burst, a momentary, blinding flash of light sparked above her, as if the universe were snapping a picture of her dilemma. Within seconds of the spark of light, a sound descended. *Church bells?* The reverberation of a thousand muted bells soothed her nerves and curled around her like a warm blanket after a nightmare. The unearthly noise filled her ears, a beautiful hum closing her in. But the tempo rose higher and higher it until it caused the backs of her eyes to throb.

The dog-wolves began to moan. She glanced back — the four monsters had crumbled to the ground, their taut, muscled legs folding beneath them. One raked his head in the dirt and grass, his massive paw clawing brutally at his ear. *The sound.* Convulsing and groaning, their desperate plea to escape the melodic cry of the bells filled the air around her. Nikki took in short puffs, knees nearly buckling beneath her where she'd slid to a stop. The first flicker of relief tried to manifest, but Nikki knew she wasn't out of trouble yet. Her mind reeled, searching for a feasible escape. But her eyes watered, causing her to press a flat palm to her temple where it throbbed from the wind song.

Wind song; that's all she could think to call it. And right now — whether causing a killer migraine or not — anything able to stop the ugly wolves ranked at the top of Nikki's new favorite things list. The pain intensified, but she still kept her attention riveted on the wolves. *Were* they wolves? She still wasn't sure. Each one was dark as a black hole, with hollow eyes she couldn't seem to look into directly. When she forced herself to lock eyes with one of the beasts, a cold river of pure fear streaked down her spine as if the wolf seized her very soul, choking out life and leaving a tormenting void.

The creatures' legs had folded and twisted into awkward positions, claws scraping at the ground, then at their ears. *Wait, that's not mud on the dogs. It's ... dried blood.* Her eyes blurred, causing her sense of survival to kick in. Head still throbbing like a bass guitar at a concert and with one hand at the side of her face, she ran. Through the tree line she caught a glimpse of silver. *Yes! The gate to the football field.* She'd make it to the other side and this nightmare would be over.

Was it just a nightmare? Some indigestion-induced dream? She could have fallen asleep in the woods while she drew the picture of ...

What had she been drawing? She couldn't remember.

But this was no dream. She was awake. Awake and aware of the spongy grass collapsing beneath her feet, aware of the scent of moist pine hanging on the forest walls. Aware of the searing sensation in her calf where *the thing* had sunk its teeth.

Eyes fixed on the fence, she tried to take a breath but managed only tiny gasps. *Get to the gate. Just get to the gate.* As if the deserted football field on the other side could somehow offer safety. Four dog-wolf-things had chased her through a quarter of a mile of woods; why would five feet of chain link stop them? She pushed on, leaping over rotting tree roots protruding from the earth like the twisted fingers of a witch. She imagined her legs getting tangled in the mass of vines, imagined the weathered roots reaching for her as she bounded past. Determination swept into her soul. With sickening certainty, Nikki knew she was racing for her life.

And more. Things, big things, *world changing* things factored into her circumstance. She didn't know how she knew it. But she did. And for the first time in her seventeen years of life, Nikki felt a destiny awaiting her. Fear and dread careening in her soul, and deadly hounds at her back, Nikki felt alive.

"Raven, the song is hurting her too," Mace said, anxiety creeping into his words as he peered over the rock ledge.

Raven scowled through his too-long bangs. "The Angel Song doesn't hurt humans. It only affects the evil within."

"Then you should be writhing on the ground with the hounds," Mace mumbled.

Raven chuckled and sank his hands into the pockets of his jeans.

Mace shifted his weight and slid his hands down his thighs. "It's time to intervene." If Raven thought he was going to torture this girl for fun, he was dead wrong. What made him think he was in charge, anyway? Just because he'd been on more journeys, and was the oldest of the three Lost Boys? So what. Experience didn't make a capable leader. The best leaders were those who put the welfare of their soldiers before their own. Anyone who knew Raven knew he only looked out for himself.

Beside him, Mace felt Vine's apprehension rise. For a quick moment, he closed off the noisy world and quieted his own soul, tuning into Vine's heart rate. Mace's gaze narrowed slightly as he listened to the kid's breathing pattern. Inhale. Exhale. All in check. Just first-time jitters.

Assured Vine was okay and ready for the fight, Mace's gaze returned to the pretty teenage girl trying to escape a nightmare sent directly from the pit. Her name echoed in his head: *Nikki Youngblood*. He'd known her name instantly. They all had. One of the perks of being a Halfling. Her shoulders were narrow, arms thin, but looked tone beneath her snug windbreaker. A small, straight nose rested above full lips that remained parted as she panted with each pounding step. Large eyes stayed focused on the field before her. Maybe pretty was an under-statement. There was something … captivating about her. It wasn't her face. It wasn't the long train of golden-brown hair that trailed behind her as she ran. It was her absolute tenac-ity to outrun her pursuers, her determination to survive. He'd watched grown men crumble at the sight of a single hell hound; she was chased by four. And *crumbling* didn't seem to be in her list of options. She'd kicked free from the hound when it bit into her calf muscle, then with a limp bolted for the gate of the football field, and he could sense as well as smell her resolve. But a mere human girl against four hell hounds? Zero chance for survival there.

"Haven't you seen enough?" Mace spat.

Raven gave a noncommittal shrug and finger-combed his hair away from his eyes. "What's your rush?"

Mace glanced fifty feet below — first at the girl, then the hounds. "She's terrified."

"Yeah," Vine agreed. "She looks really scared."

Raven smiled, white teeth shining in the disappearing light. "So?"

"You're a jerk." Mace spread his arms and prepared to

descend. One of the benefits of being a Halfling: a fifty-foot drop was nothing. He snapped his wings open to swoop down, but before he could drop off the ledge something hit him square across the chest. Air whooshed from his lungs as he landed with a thud.

"She'll see you," Raven snapped. As he stared down at the girl, a surprising—almost tender—look crossed his face, only to be whisked away by his normal demeanor of cold detachment. But Mace had seen it, and the flash of compassion shocked him.

"You're not in charge, Raven." Mace said, rising from the rocky terrain. Once on his feet he dusted his rear end, partly to remove the dirt, partly to keep his hands busy so they wouldn't ball into fists and pound Raven into the ground.

"Be patient." Raven's voice lowered to a purr.

Mace's jaw clenched. He hated this part of an assignment. Yes, okay, sometimes it was important to let things play out a little, to not sail in and rescue too quickly. But the human side of Mace despised it. The angelic side of him ... well, the more journeys he completed, the less human he felt. Just as well. It was a world out of reach, and he needed to remember that.

He knew Raven would only allow intervention at the last possible moment. Mace felt the short hairs on the back of his neck rise along with the anger crawling up his spine. "Why would we have been sent if we weren't going to be utilized?"

Raven's eyes flashed fascination. "Maybe just for entertainment?"

Vine's mouth dropped open, his white-blond hair falling forward. "*Entertainment?*" He shot a quick, questioning look to Mace. "Does that happen? I mean, are we sent to just *watch* stuff like this?" Trepidation clouded those naive blue-gray eyes.

Mace sometimes marveled at the fact Vine was only two

earth years younger than him; his innocence glowed like morning dew, quickly visible and quickly trampled into the mud.

Raven's mouth twisted. "Our kind does it all the time." No dew softened Raven's stark features and face cut into strong angles. His eyes, once bright blue, had darkened to midnight in recent years, which didn't bode well. "You know, earth girls are hot when they're running for their lives."

That was it. Mace dove for Raven, sick of his antics and, well, sick of him in general. Raven sidestepped and in an instant the two were nose-to-nose, fists drawn.

Mace cast a glance to Vine. For the first time, the kid looked like a warrior. Ready to step in if the two older boys came to blows. *Go, Vine.*

Mace exhaled a long breath and lowered his hands. Adrenaline surged into his muscles and pulled every ligament into a tight cord.

Cool confidence oozed from Raven as he tilted his chin into the sun, as if daring Mace to strike.

"I won't fight you, Raven," Mace said. *Vine needs some sort of role model. Which he'll never have if I keep getting sucked in by Raven's games.* He forced his attention away from the Halfling and focused on the pitiful scene unfolding beneath them. A fist fight wouldn't help the girl either.

Long hair floated behind her. Strands matted across her delicate face where her skin glistened with a silky sheen of sweat. She smelled like fear. The scent curled into the wind and rose on pleading wings, calling to him.

When she reached the fence, her golden eyes flashed relief. Mace watched a moment longer. "Raven, there's nothing to learn. Look at her." He gestured toward Nikki Youngblood and the hell hounds no longer chasing her. The four beasts whimpered, trying to escape the Angel Song drifting around them. Nikki trembled at the gate to the football field, hands shaking when she spotted the padlock secured with a thick chain.

"She's here for a reason, Mace. We have to find out what it is." With a twinkle in his eye, Raven clapped his hands and the Angel Song died. "Time to party."

Sometimes the worst part of being a Halfling was standing aside and letting events happen as they're supposed to. Maybe that was the worst part of being any created being. Mace's eyes drifted shut. Without the Angel Song to torture them, the hounds would once again be on the hunt. And Nikki Youngblood would be as good as dead.

"Come on," Nikki pleaded, willing her hands to stop quaking. Her fingers bled where she'd slammed them into the fence. She jerked back and forth on the entrance, a vain attempt to break the lock, and hopelessness born of despair slipped down her body like deadwood slipping into the sea after a storm. She was trapped. Blood began to work its way through her veins but brought with it a new form of torture. Splinters rather than blood seemed to course through her while her head pounded rhythmically.

Then the wind song disappeared.

The dogs stopped groaning. The forest dropped to a dead, graveyard quiet. No little bunnies or squirrels rambling through the fallen leaves. Just stillness. Just the promise of death.

A rustle behind her evoked a fresh wave of nausea. Desperate hands tightened on the crisscrosses of chain link. If she had the energy, she'd climb. But fear and torment had stolen the last shreds of her strength, leaving nothing but a bundle of exhausted nerves.

She dropped her head to her hands and closed her eyes. A twig snapped, forcing her head up. She tried to swallow, but her mouth and throat were cotton.

As a breeze skirted through the trees, cooling the sweat on her face, Nikki cast a reluctant glance over her shoulder.

The lead dog-wolf moved toward her methodically, a long bead of saliva dripping from his mouth. She watched as each paw landed on the ground. Nikki frowned. He seemed almost ... fearful as well. Was he scared of her? She turned, chin jutting forward. "What?" she spat, addressing the hound. "You afraid I might pop the cork on a bottle of screaming bell song again?"

Head dropping between his wide shoulder blades, he stared at her with those empty eyes. She hated that posture, that stalking, ready-to-lunge stance. Wolves at the zoo did the same thing and it freaked her out even though they were on one side of the enclosure and she on the other. She didn't even like to see her dog Bo stand like that. It was too predatory, too anxious to kill.

"Oh man," she mumbled. *What did I just do?* Her valor dissolved at her feet as the breeze moved again, this time pushing a rotten scent toward her. Nikki nearly gagged on the putrid odor. *Rancid meat has nothing on these wolves.* Years ago, some boys at her school had put a dead pig inside a car and locked it in a garage of an empty house. Weeks of scorching heat not only ruined the car, the house had to be demolished as well. When the vehicle was opened, the stench fetid animal threaded through several blocks of her neighborhood. At the time, she thought she'd never again smell anything so foul. She was wrong.

The beast growled deep in his throat and the sound invaded every cell of her being. Black lips curled back to expose yellowed fangs. Round eyes grabbed and swallowed light into the empty, soulless pits that were its sockets.

She pressed her back into the chain links. Tears rushed to her eyes as the other hounds appeared from the woods, leaving no way to escape.

The hunt was over. This is where she'd die.

Wiggling on his back haunches, the wolf leapt.

She cupped her hands over her head for protection, watching through the crook of her arm as the animal attacked. Scarred paws stretched toward her, razor-sharp claws seeming to grow larger and larger as they filled her vision. Why wouldn't the song return? Frantic, Nikki cried, "God, help me!"

A whoosh of cool air blasted her body and an explosion of light soared past. An instant later something solid slammed against her, shoving her to the ground. Her head thundered on impact. As she fought to take in air, white sparked above. She could hear voices, and the wolf's growl, but remained unable to focus her eyes or attention.

White again. With it, the dog creature screeched. A sickening voice entered her ears, whispering, hissing like a hundred snakes. It referred to something as sons of God.

Was the wolf talking? She couldn't see. White—white everywhere. Her mind whirred as an electrical current ran the length of her being: head to foot, foot to head, zipping through her, electrifying and depriving her muscles of movement.

Consciousness slipped away. As her eyes closed for the final time, a velvet voice soothed, "You're safe now, daughter of man."

Chapter
2

"And why did you bring her here?" Will asked.

Their caregiver donned the fatherly posture he'd cultivated from watching family sitcoms. Mace, Raven, and Vine gathered near Nikki and awaited the tongue-lashing they'd expected since arriving back at Pine Boulevard and their new two-story, Victorian-style home for the moment.

"She's injured," Mace said. *It's partially true, at least.* He glanced down at Nikki—passed out on the couch—and his heart flopped. Since encountering this girl, he'd been trying to figure her out.

It was a useless attempt. He didn't *get* her. One second she's shaking the gate with the full force of her body, hair whipping in an *S* pattern, the next she's crying, and the next, she's screaming at the hell hound in what he'd describe as a taunt.

Maybe hysteria did strange things to the brain—he could understand that. But when the hound leapt at her, she kept her eyes wide open and peered through the bend in her arm. She'd *actually intended to watch the attack.*

"Did you *see* what we *did*?" Vine asked for the thousandth time. "That's what I'm talking about! Those hell hounds were nothing. When do I get to face a wraith?"

Will groaned.

Mace cast a furtive smile to Vine. *Newbie.* He still remembered his first assignment, his first shot at hero work. *If only that excitement lasted forever.*

Uncle Will — or so they called him — pursed his lips. Mace had to bite his cheek to keep his mouth straight. Though Will was over six foot five and built like a Mack truck, the deep dimples and puff of curly brown hair — as well as his animated, bright blue eyes — weakened the intimidation factor.

"Can we keep her?" Vine asked, voice lilting like a child's.

"She's not a pet, Bloom. She's an assignment," Will said. "And facing off with wraiths should be neither a desire nor a source of excitement."

"I'm not the bloom. I'm the Vine!" He tried to frown, but a quick smile betrayed him.

Mace knew Vine loved the nickname he'd gotten from developing his power at an unprecedented young age. Nicknames were what families had for one another. Real families. Though Will tried his best, Mace often wondered what it would have been like to be raised by his real parents, instead of separated from them at birth as was the custom for beings like him — for his protection, of course.

His younger "brother's" eager voice knocked him out of his thoughts.

"I've got a question," Vine said. "Why would the Throne have sent us to protect some teenager? I mean, aren't our assignments ... you know, about important people?"

Will nodded toward the girl, who still lay unconscious. "Do you not consider her important?"

Vine rolled his blue-gray eyes. "Everyone's important. But, I mean, she's just a kid."

Will smiled. "Like the three of you?"

"Yeah." A frown furrowed Vine's smooth brow. "Didn't Raven have an assignment once where he protected some political dude?"

Raven gave a curt nod. "He was a world leader, and thanks to me he's still alive today."

Vine pointed at him. "Yeah, that's what I mean. I expected to be assigned to, like, D.C. or New York or something."

Mace took a step toward Vine, blocking Raven from his field of vision. He was still ticked at the brooding creep for baiting him in the woods. No, Mace was angry at himself for *letting* Raven bait him. Mistakes like that could cost lives. "Vine, we don't always know why we're protecting a person. This isn't the Secret Service. We're not CIA or FBI. And our instructions don't come from the limited knowledge of an earthly man." He nodded toward Nikki. "It may not be about who she is right now. It's possible that ..." He shook his head and shrugged. "Maybe she's going to be the scientist who discovers a cure for cancer."

"Or solves world hunger," Will added.

Raven scoffed. "Or maybe she's going to do something really important, like figure out how to get the DVD player to stop flashing twelve o'clock."

"Whatever it is, the enemy isn't wasting any time." Will lifted the girl's arm, his giant palm swallowing her dainty hand. "You say she was being chased by hell hounds?"

The sight of her dodging the predators was forever carved

into his mind while the gratitude in her glassy eyes when he scooped her into his arms was imprinted in his heart. His pulse accelerated. "There were four."

Will's eyes narrowed in concentration. "Doesn't make sense." He examined the cuts and scratches on her fingers. "Hounds coming after a human. You're sure?" A crystal-clear gaze questioned them, drifting from one boy to the next.

Mace crossed his arms over his chest. "Uh, yeah. We got an up-close, personal look at them. Rotting flesh with a sole purpose. To kill Nikki Youngblood."

"Someone wants her dead," Raven said, bending his fingers so they resembled a gun. He pointed it at the girl's head and pulled the trigger by clicking his thumb.

Mace shot him a dirty look.

"What?" Raven's voice oozed innocence.

"How'd the hounds get here?" Vine interrupted.

"The same way we got here, moron," Raven said. "You know, the midplane? The safe zone between heaven and earth where all of us misfits roam? Someone hasn't been paying attention in class."

Vine's lips pressed together, embarrassment splashed all over his face.

Mace's heart ached for Vine. The first journey was always the toughest. Lost Boys, Halflings: no matter what you called yourself, you were still an outcast in both the heavenly and earthly realms. Who thought up *that* brilliant idea? An emissary of heaven to an earth you can never have.

Not that journeys were not important. Mace himself had been sent on several. He'd saved lives and had hopefully pushed himself away from eternity's cliff edge named Scary Beyond

All Stinkin' Reason. Quiet and peaceful eternity sounded *so* much better.

"This is a surprising card for the enemy to play. What does he know about this girl that we don't?" Will stepped away from where Nikki rested. Hands on hips again, he searched the street beyond the bay window. "Four hounds pursuing one young girl?" he repeated. Sunlight streamed in and illuminated the side of his face. He pitched a glance toward the boys, gaze locking with Mace's.

A fatherly smile formed and almost hid the apprehension. Almost. Worry clung to Uncle Will's expression. Mace knew he agonized about his boys, even though he wasn't supposed to be equipped with sticky emotions like worry, happiness, or sorrow. *Hiding your emotions ... what a human thing to do.*

The girl stirred.

All eyes went to her.

Will's clear, penetrating look shot through Mace like a lightning bolt. "She's the only clue we have to why we've been sent. I'm glad you found her when you did. Those hounds would have shredded her." Will shuddered, then resumed his authoritative posture. "Since we just arrived from the midplane, I don't want any of you outside again for a couple days. You all need time to adjust to this realm. That means beginning Monday morning, you'll be keeping a close watch on her. Should be easy enough; I've enrolled you at Waterside High School."

Moans emanated from Raven and Mace. "Not high school," Raven groaned.

"Really?" Vine swiped at a dirt smudge on his T-shirt and chewed on a Twizzler he'd snagged from the foyer table. "That'll be cool."

"But right now, you'd better get her home." Will returned

from the window and leaned over the couch. He placed his hands on Nikki's. "The longer she stays in our presence, the more she'll be able to tolerate our atmosphere, and we don't want her waking up to four unnatural creatures hovering over her."

"No," Mace agreed. "That's actually how she passed out in the first place."

Vine questioned him with a look.

"But those four were stinking hell hounds," Mace said.

Vine raised a finger. "Actually, she didn't pass out until you picked her up. Remember? She looked right in your eyes and—"

Raven coughed, stifling a laugh.

Will's face turned to fury. "She *saw* you in the forest?" His stormy, silver eyes shot icy daggers at Mace. *That's one emotion Will really shouldn't be equipped with.*

Out of the corner of his eye, Mace watched as the muscles in Vine's face collapsed, leaving a gaping mouth.

"We didn't mean for her to see us. We were waiting for her to close her eyes or turn away from the attack." Mace's heart pounded. If he'd blown this assignment already, he'd never forgive himself. He chucked a frustrated hand toward Nikki. "She just kept watching, Will."

"What?"

"She kept watching. The attack."

Will's eyes dropped to Nikki and held for a long time.

Mace thought he heard him mumble something about a mark of fearlessness.

Finally, Will spoke. "The world balances on a pinhead, and its fate rests in the hands of teenagers."

The cloud of uncertainty surrounding Nikki unnerved

him, Mace could tell. Will was a true warrior, and right now the fighter within was being stirred.

"Time is short," Will said. "I wouldn't be surprised to see an untapped weapon hidden in her mortal bones. Though she looks like a mere teenage girl, I think her heart beats with the strength of a warrior's spirit. Queen Esther comes to mind."

"Huh?" Vine said, his head tilted and his face twisted into a quizzical expression. Actually, Will's little monologue had sort of lost Mace too. As an eternal being, Will often sensed things the boys couldn't, but was prone to voicing it in grand terms.

Raven had been around the longest; maybe he understood what Will was mumbling about. But he stared straight ahead, hands locked across his chest as if bored with the whole conversation. On cue, he yawned.

Will knelt beside the girl. Squeezing her hands gently, liquid gold oozed from his palms and covered hers. The pure aroma of Gilead's Balm — heaven's Neosporin — filled the room. They each savored it. Nothing was sweeter — except the breath of life.

"Whoa," Vine said, eyes darting to Mace. "We're, um, seeing in both realms right now?"

Mace smiled at his young counterpart. "You ain't seen nothin' yet."

Nikki awoke in her own bed. She sat straight up and shook off the sleep. Fragments of memory bounced in her head. Running … the fence … the wolves. Voices.

And deep, blue-green eyes. Cerulean blue. The color of the glistening Mediterranean Sea capturing the sun's reflection. Even as she remembered the horror, her heart calmed, imagining those pools of safety. And a face. There was a face attached to those eyes. Angular. Strong.

Rich words had rolled off his tongue: "You're safe now, daughter of man." Then all had faded, except those round, cerulean eyes. No other shade on her artist's palette captivated her like cerulean. And no other eyes captivated her at all.

But it had just been a dream, right? She lifted her arm from under the covers and ran a hand through her hair. As she did, she noticed her arm was still in the vintage T-shirt she'd worn yesterday. She wiggled her legs. Yep, jeans. Panic crept in and she suddenly wanted to get out of the clothes she had on.

She jumped from the bed, and the room spun around her. "Whoa," she muttered as fingers scrambled for the bedpost, holding on with white-knuckled determination until the walls slowly sharpened into focus.

In the dream, she hit the fence. She remembered the slicing pain when the chain links cut into her flesh. Lifting her hands, she examined them, front and back.

Nothing. Not a scratch on her fingers, not a cut on her hands. And no jacket. Nikki's mind raced. She had her jacket on in the dream and it snagged and tore on a branch. Her gaze darted from the small bistro table sitting in one corner to her laptop in the other corner, but no sign of her light coat. The room whirled again. Nikki sank to the bed and her hair fell across her face. A few calming breaths later, she shoved the loose strands back as the nausea passed.

"It had to be a dream," she whispered.

No, the hounds were real.

And those beautiful eyes, they *had* to be real. She rolled her pant leg and searched for the mark the monster dog left. Twisting, she squeezed her calf. No wound. No pain. As she unrolled the material, however, a spot of blood appeared on the denim. She unsnapped and unzipped her jeans and dragged them from her body, turning them inside out. Skin exposed, goose bumps spread along her thighs.

The spot on her jeans was larger on the inside than on the outside, making it clear the dried blood had come from her. Using one hand to tug her hair over her shoulder and out of the way, she propped her foot on the bed and examined her calf again.

Nada. She poked at the spot where the bite mark should have been. *Not even sore.* She lifted the jeans for closer inspection. Just above the dried blood, a tiny hole. Frantically, she brought the material to her face and searched. A black hair was partially buried in the blood. Clasping the thing between her finger and thumbnail, she tugged it from its cocoon, finding it half an inch in length and ... wiry. She placed it on her nightstand and repeatedly wiped her hand against the bed, removing the dead sensation the hair created.

Standing on shaky legs, she peeked from her bedroom window. A cloudless Missouri sky hovered above the world, *her* world, and the home she'd known since birth. She took in the room that had grown with her, first filled with baby dolls and teddy bears, then Barbie and the preferred G.I. Joes; now replaced with karate trophies and artwork. All of her favorites splashed across her walls, with *Starry Night*'s swirls shimmering down on her. And somewhere in the deepest corner of her closet her much-loved teddy rested in a box. Yes, this was her world. Safe. Normal. Without wolf-dogs.

In the kitchen, her mother was probably baking as she did every Saturday morning, while her dad puttered around in the garage playing with ancient swords and daggers. As antique weapons dealers, her parents' passion for history had always fascinated Nikki, and likely spawned her interest in art. They'd taught her beauty was often hidden in ordinary items, but with the right amount of care, patience, and a dose of determination, what most see as junk could become a treasure.

She drew a breath and started to turn from the window, but something flashed in the fringe of woods alongside her house.

Cold chills ran up and down her spine as she squinted into the darkened edge of trees. Off to the right, movement. She tried to swallow against the desert growing in her throat, but gulped down only hot, sticky air. Her hand trembled, squeezing the curtain with such force she felt each pulse of blood pumping through her closed fingers.

Something was lurking in the shadows. And it was waiting for her.

"So, can you give me a reason why you're so distracted today?" Krissy asked, batting thick lashes at her while sinking into the coffee shop seat.

Nikki pulled the latte to her lips and took a long, lingering drink. Explain? *I wouldn't know where to begin.*

Krissy used the end of her green straw to toy with the chocolate-striped whipped cream on the top of her iced drink. "Look, I know you hate shopping. But you promised to at least have a good attitude."

Nikki sighed deeply. *What kind of a friend am I?* "I'm sorry Krissy. It's not the shopping. I'm excited about it, really."

"As is evidenced by your wide eyes and bobbing head. You know I live for these chances to see you in real clothes. Not your customary boyfriend-fit jeans and vintage T-shirts. I mean, they're cute every once in a while, but would it kill you to wear a skirt?" Krissy slurped some of her drink, but stopped and wiped her mouth when two guys passed by their table. A toothy smile and a flirtatious head toss, and the guys were sitting across the coffee shop with eyes glued.

Nikki cast a glance behind her to the boys. "You're unbelievable."

"It's just a game. I happen to be a good player." Krissy beamed and motioned with her free hand, careful the boys wouldn't see. "Look, look, look! They're totally coming over here."

Nikki panicked and grabbed Krissy's arm in a death grip. "No."

"Let's invite them to sit down."

"Krissy, please." She squeezed tighter. "Look, if you'll get rid of them, I'll tell you what's going on."

Blue eyes narrowed, the telltale signal she was unable to resist the intrigue. "You'll tell me why you're so jacked up today?"

Nikki felt the boys bearing down on her. "Yes, I promise. I'll tell you everything." Her cheeks felt like they were burning.

Krissy sighed and shifted into catch and release mode. "Fine."

When the two teen boys stopped at the table, Nikki tried to offer a tentative smile, but figured it looked more like constipation.

They greeted, and Nikki mumbled a greeting in return. Then Krissy kicked into full gear. "So, I noticed you guys go by and I was thinking, you two look just like a couple of my little brother's friends. His name is Jeff and he goes to Waterside Middle School."

The boy's faces crumbled.

Oh, dear Lord, just kill them now and save them from this embarrassment.

But Krissy soldiered on. "I don't know all his friends, but I remember meeting some of them at Chunky Monkey Ice Cream Shop when we had his birthday party."

Nikki sank deeper into the chair sure the boys' egos weren't likely to recover in this millennium.

Within moments — though it felt like several lifetimes — they disappeared.

"Krissy! That was mean," Nikki scolded and threw a glance over her shoulder.

But the petite blonde gave her a dead stare. "You've got info. And I don't want to be distracted by some cute guy hanging around while I hear it."

Nikki could relate. All morning her thoughts had strayed to the ocean blue eyes and the velvet voice that had soothed and protected her in the dream. Yes, she'd determined it had to be a dream. Otherwise, she had to admit the very distinct possibility she was going nuts.

Krissy listened intently as Nikki filled her in. "And that's it. I woke up in my clothes in my own bed."

"Wow."

Nikki dropped her hands flat on the table and blinked at her friend. "*Wow?* That's it?" Krissy had an opinion on absolutely everything.

She waved a hand in the air. "Give me a minute, I'm thinking." Her lips puckered slightly and her straw plunged repeatedly into the depths of her iced mocha. "You're being chased. That means something in dreams, but I can't remember what. Then a fence." She snapped her fingers. "What could a fence mean? And there were wolves? That means something too, but …"

Nikki's head dropped to the table. "Let me guess. You can't remember what."

Krissy nodded, ignoring the monotone remark. "What else stands out?"

Cerulean eyes. So filled with color and life, it was as if pure pigment had created them and trapped a beam of sunlight just beneath their depths. Nikki squeezed her eyes shut. "The guy."

"Oh. Ohhh." Krissy nodded. "Now we're getting somewhere. It's simple. You want someone to rescue you. You want — no, wait, you *need* a knight in shining armor to come and save you from the dragon."

What? That was the stupidest thing she'd ever heard. And yet … She rejected the thought. *I don't need some guy.* From her karate to her artwork, from her choice of clothing to her choice of transportation, she had it all together. She was a girl who knew exactly what she wanted. Except she didn't.

In fact, she felt like the most conflicted person on the planet. She couldn't even decide on a career path. Business for becoming a karate instructor and own her own dojo someday, or art school? They both fit like a shrunken sweater: a past favorite, and the other certainly not a choice one could live with forever. It was as if a huge part of Nikki had gone missing long ago and she didn't know how to find it … or if she'd ever had it to begin with. Could her best friend actually be right? "What? What's the dragon?"

Krissy threw her hands into the air. "Who knows? It could be anything. Science class, the MCAT, green Jell-O."

Nikki drew her brows together in a deep frown.

"The dragon is whatever terrifies you. It's whatever you're scared of."

Myself, Nikki thought. *I'm scared of myself. What I can't do. What I can do. Why I don't know who I am.* A rock sat on her chest, making it hard to breathe. She forced a laugh, but there was no humor in it. "I'm pretty sure it's green Jell-O."

Krissy pointed at her. "You need a man. That's all."

One split second later, two new victims entered the coffee shop. Nikki groaned and grabbed her backpack-style purse. "Let's go. I don't want you fixing me up. Besides, there are clothes waiting for us!"

Krissy squealed and clapped her hands together. "Yay! Shopping."

Nikki hung her new clothes in her closet, her eyes stopping at the black cocktail-style dress Krissy talked her into buying. She ran a hand over the soft, shimmery material. She chewed her lip. It really was a beautiful garment. And she *did* have the art gallery showing in a few days. She should have a grown-up dress, or as Krissy called it, a little black dress destined to be a girl's best friend. Admittedly, it had been gorgeous when she tried it on, but now, hanging in her closet, it looked ridiculous amongst the jeans, T-shirts, riding boots, and flip-flops.

Shopping was always exhausting on a deep level and her constant apprehension about rabid wolves finding her in the dressing room and chasing her through the mall in her underwear didn't help. *All day it was like eyes were on me.* It was nearly evening now, and she had to get out, clear her mind. She shoved the black dress to the back of her closet and slammed the door, flying down the stairs in a desperate attempt to outrun such adult clothing. Sprawled in the family room, she caught a glimpse of yellow fur beneath the coffee table. It whimpered. She dropped to her haunches at the table's edge and cooed, "Who's a good dog?"

A massive head plopped onto her thighs. Innocent brown eyes blinked their adoration.

She scratched his head between his ears, and the yellow lab stretched, arching his back, long gawky legs straightening like boards.

Already feeling better, Nikki strolled into the kitchen and snagged a piece of fruit.

"Getting hungry? I'm going to start dinner soon," Mom said over her shoulder.

"Nah, I'm good. I'm leaving for a while."

"Where are you going?"

"Just for a ride."

Her mom frowned. "Alone?"

Nikki cast her eyes heavenward. "Yes, alone, but I'll be fine. You'd think I'd just gotten the bike a week ago."

"I just like it better when someone goes with you."

Must we go through this every time? "Well, I've put in an application to join the Swamp Rider's Biker Club, but I haven't heard from them yet."

Her mom swatted at her with a dish towel. "That's not funny. Oh, before I forget, we have to be gone Monday night — your father has an auction in St. Louis. We'll be finishing late, so he's planning on spending the night and driving home Tuesday morning." Her mother's dark brows scrunched inward. "Actually, we could cancel the room and drive home Monday so you're not alone."

Nikki groaned. "Mom, I'll be fine. I'm seventeen. I think I can survive one night without you here."

"All grown up," her mother said, and closed the distance to pull Nikki into a tight mom hug. "Speaking of grown-up events, did you find a dress for the gallery?"

Nikki groaned again and sank onto her mom's shoulder.

"Did I say the wrong thing?"

"No, Mom. Everything's fine." But her mom pulled her closer, nearly squeezing the breath from her lungs.

"That's right, Nikki. Everything *is* fine." When she drew away, something glistened in her mom's gaze. Something unsettling.

Nikki smiled and refused the voice that told her life as she knew it was about to end.

She flew down the highway with wind rushing past, enjoying the whine of the Kawasaki Ninja 600's engine. Her mood lifted with each rev. The nightmare of last evening jettisoned away as she gripped the clutch and relished the feel of her bike beneath her. Or certain-death crotch-rocket, as her mom called it. She still remembered the fights when she'd asked her parents for the motorcycle for her sixteenth birthday—and how her dad had worked around her mom's no-sixteen-year-old-of-mine ultimatum by presenting the bike a year later. Eight inches of hair flapped below the helmet she'd promised her mother she'd always wear. So far, she'd honored that vow, but warm Saturday afternoons encouraged long drives. She'd often end up in Arkansas where there was no helmet law. The temptation was great.

She stopped for gas and filled the tank. Six bucks. Beside her, a thirty-something-year-old guy filled an SUV. Nikki stifled a grin as he poured in numerous gallons of gas. Yes, life was good and it was beginning to feel normal again.

The guy shoved the gas pump back into the holder and caught her gaze. It stopped his momentum and he stared straight at her without moving.

Nikki swallowed and gave a nod toward him, but before she could turn away his eyes changed. A shadow closed over his features, then seemed to disappear. The guy blinked a few times and mumbled some angry words, then wiped his hand across an already dirty flannel shirt. But he never took his eyes off her.

She flashed a quick smile and dropped her gaze. When he slammed the hatch to his gas tank, Nikki jumped.

Seeming pleased with her reaction, he watched as she replaced her gas lid.

"I said I'm talking to you," he growled.

She hung up the pump. "Excuse me?" Looking down at her gas cap, she noticed her hands were trembling. Her teeth clenched. *What's happening? I never walk around this afraid. Plus, I could take this guy if I had to.* The answer wasn't long in coming. Last night's brush with ... well, with whatever it was, left her more than a bit uncomfortable. And grungy flannel shirt guy with the SUV wasn't helping.

"Stupid teenager," he grumbled.

Nikki donned her helmet, snagged her receipt, then threw a leg over her bike. "I didn't do anything," she said in the safety of her full-coverage helmet.

"What?" His face reddened, and he took a step closer. "What did you say?"

Twisting her wrist, she sped out of the parking lot. "Okay, that was weird," she muttered. The guy had seemed fine when she first pulled up.

Trees and hills disappeared past as she zipped down Farm Road 211. But her nerves were raw so she slowed down. The speedometer read fifty, and she held steady there until she saw the grill of a vehicle inching closer in her small, round rearview mirror.

From a half-mile away she could plainly see the acceleration as the SUV moved closer, faster. She blinked repeatedly, fighting panic — it was the same vehicle from the gas station. Glancing alongside the road, she searched for a place to pull off and hide or turn around, but no decent option presented itself. Hands sweaty, she accelerated again.

The dark SUV closed the distance. She could outrun him — sport bikes were known for their speed. But they were also known for hitting loose gravel and tumbling end over end. Every time she tried to accelerate beyond a safe speed, the rear end shimmied, losing traction. *Road rash? No, thank you.* Nikki held firm at sixty, and didn't dare push it even though every synapse in her body begged her to let loose. The two vehicles sped down the empty stretch of road, the SUV now mere feet away.

In her mirror she made out his face, still red but now smiling as if enjoying the chase. Nikki willed her mind to concentrate on riding, instead of imagining what Nikki roadkill would look like. More than once she swerved into the empty oncoming lane to keep his front bumper from making contact with her back tire. If the two touched, it would catapult her from the bike like a ragdoll.

Her secret weapon was she knew this road by heart, could probably drive it with her eyes shut. Up ahead, a tight turn waited. Nikki formed a plan.

Chapter
3

Mace snuck from the house for the second time on Saturday. Keeping a safe distance, he'd watched Nikki and her friend meander through stores at the mall with a mammoth battle raging in his gut. Will had given an order — a direct and very specific order — and he was breaking it. It was a huge risk to move among humans while he still looked, smelled, felt, and, as he'd discovered, *tasted* otherworldly. The problem was, he simply couldn't wait two more days to see Nikki Youngblood again.

He'd messed up on this journey already by letting the girl see him in the forest. It had been a stupid mistake, one that could cause questions later. Guys don't just appear out of nowhere. *Of course, neither do hell hounds.* None of it would make sense to her. Then again, nothing about this journey made sense to him, either. Especially the way he couldn't stop himself from scooping the girl into his arms.

Raven had watched with the interest of an alligator waiting

for a victim to pass by. He'd probably intended to tuck away Mace's mistake and pull it out when it could do the most damage. He couldn't afford to give Raven such leverage.

Yet here he was on Saturday evening, tailing Nikki Youngblood as if he'd been instructed to do so. Stupid.

And necessary. Something inside told him she needed a constant watchman. Not that his services had been helpful. She'd spent the day shopping, and though he'd managed to stay off her radar, every now and then she'd pause and scan the area around her like she knew he was there. Hiding. Waiting. Watching.

Like he was doing now. He'd nearly turned back and headed home but as he banked, wings spread above the motorcycle and the girl riding it, he'd noticed the SUV. It pulled into the road and gunned the engine, causing Mace's wing feathers to prickle the way they did when demons were around. He tilted down for a closer inspection of the driver. No demon, just some guy who'd been rude to Nikki at the gas station. Nonetheless, Mace kept his speed up to keep from being seen, moving so fast his molecules disappeared and no human would see him coming. Nothing like having angelic powers on hand when spying on someone.

He hovered above a row of trees. Judging by what was happening on the road, it was a good thing he'd disobeyed Will's rules.

The girl was being chased by a human, but one under evil control. *Darkness wastes no time.* Well, then he would step up the game as well. Uncle Will wouldn't approve, and neither would Raven, who despite his experience — or maybe because of it — had the most contempt for their charges. *Will I grow as callous over time? Will these journeys in this realm create shad-*

ows in my heart? Raven hadn't always had the darkness that now glimmered in his eyes.

Will's constant reminder drifted thought Mace's thoughts. *Never forget your origin.* Born in rebellion, marked for eternity, and rejected as outcasts. And meant to keep the realms in peace.

His eyes fanned to the corner ahead, where the street bike and the SUV were moving too fast for the turn. Mace waited while seconds stretched, each one lasting an eternity. This couldn't end well.

He'd promised himself he'd simply observe, not interact. Yeah, right. *If Nikki's truly in danger, I shovel her into my arms before a single scratch marks her skin.* And he believed that single fact alone made him a dangerous choice — and the right choice — for this journey.

Thankfully, she slowed as she reached the tight corner. The SUV's engine wound down in response. For a brief instant Mace thought she'd make it, but loose gravel connected with her tires, throwing her into a fishtail. She zigzagged one way then the other, along with his stomach. The bike tilted closer to the ground with each swerve. Momentum drove the bike, and though he could tell Nikki was a capable rider, a hundred pound girl was no match for an out-of-control seven-hundred-pound machine. Gravel sprayed from one side then the other as if created by a water skier in perfect form.

Mace's muscles tensed with each swerve of her front wheel. Rules or not, if he didn't interfere she'd never survive the fall.

In less than a heartbeat he was at the back of her bike. He lifted the back end gently, keeping it an inch off the ground until Nikki cleared the dangerous corner. Behind him the SUV squealed.

Please tell me he didn't see the golden glow . . .

Mace reached around the girl and held her against him in a bear hug, unsure if the vehicle behind might make contact. He longed to snap his wings open and lift her to safety, but that would definitely get him replaced on this journey and it would certainly trash her bike. No, he'd wrap his body around hers and take the hit himself, gravel blanket and all. If tumbling along the road was his fate, he'd seize it, as long as he protected Nikki.

His heart jolted again when her reflection flashed in the side view mirror, face covered by her helmet save for her caramel eyes now filled with terror. He wasn't the SUV she'd been expecting.

"Great," he mumbled. *How am I gonna explain this to Uncle Will?*

Recognition filled her gaze and her eyes melted into peace, proving his cover was blown. Mace knew he should be admonishing himself for landing directly behind his target — even Vine knew better than to *stop* when you wanted to stay invisible — but instead his heart hammered with an uncommon sensation. Something in his very soul reached out for her. And the really scary thing was . . . it felt like something in her soul was reaching for him.

Behind them the SUV shuddered, wheels catching and releasing the road. It squealed again before shooting into a field like a rocket and disappearing.

Mace's muscles released marginally, causing a new awareness of where her body touched his. The inside of his arms, moments ago simply a place of absolute safety for her, were now on fire. His arms and chest tingled. He felt like a rod of metal in a lightning storm, or a cord of frayed wires plugged into a socket and scattering sparks. He was in trouble.

As if awaking from her trance, Nikki squeezed the brake and they slid to a stop. She leapt off the bike and spun to face him. But instead of the fiery speech, she faltered, grabbing for air. Her eyes rolled and she collapsed.

Slipping behind her, he caught her weight. He noticed her scent as he lowered her gently — clean and alive like flowers sprinkled on the wind. Her fear blended with and only intensified the sweet smell. Strands of hair pressed against her forehead where her helmet held them in place, trapped like butterflies under glass. Before he had her all the way to the ground, he unfastened the strap beneath her chin, needing to see all of her features.

A blanket of her silky, dark hair covered his legs once he knelt down. A breeze blew across her, setting the butterflies free and allowing long strands to dance slowly in the current of air. Her eyes fluttered open, dark lashes framing irises of warm honey.

"I know you," she whispered then passed out again.

For an eternity he held her while the wind grabbed leaves and waltzed them across the road. Mace couldn't stop his fingers from reaching to touch the skin on her cheek. *Ah. Angel skin.* It struck him as odd that though he was the half heavenly being, it was her flesh that carried unearthly softness. Maybe all daughters of man felt that way. He didn't know, since he'd never spent time so near earth girls.

Nor would he.

Mace snatched his hand from her face as if it burned. But when she pulled a deep breath and seemed to snuggle into his lap, tension dissolved from him. *Admire*, he told himself. *But admire from a safe distance.*

He bit his cheek hard to keep from pulling her closer.

Stillness seemed an unnatural state for her. She'd been halted, stopped by possibly the only thing that could stop her. Mace's face creaked into a smile. It only took a blast of heavenly electricity to slow her down. The mere fact *he'd* been the force powerful enough to stop her played havoc with his senses. *Get a grip.* He drew a deep, cleansing breath.

Her scent assaulted him again.

Above them thunder rumbled, the heavens sending a warning of their own. Mace glanced at the sky; dark clouds swirled, announcing an oncoming storm. Across the road, a barn anchored an overgrown cornfield and an ancient farmhouse sagged at the edge of the street. Mace scanned the buildings with narrowed eyes. No one outside. No one inside. The entire area seemed uninhabited, absent of even a skittering rodent.

Will and Raven won't find out. He slid a hand beneath her knees and effortlessly lifted her into his arms. Smooth steps carried them toward the house. Less than two hundred feet away, he stopped.

Alarm prickled across his shoulders, heightening his already-tuned senses. The cold of death, torment, and evil swept past. He angled away from the house and toward the barn as thunderheads rolled closer.

He shifted her weight as angry, fat drops fell from the sky only feet from the entrance. When he fumbled for the door handle, she stirred. Her head fell back and a tiny moan escaped her lips. Her breath feathered across his face.

Mace staggered. He pulled the sugar-sweet aroma into his being. The breath of life. As a boy, Mace carried the scent — all

Halflings did. But as he'd gained his angelic power, the breath of life disappeared. One more reminder that earth was not his home.

Leaning against the doorframe for support, he inched his face closer to hers. Again, her breath fanned him, weakening his strength and reminding him of all he could never have. Deep yearnings drove him to close the distance to her mouth where the cloying air hissed from her lips. Nothing smelled so satisfying, so alive — or so unattainable. And at the moment, nothing looked so inviting.

Only inches from kissing her, her eyes flittered open. The faintest smile touched soft, pink lips. "I'm floating in a pool of blue-green water," she whispered, "drawn from the Mediterranean Sea." Her eyes blinked, still glassy but concentrated. "You know what?"

He shook his head.

"The water is perfect." Lashes fluttered. She slumped against his chest.

Mace had to draw several calming gulps of air before attempting to transport her into the barn. Admire, but from a safe distance. *I've already wrecked that plan.* He tried to remind himself of all that was on the line. Normally, he liked boundaries. Boundaries were the safety net. Boundaries kept people on the right path. But right now, he felt like rules were made to be broken and consequences were miles and miles away.

If journeys came with rulebooks, he'd probably just disobeyed every word.

Chapter
4

Raven stretched out on the bed and locked his hands behind his head. Heavy rock rumbled from a stereo in the corner, though he'd turned it down to insure he'd hear the footsteps — and the explosion — he was waiting for.

When the giant started up the stairs, Raven couldn't help but smirk. The booming footsteps halted at Mace's door. *Let the fun begin.* He jumped from the bed and swung his door open to watch the fireworks in the next room.

Without pausing to knock, Will threw open the door to Mace's room.

Raven stepped into the hallway from his own domain and followed Will's gaze into the empty space. Trying, really trying, not to laugh, he mumbled, "He's so busted."

Will spun and took a menacing step toward Raven. *Ooh, scary.* "From the time the Ancient of Days created me, I've roamed first the heavens, then the earth. I've comfortably breathed both the scent of death and that of life. I have endured multiple generations. But one thing I cannot abide is insubordination."

Raven sighed, simulating heartfelt sorrow. "I understand completely."

Will darkened. "When I give an order, I expect it to be respected."

"Yeah, I feel ya." Hand flat on the doorjamb, Raven shook his head as if disappointed. "Where'd we go wrong? I thought we'd raised him better."

Will's eyes blazed. "And when I lead, I expect those under my command to resist mockery."

Uh-oh. Should have left it at concerned brother. Raven flashed a brilliant smile and shrugged.

With no Mace present to absorb his frustration, Will returned his attention to the empty space. There was only one likely explanation: Nikki Youngblood. Raven could practically feel the concern crawling up Will's neck. The giant's wings fluttered at the tips, each feather rising like hair on a dog's back.

Will's reaction zapped the fun of watching Mace — the *good* one — bumbling into mistake after mistake. Though Will had faced all manner of disaster throughout millennia, Raven couldn't ignore the apprehension — so thick it spiked from Will's flesh — that signaled trouble surrounded Nikki Youngblood.

When Will turned to face Raven, a cold chill scraped the length of his spine. In the depths of Will's lightning blue eyes, a painful secret rested. And Raven was pretty sure it said this journey would take the life of one of the Lost Boys.

A crash of thunder woke Nikki. Foggy headed, she tried to grasp and hold the edges of her reason. *Where am I?*

Heaviness filled her body, making it almost impossible to rise from the floor. Eyes still unfocused, she teetered on panic until those cool, cerulean orbs filled her vision. Was she dreaming again? Everything seemed to be melting around her as if the world was made of carnival glass and she could only view it through a rain-streaked window.

"You're safe," the voice said.

She'd heard that deep, velvet voice before. She'd even heard those exact words, but where? *Why can't I concentrate?*

An arm slipped around her shoulders and pulled her to a seated position, where she could see his face. He possessed a sculpted jawline and a perfect nose that seemed to be crafted by Michelangelo himself. Two high cheekbones rested above a mouth that looked capable of pleasing any girl's lips, but also able to draw into a tight line of defense when necessary. And then there were those lose-yourself-in eyes. Though he appeared to be her age, she'd never seen anyone like him. Even his knees, visible through the holes in his faded jeans, seemed perfect.

But it was his eyes that begged trust. Each time she looked at them, a little more tension eased from her muscles. "What happened?" She glanced up. Above, a giant dome of wood slats cupped around them. The sweet smell of hay hovered in the space. *Are we in a barn?*

"You spun around the corner and lost control of your bike," he said.

A frown slashed her forehead. "I wrecked?"

"No, you spun out but you didn't crash. You did lay the bike over, though. It's at the edge of a field."

She stiffened. This was wrong. Why was she *in here* and why were they alone and why did she feel drugged?

"It's okay. I made sure it was off the road, and I doubt anyone can even see it."

That bit of information didn't inspire confidence. If no one could see her bike from the road, no one would be looking for her. Her eyes shot around the barn, things beginning to sharpen into focus. "What am I doing here?" She eased away from him, hands pushing against the hay-strewn ground.

Lightning, accompanied by a blast of thunder, answered her question.

He gestured toward a window. "Storm. A serious one." His shoulder tipped into a tentative shrug and she had to marvel at the sudden vulnerability he seemed to exude. She really *did* feel safe with him.

Bursts of angry light flashed through the barn's slat walls, scattering blue-white beams in all directions and fracturing her short-lived confidence. *You're still in a barn with a guy you don't know and you have no recollection of getting here.* "They're all serious ones in Missouri," she said, hoping to engage him in conversation until she could determine the best course of action. She needed to get out.

"So I hear," he said.

"You're new?" she asked, forcing her shoulders to relax.

"Just moved here."

His face was so very alive. Like moonbeams captured in flesh. She tried to separate her emotions from her sanity, because the two seemed at odds. Then the room spun. The blood supply to her brain careened first to her stomach, then down to her feet. In what was becoming a habit, she dropped her face into her hands, where all thought of action, escape — and boys too cute to be lurking in abandoned barns — faded.

"Are you all right?" he asked.

"Yeah," she managed, but it was a pitiful reply. "No." She pressed her palms into her eyes. "It's weird, like my strength is being zapped." It reminded her of when she was twelve and had laid her hand against an open light socket while helping her dad fix a broken switch. It had caused her muscles to falter throughout her entire body. While she barely remembered the incident, she remembered that strange weakened-feeling vividly. She also recalled the next hour. After some argument, her parents called a family friend rather than the paramedics, which Nikki had always thought weird. She remembered the dark-haired, dark-eyed man who had hovered above her like a watchful mother hen. After several minutes, he announced her fit and life returned to normal.

This sensation was different, somehow more internal and less harmful than the jolts of electric current. But she still had the sense something freaky was going on.

The boy moved closer to her, scooting across the dirt floor. "Here, lean on me." Her trepidation again waned as the soothing vibrations of his voice filled her ears.

Her head returned to the spin cycle, and she collapsed toward him, tucking her shoulder beneath his arm. His chest was a breathing concrete wall against her cheek, and she thought she felt him shudder. She felt herself weaken even more but couldn't muster the energy to mind. Heat rose from his thin T-shirt, warming the side of her face.

Low volts zapped her, causing drowsy, hazy flashes in her mind. This was how she'd felt yesterday. *He'd been there.* Him and a pack of wolf-things. As if every synapse were suddenly aflame, Nikki pushed away from the stranger.

He tensed. "What?"

"Who are you?" she demanded, rolling onto her knees to

make it easier to stand. But he was still too close. A balmy hand fell on her shoulder.

"Don't worry, Nikki. I'm not going to hurt you."

She'd studied six years of martial arts, ensuring no man on the planet could hurt her. She backed away from him, his touch, his warm body, and stood on *al dente* spaghetti legs. *Right, like I could throw a punch or land a kick right now.* The first sign of potential support was the wall near the barn door. Surely her legs could carry her that far. She stumbled toward it and dropped her hand to the slat handle to stay upright. And to make a quick exit. As soon as she could walk without staggering, she'd make a run for it. Until then, she'd get answers. "How do you know my name? Who *are* you?"

"My name is Mace." He stood and attempted a tentative step in her direction, as if trying to corner a skittish cat.

To which she shook her head. Adrenaline coursed and Nikki drew on its potency. Her hands opened from the fisted position they'd maintained while vulnerable. Open hands were hands of war, hands of control and conviction.

Mace frowned, recognition seeming to register in his eyes.

Determined to avert her gaze from the blue-green sea, her right foot slid back, knees bent, weight shifted, left foot ready to strike. Ridged hand ready to follow. Fact was, she really, *really* didn't want to fight the cutest guy she'd ever met. The fact that she'd noticed he was cute was a big deal. She usually stayed oblivious since they seemed an immature lot. One she rarely had the time or inclination to indulge. Her best friend Krissy referred to her love life as the black hole, where possibilities were devoured by its bleakness. *Why, in the midst of a potential attack, am I thinking about my love life?* Lack of blood flow to the brain, no doubt.

The boy took a step back, his jeans shifting over muscled thighs. He lifted his hands, palms facing her. "Look, you don't have to be afraid."

"I'm not afraid," she said with a voice sounding much more confident than she felt.

He raked a hand through his dark blond hair. "Whatever. I brought you in here so you wouldn't get drenched."

She nodded, heart hammering. "Right. You could have just called for help, you know." She tossed a glance through the window. "In the time it took you to drag me here, the police would have arrived."

"Have you watched too many horror flicks?" His eyes narrowed. "I didn't *drag* you here. I carried you because you couldn't walk. And just how would I have called the police?"

Seriously? She pinned him with a dead stare. "You own a cell phone, don't you?"

"Uh." His cheeks flushed and he looked down, intensely examining the barn floor then several steps away to the spot where her helmet had been neatly placed on a hay bale.

She'd caught him off guard. Interesting. But he had her on the edge too. In fact, as she studied him, it seemed like the uncertainty between them created a canyon of doubt, but there was a curiosity that forged a bridge neither seemed able to completely ignore.

A chuckle slipped from her lips, surprising them both. "No cell phone? Are you, like, Amish or something?"

His hands came together, fingers interlocked at his waist.

The term *little boy lost* slid into her mind. Good. She had the upper hand after all. Confidence renewed, she pulled her phone from her front pocket and flipped it open. She pretended to mash buttons.

He raised a hand. "Nikki, wait."

His eyes pleaded. Her heart fluttered. And suddenly, the thought of being locked in a hand-to-hand scuffle with him seemed a gratifying way to spend a rainy afternoon. Alone in a barn.

Whoa there.

"Please, wait." Again, his lean, strong fingers slid through hair cut into a shaggy style that fell into exact position. Exact order. Yes, there was something decidedly ordered about him. Like he wasn't used to breaking rules but had recently found himself unable to keep them. He was as out of place in the barn as she was, and again this gave her the edge.

Well, kind of. She found herself fixated on the long bangs that dusted his forehead, slightly creased by a distant frown. Apart from the uncertainty he exuded, his chiseled bone structure and smooth skin radiated perfection.

The idea of sketching him whipped into her mind. Charcoal, maybe. To capture the light and shadow of his carved features. But a shadow hid his heart as well, of that she was certain, and she had no idea how to depict that with paper and pencils — or even what it was for that matter.

He took a step closer.

Her jaw shifted, her eyes splitting glances between him and her cell phone. "I want to know what's going on."

Mace's shoulders slumped. "I'll explain what I can." He seemed to catch himself. "I'll, uh, explain what I know."

A peculiar sadness entered his gaze. Beyond little boy lost. Little boy … never to be found. Again, her heart reacted.

"First, about the accident." He stumbled over the words. "Not really an accident. I mean, your bike's fine. Some jerk was chasing you in an SUV."

The incident flooded her mind. Gas station. Crazed guy. Red, smiling face. Flash of light, and … Mace … sitting behind her on the bike. Her cell phone dropped from her hand and landed on the ground with a thud and a dust puff.

Her knees buckled and once again the world went liquid. She glanced down at her phone, how it had fallen; she was bound to trace its path and land on the barn floor. Sliding, sliding her back against the wall … then a sudden stop. Mace's face once again was before her; he'd caught her and trapped her between the barn wall and himself. Her world darkened to a tiny tunnel of light. Everything faded except cerulean eyes.

"No," she whispered. Then, she saw nothing at all.

Chapter
5

This is so bad — *Uncle Will's going to kill me.* His warning echoed in Mace's head: "The longer she's around us, the more she can tolerate our atmosphere."

Well, that didn't seem the case. She'd fainted, like, fifty times, and was completely out. Mace's hands rested flat against the wall, keeping her arms draped over his as they stood face-to-face. With no one watching he could take a minute to study her. He could find interest in a spider on a web if he gazed at it long enough, though Nikki Youngblood was far more interesting — and even more dangerous — than any web or poisonous spider this world could offer. And the danger lingered on two levels: first, because he seemed unable to stay on task whenever she looked at him; and second, because he was sent to protect her, and it was quite obvious by her attitude Nikki didn't feel she needed any protection but her own.

He willed her to exhale. Just one more breath. Again, his lips hovered only a few inches from hers. Sculpted brows framed her eyes, now closed but no less beautiful with their thick crescent moons of dark lashes. A small nose, turned up slightly at the tip, and pink lips. Artist's hands had sculpted this daughter of man.

He had to grin at her vintage T-shirt. He'd always felt that retro clothing hinted at some deep appreciation for the past, for history and its richness. She wore a light vanilla-scented fragrance, but it paled to the aroma of Nikki. Clear, alive. Wind and fire.

When she opened her eyes again, he smiled. "Welcome back."

Glancing down at her predicament, she exhaled a long breath as if surrendering.

Mace's heart responded with a series of fierce beats.

Her head tipped back, resting against the barn wall and mashing her long hair. A strand flittered across his arms, and he hoped she didn't notice his skin reacting to the feathery touch.

"What's wrong with me?" she said in a small voice.

Finally, the fighter in her had conceded. He needed to seize the moment. "I want to ask you something."

She nodded, and the tips of her hair danced over his skin. *She's making it monumentally difficult to concentrate.*

He opened his eyes wide, allowing her to read his intention. The eyes were the mirrors of the soul, after all. "Can you trust me?"

For a long time, they gazed at one another, and Mace wondered if the contact was playing havoc with her the same way it was with him.

"Yes," she said, and it seemed to surprise her. One side of her mouth skewed upward. "I can."

Mace inched closer, watching for any hesitation as he drew near. This was a mistake; he could completely short-circuit her and she'd end up passed out on the barn floor again. *But really, what do I have to lose?* Either way, he was with Nikki Youngblood, and though his mind sought to remind him of the trouble he'd be in if Will knew, he doused that voice when she didn't stiffen or try to shrink away. "I'm going to hug you," he said.

She bristled then, as if wanting to retreat ... and possibly embrace his movement. Mace could hear her heartbeat quicken, then slow, and her breathing seemed to match. Neither seemed rooted in fear, but how much of her reaction was due to his aura over her?

"Nikki, is it okay if I come a little closer?"

She dropped her eyes toward the floor and swallowed. "I-I think so. As long as it's just a hug."

His hands slid off the barn wall and lightly touched her back. His arms, moving in response, closed around her and drew him into her warmth . When their bodies met in the embrace, she sucked in a breath. Her back arched as her body stiffened for a moment, then melted like butter. And for an interlude that could have been a lifetime, they hung there, drifting between two worlds.

Her eyes flew open and she tilted back enough to look at him. Both exhilaration and wonder lit her features in equal measure. She searched his face. "What just happened?"

"I hugged you," he said, voice jagged from the contact. He fought the urge to pull her closer.

"What else?" she said, her breath light. "I feel ... stronger. It's like that hug energized me."

This was a bad, bad, bad idea.

But he was smiling like an idiot. He *was* an idiot. When she fully came to her senses, she'd know she'd been in contact with something unearthly. Something beyond this realm, and outside the scope of normalcy. "You said you trust me."

Her eyes narrowed playfully. "And you said you'd explain."

"About the *accident*," he said.

"There was no accident, remember?" All her previous fear and panic had drained, leaving only confidence. Her gaze dropped to his lips, then flashed back up to meet his eyes. "I saw you. You were on my bike."

This was spiraling out of control. He fought for an explanation ... but had she bit her lip when she'd glanced down at his mouth? *Heaven help me.* "You saw me on the side of the road in your side view mirror."

A coy grin slanted her cheeks. "Who said I saw you in the side view mirror?"

Oops. Mace clenched his jaw and began to draw away from her.

But her fingers found their way up his shoulders to the back of his neck. "Wait," she said, the slight squeeze of her fingertips stopping him cold. Or hot. It was a strange mix of sensations, the play of her fingertips against his skin, the mounting pressure on his chest.

Nikki smiled sweetly. "You saved my life. Thank you."

Ugh. That little announcement landed like a rock in the pit of his stomach. "Don't mention it. Really, don't," he said.

One brow notched up. "You're a strange guy, Mace."

"So they tell me," he said. Still, her hands remained closed on him like she didn't want to let go. He felt her pulse in each fingertip.

When the moment drifted toward the awkward, she released her grip and slipped her arms off his.

"Feeling better?" he asked.

"Yeah, almost normal. In fact, better than normal. This is bizarre, but it feels like there are really low volts of electricity drifting through my body." Nikki grimaced. "That sounds crazy, doesn't it?"

"No." He rummaged his memory bank. He'd had to explain the "electricity" a few times before. Never to a gorgeous earth girl, but hey, first for everything. He nodded toward the window. "I'm sure it's just the storm. Electricity fills the air with ionized particles. That's part of what makes lightning storms so dangerous."

"Ionized particles, huh?"

"Yeah," he said, and stopped nodding his head like a bobblehead doll. He wasn't so good with lying.

She tossed dark brown hair over her shoulder. "Thank you, Professor Mace. What about yesterday? There was no lightning and no storm, just some crazy dogs chasing me, and I felt the same jolts. I saw you there too." A cold wind whistled through the slat wall, momentarily stealing her focus. When the beams above groaned in protest, Nikki hugged herself.

Mace stole the opportunity to move away. He surveyed the surroundings. "I don't know what you're talking about — and you're shivering. I'll find a blanket or something for you." He'd hoped yesterday would be enough of a blur that she'd assume it'd been a nightmare. No such luck.

She closed the distance and spun him around to face her. "You still haven't explained what happened. *Really* explained."

"And, must I remind you, I said I would explain *what I could*," he countered, voice rising as he realized just how huge of a mistake he'd made.

Her unrelenting, golden-brown eyes devoured his composure. Apparently, earth girls had their own brand of electricity, and males were susceptible no matter what realm they hailed from. Will had never told him what to do if he was taken in by her atmosphere.

"I don't even know you," she said. "In the last two days, I was nearly mauled by rabid dogs and ran down by a whack-job SUV driver. And you showed up both places. How do I know you didn't stage both those attacks?"

Appalled, his head jutted forward. "What? Now you sound crazy. Why would I do that?"

She lifted her hands then let them fall to her thighs with a slap. "I don't know, freak. You tell me."

Freak. So true, but hurt twisted his chest — a deep, slow burn that ached until it seemed his very heart would explode. The pain slid like morning fog into his being, then burned like the poison from a hell hound's bite. Shoulders curled forward, he gave a slight nod. "Your bike is across the road. You'll see it." He took a tentative step toward the door.

"Wait," she said.

Regret crossed the valley of hay and hurt to catch him as he reached for the slat handle. But it was too late. In one word — *freak* — she'd summarized him. What he was. What he'd always be.

"Don't leave." Almost a plea.

But it didn't matter. He'd already caused such a mess there may be no hope of repair.

Muted light flooded the space as he tugged on the barn door. Tiny, singular peaks of moist straw lay in lonely clumps around the opening, separated by mud holes and dirt trenches of unabsorbed rain water. His eyes scanned the perimeter. "You'll be okay," he said, not bothering to turn and look at her. "Just get home." His fingers tightened on the door. "And Nikki?"

She shuffled closer. "Yes?"

The storm had abated both inside and outside the barn. Tiny shafts of sunlight tried to puncture through the weighty wall of clouds. "From now on, be careful." Mace slammed the door behind him, solidifying his resolve to never, ever again break Will's rules. No one was worth the consequences, especially a human girl whose words could rival the bite of any deadly spider.

Chapter
6

Raven sauntered down the long hall of Waterside High School. Same sights, same sounds as the last dozen times at the last dozen schools. Same female eyes tightly glued to his back. *Huh, never gets old.* He sniffed the air, aware of Nikki Youngblood somewhere nearby. Her scent filled his nose and he caught himself pulling it deeper into his lungs above the institutional smells of floor varnish, leather tennis shoes, and girls trying too hard to smell good.

A cute redhead crossed too close in front of him, then hugged her notebook and threw a flirty, "Oops, sorry," back at him.

He graced her with a nod and allowed one corner of his mouth to grin in that "Hey, babe, no problem" way he'd perfected.

High school could actually be fun if he let himself enjoy it. *If. When was the last time I really enjoyed anything?* A cloud fell over him, one he'd learned to live with. Before he spent another moment seeking self-pity — for that's all it was — he returned to the game at hand.

His eyes fell to his schedule. He'd memorized it, of course, but the slight hesitation in his steps gave proof of just how many people were watching. Three feminine voices spoke up at once, blending in a mix of words that flew toward him at barrel-neck speed. "Are you lost?" "I can help you find —" and "I think we have the next class together."

Too easy.

He checked out each face and settled on the cute redhead that had bumped into him moments before. She'd continued her hunt by lingering at a locker until a geeky guy asked her to move. She shot him a look that reminded him of a shark facing down its prey. The poor kid shrank visibly, turtling into his oversized polyester shirt.

So, she was a mean girl. That suited Raven fine. He didn't need any romantic involvement, just some pretty eye candy to decorate his arm now and then. Mean girls, he'd discovered, harbored an amazing power to bounce back. Like him, they didn't seem to feel much. No broken hearts when the game ended.

Just enjoy it, he told himself. He offered his arm, and she laced hers through and gave the other girls a victorious — albeit vicious — smile followed by a "try to touch him again and you're dead" glare.

Like the turtle-geek, the girls shrank away wordlessly.

Krissy Cunningham hugged her notebook, her cheeks shimmering with a perky peach hue. "Don't you see? You are our ticket to Coolsville."

"Did you just say *Coolsville*?" Nikki slammed her locker then placed a finger in her open mouth and made a gagging sound. "Never, ever say that again."

"Seriously." Krissy propped her weight against the lockers and inspected her strappy sandals for a moment. "This is a new year. A chance to make a change, a fresh start. I know you're the self-proclaimed brooding-artist type. But you know what happens to them? They all cut off their ears. Think about it. You'll end up with *no ears*, living in a trailer house eating cat food. Not a pretty picture."

Nikki tried to keep her eyes from rolling at her petite, blonde best friend. Good thing, because Krissy then raked her eyes over Nikki. "And what happened to the clothes we bought? You swore you'd wear them. A best friend oath is nothing to trifle with, Miss Thang."

Nikki fingered the corner of her science book. "The jeans are uncomfortable and the shirts you insisted I buy are too tight." She started walking and motioned for Krissy to follow.

"Ugh. What am I going to do with you? Anything would be uncomfortable after living in boyfriend jeans and threadbare T-shirts. And isn't there some unwritten rule about *having* a boyfriend before you wear his jeans?"

Nikki shrugged. "There wasn't a tag or anything when I bought them."

Krissy tipped her head. "It's bad luck."

"I don't believe in luck."

Krissy countered, "Do you believe in fate? Because I think she's going to have to work overtime to find your dragon slayer if you don't start cooperating."

"I don't believe in fate. And I don't think I'm scared of green Jell-O anymore."

Krissy rolled her contact lens – enhanced blue eyes. "You know what? I think it would be easier to have the Grinch as a best friend. Fashion isn't always comfortable, but you get used to it. It's the price of looking good. And speaking of looking good, have you seen the new hotties?"

Nikki frowned.

"Three blond, gorgeous brothers, though there's a rumor they're cousins. One has this long white-blond hair. It's amazing. You can't stop staring at it." She wiggled her fingers in the air. "You just want to touch it, ya know? Blondish-brown hair on the other two. I don't know how they're related, but as long as one is interested in me …" Krissy said, traipsing down the hall all but lost in her boy dreaming.

Nikki stopped, causing a traffic jam behind her. "Do you think about anything but boys?"

Krissy blinked. "Do you *ever* think about boys?"

An azure gaze materialized in Nikki's mind. Yes, she'd met one of the new hotties. In fact, in the deepest part of her mind she felt as though she'd been in contact with all three. But her mind was a hazy and foggy dream she couldn't reach. "I don't want to wear clothes I can't breathe in."

"It's part of being a woman, so just deal." Krissy flashed a megawatt smile as a guy in a football jersey ran past.

"I don't want to be a woman. I want to be an artist," Nikki complained. Around them, locker doors squealed open and slammed shut.

"You're a junior. Only two more years, then college." Krissy's voice rose.

"News flash. Everyone wears sweats in college," Nikki said. "I'll have to be deconstructed just to fit in."

"News flash for you. I'm sorry, but motorcycle-riding pretty brunettes that are black belts don't fit in anywhere."

Nikki chewed on this truth a moment. Krissy hadn't meant anything by it, but she'd hit pretty close to home. "Wait a minute! There is somewhere."

Krissy waited.

"Japan. Lots of pretty brunettes there are black belts, and I'm sure at least some of them ride motorcycles."

Krissy's entire body radiated exasperation. She raised a hand. "Stop it. Stop it right now. I refuse to have this conversation with you. And most black belt moto-chicks would be jealous of your curves, so I don't think you'll find a line waiting to be your best friend. You don't even maximize your shape. Do you know what I'd do to have curves?"

"Shut up. You have a great body," Nikki said.

"Yeah, if you like two-by-fours. I'm a stick. But you ..." She gestured over Nikki's form with an open hand. "Besides, you made a promise about the clothes."

It was true, but she'd only promised to try. Which she had. She put the pencil-thin jeans on with the dark blue blouse Krissy picked out because some rock star wore it when she performed at Madison Square Garden. Krissy had bought the concert on pay-per-view and freaked when she spotted the shirt at the mall.

"Why do I have to change? Who makes these rules? Why can't I just be me?" Nikki pleaded.

Krissy stepped behind Nikki and shoved her toward science class. "You're going to be you," she grunted. "Just you in amazing clothes. You *promised*, Nikki. Breaking a best friend promise is like a curse that plagues you for life."

"You're making that up," Nikki said.

"Am not. Check the internet."

Krissy: Her personal hero. Her personal bulldog. Her personal pain in the neck.

What wasn't to love about a best friend?

Raven stepped into the classroom, where a friendly smile greeted him. Dr. Richmond, science teacher extraordinaire. Blah, blah. Who cared?

At the doorway of the classroom, the redhead seemed reluctant to leave. *Okay, one thing I don't need is a lost puppy following me everywhere.* He flashed her a quick smile then looked away to concentrate on his reflection in the mirrored window. Oh, yeah. He looked good. Dark jeans, graphic T — with wings on the shoulder blades. *If they only knew.* And to really get the girls' hearts beating, he'd jelled and clumped his blond hair into long spikes around his face.

Though in the glass, his eyes seemed darker, a harsh reminder of the penalty for playing the game but tossing the rulebook. He swallowed past the lump. Would his eyes completely blacken one day? Would he wake one morning and find himself on the enemy's team? Chewing his lip, he dropped into a seat near the window and turned from the perfect reflection of himself.

Best not to linger on it.

Nikki Youngblood entered the room, and he silently gave thanks for an enjoyable assignment. Pretty, really pretty, but moving like she didn't know it. She and the science teacher greeted each other warmly as if friends. *Friends. What a human idea.* Sappy and sentimental. Shallow and stupid. Raven didn't need friends, he needed subjects. Minions. He bit his cheek to minimize the smirk toying with his mouth.

When she sat beside him and tossed her hair in the opposite direction, he looked over.

A devious grin materialized on her face. "I know you," she mouthed.

Her eyes were the color of a morning blaze. They narrowed

playfully and his heart did a flop. Okaaay, that was unexpected. He found himself not quite sure what to do with it or with the fact that his palms had gone sweaty; definitely a new sensation.

Minions. And possibly a girlfriend. One who actually smiled.

"Nikki." Dr. Richmond let the bifocals slide to the end of his nose. "Or are you going by Nicole this year?"

"Nikki's fine. The answer is electricity." Her eyes trailed back to Raven, whom Dr. Richmond had introduced at the beginning of class. Raven draped the desk like a hip-hop star. All the girls in the room seemed to be pining for him, sucking in their stomachs and pushing out their chests at his slightest glance in their direction. Pathetic. Okay, so she had to admit he was hot. He had the same chiseled perfection as Mace, but coupled with a troubled demeanor that made him that much more appealing. Appropriately, his hair was darker: still blond, but dirtier, almost brown.

She felt stronger today, and her world was under her control once again. But her eyes remained on the brooding next to her while she answered the teacher, searching for a sign, a clue, anything that might offer some explanation of these guys and why they made her world spin. "You see, electricity causes ionized particles in the air."

Raven's head whipped around and he shot her a confused look.

Busted! Apparently Mace wasn't the only one who'd tried that line. How often had these tall, beautiful golden boys tried to minimize the fact that tiny bits of lightning seemed to follow them — or, rather, radiate *from* them?

Satisfied, she smiled at him.

64

Looking a bit off his game, he blinked, midnight-blue eyes swimming with questions.

Oh, this was fuuuun. She winked and heard the snickers around the room, but she didn't care. Once again, she'd bested the enemy.

"Uh," Dr. Richmond interrupted. "Okay, that's a good explanation for lightning, but it doesn't really have anything to do with what I asked."

She batted innocent eyes at the teacher. What on earth had just happened to her? She wasn't this forward, this brazen. This … *Krissyish*. "Oh, I'm sorry. I must have misunderstood. Could you repeat the question?"

When class ended, Krissy barreled toward her. "Excuse me," she said in a stage whisper. "What was that?"

"What?" Nikki asked, all innocent and sweet, but in no mood to try to explain to Krissy. How could she put it into words?

"That little exchange between you and the Greek god over there." Krissy followed Nikki to the back of the room, where she dropped her textbook on the shelf.

Nikki rolled her eyes. "Nothing. I didn't even talk to him." Inside she was celebrating, reveling in a victory she had no hope of comprehending.

"Look." She poked a peach-polished fingernail into Nikki's shoulder, backing her into a corner. "I saw it. You were like blah, blah, blah *ionized electricity*. And you knew he was going to look at you. And he did." Krissy shook her head, squeezing her eyes shut. "And you *winked* at him. Don't even try to deny it, Ni — Ah!" Krissy hollered as powerful arms draped her shoulders.

"Nice off-the-cuff answer," Raven said.

Krissy's mouth gaped and she seemed to be frozen in place. Raven's arms hung on her like a letterman's jacket, his head tilted over her shoulder though a good foot above. Nikki marveled at his lack of respect for personal space. Head that close to Krissy's, they had to be breathing each other's exhales. Not that Krissy seemed to mind. In fact, she'd gone a lovely shade of russet, one that clashed with her soft peach lips and nails.

"Breathe, Krissy," Nikki whispered.

One giant breath in, and Krissy was off. "So, um, your name is Raven, right? That's cool. Seems like your hair would be black. You know, 'cause ravens are black." She tossed blonde curls and angled her head to look at him without moving an inch of the rest of her body. "I've never known anyone named Raven before. And I guess you have brothers? It's not like I was trying to find out or anything, I mean, it's a fairly small school so, when someone new comes ... But we're not like totally backward or anything. It's pretty cool here. So, your brothers, are they as, um, tall as you are?"

Raven's eyes fanned to Nikki. "Does she ever shut up?"

Nikki smiled. "She hasn't yet, but we're still hoping."

"Oh." Krissy flashed white teeth. "That's funny. I bet you guys play football. I didn't see any of your names on the list, but you have to, right? You're totally built for it."

His eyes widened.

"Did I just say you're totally built? I *meant* for football. Anyway, what're your brothers like? Now that I think of it, maybe you'd be more suited to baseball or something. You know, long and lean. Do you play baseball?"

Again, he directed the question to Nikki. "Which question should I answer first?"

"How about mine?" Nikki said.

Raven stiffened. "You never asked a question."

"Sure I did. You just weren't paying attention to how it was asked. What *else* besides electricity causes ionized particles to fill the air?"

He blanched, tensed, and any hint of a smile faded from his features.

Krissy panicked. "We should all have lunch together. That way Nikki and I can fill you in about the school and town and stuff. Lots of people are planning to go bowling. It's sort of a beginning-of-the-year tradition. You're going, right, Nikki?"

"No," Nikki said.

Krissy gasped. "Well, I'm sure Raven's going to go, right?"

He dropped his hands. "Whatever."

Krissy stood between Raven and Nikki, and Nikki was sure her friend could sense the sparks that flew freely. *She* could certainly sense them.

But this time she wouldn't get weak and wind up a gelatinous pool on the floor. Nikki'd thrown him off base with the ionized air comment, so she took the advantage and really examined the boy before her. Like with Mace, Raven's gaze drew her focus. His eyes were an unusual shade and tinged with trouble. They were eyes that hid secrets and maybe a fair portion of pain.

Just as Nikki was about to ask Raven to walk them to their next class, something flashed in the depths of those midnight eyes, distracting him from the banter. Though he didn't stir a muscle, she could tell his attention shifted elsewhere.

A strange sensation swept Nikki as she watched him. Time seemed to freeze as his body reacted to whatever had drawn his concentration. Moments later, she heard heated voices drifting from the teacher's desk. The words grew in intensity, but her focus remained on Raven, who remained statue still — he didn't even breathe. The thought *predator* suddenly careened into her mind. He looked like an animal getting ready to make a kill.

Nikki swallowed hard while prickly gooseflesh spread across her arms.

He wasn't human. And she wanted to get away.

Tearing her gaze from him, she glanced at Krissy, who'd quieted but didn't seem to notice any change in Raven.

Finally, Nikki turned to see what had caused him to react. Two guys were arguing by the desk at the front of the class: one was dressed in camouflage and looked like he'd just come in from deer hunting. Nikki remembered him from last year. Joey-something. As she tried to recall his last name, he reached under his jacket to the small of his back.

Nikki knew that posture. Her heart dropped. "No!" she screamed, flying to the front of the room as Dr. Richmond's face turned to horror and he stepped between the two boys. Joey shoved the portly teacher and Dr. Richmond tumbled backward, teetering beside the second boy.

The rest was a flash. First, the glint of steel passing camouflage clothing, a scream from somewhere, blade jutting forth, then Raven. He blocked her vision, moving in long, deft swift motions more graceful than any dancer she'd ever seen.

Nikki tried to close the distance to the knife-wielding Joey, but couldn't reach him in time to stop the blade's trajectory. That's when everything slowed. Almost to a halt.

Chapter
7

Raven shoved Joey down so hard his head cracked against the desk. He then turned and grabbed the blade in midair, and with his free hand snagged a falling Dr. Richmond. He leveled Richmond on his feet, let him go, and reached for the other fighter, who'd bolted for the door.

In six years of karate, numerous fighting tournaments, and watching martial arts documentaries with her father, Nikki'd never seen anyone move so quickly. It wasn't humanly possible to do what Raven had just done. Just like it wasn't *humanly* possible for Mace to appear on the back of a moving sport bike.

The entire time Raven repeatedly glanced over his shoulder at her — as if specifically making sure she was safe — and that both thrilled and terrified her.

Fear crept along her spine and settled in her neck, tightening the muscles and causing them to throb. Her fingers trembled. She raised them to eye level. When she mustered the nerve to look, she found what she'd feared: tiny sparks of electricity shot from one finger to the next. She clamped her hands into fists and prayed she wasn't losing her mind.

"So," Principal Schmidt said, directing her attention to Raven. She was using her perch on the corner of her desk to its full advantage. "You were right there but didn't see exactly what happened?"

Nikki's eyes narrowed. She liked Principal Schmidt ... usually. But the administrator had raked the boy over as soon as he entered the office. She supposed she could see why the principal had made such a quick judgment call about Raven. He definitely looked dangerous in his dark T-shirt, faded jeans that hung low on his narrow hips, and black boots only someone like him could carry off. But no matter his look, he'd quite possibly saved someone's life, maybe even that of Nikki's favorite teacher. She risked a peek at Dr. Richmond, who still looked as pale as the wall behind him.

She had to admit Raven carried himself with a little too much confidence, held his mouth in a slightly too crooked way, and stared you down in a bit too intimating a fashion. Even now, he was slumped in the chair as if the whole incident and follow-up were boring him to tears.

Schmidt's high-heeled foot tapped in frustration against her mahogany desk. Nikki understood authority and its importance in life, and tried her best to make up for Raven's deficiency. Right now, his only chance was if Dr. Richmond came to Raven's defense and let Schmidt know he was innocent. Nikki planned to stay out of it.

But as she watched the principal do her best to break him down, Nikki found it impossible to keep her mouth shut.

"Raven wasn't involved, if that's where you're headed. He was at the back of the room talking to me and Krissy. You can ask her if you like." Her tone matched her attitude, both drifting toward the defensive.

"I'll do that." Principal Schmidt's attention stayed on Nikki for a long time.

Nikki drew a deep breath and tried to explain again. But from the corner of her vision, she felt Raven's eyes on her, and a sense of appreciation — miniscule as it may be — seemed to drift from him to her. It was no big deal, but she had to wonder if he often found himself on the wrong end of the proverbial gun. And if it was a rare occasion for someone, anyone, to come to his defense. She cleared her throat. "We heard angry voices and turned. Both of us tried to get up there, but Raven's legs are longer than mine — I barely made it halfway. He shoved Joey and grabbed the knife as Joey went down." Nikki waited while the words sank in. But the principal's gaze traveled to Raven.

He lifted his hands, as if to say, "Told ya."

Schmidt shot a questioning glance to Dr. Richmond.

"It's true," he added, rising from his chair. "If Raven hadn't been there, who knows how this might have concluded." The apparent anguish over the entire situation showed on Richmond's face, deepening a frown in his forehead usually caused by intense thought. "Could have been bad." He shook his head. "Tragic, in fact."

Schmidt's posture relaxed as she spoke with the science teacher. "I'd appreciate your discretion in discussing this with anyone, Dr. Richmond. We don't want to cause a panic. I'll be making a complete statement at noon." She turned to Nikki. "As for you, Miss Youngblood, you've never been in trouble of any kind."

Nikki expelled a sharp breath. "I didn't have anything to do with this," she said, mindful being in the wrong place at the wrong time could create a guilty verdict, no matter the truth.

Richmond offered an apologetic smile to Nikki. On some deep level, she wondered if the geeky science teacher understood her. She was such a freak to most of the kids, and Krissy had unintentionally done a great job of reminding her of that before science class. *Here we are, a room full of freaks: the new good/bad boy, the black-belt artist, and the geekster science teacher. What a trio of misfits.* No wonder Schmidt was thrown off.

Schmidt stood. "I appreciate your cooperation," she said in Nikki and Richmond's direction, ignoring the large blond before her. "Still, I get the feeling you aren't telling me everything." And that's when her eyes fell to Raven.

Nikki fought the urge to look at him. But her heart was pounding. Did Schmidt *know* she was leaving vast holes in the story, like the fact that Raven had suddenly morphed into a predator with moves to rival Jason Bourne? And that her body had been sparking during the whole thing?

Schmidt tromped to the door. "I'll be keeping an eye on you," she said.

"Yes, Ma'am," both Nikki and Raven answered. Raven rolled his eyes.

"*Both* of you. If there's more to this story, I intend to find out."

If she only knew. As far as Nikki could tell, Raven and Mace — both clearly nonhuman beings — had protected her twice, Dr. Richmond once, and saved the guy ready to fight Joey from a knife wound. At the same time, she'd never had any trouble like this until they showed up. Since their uninvited arrival in her life, she'd been nearly killed twice. Were the new hotties good guys or bad guys? Too soon to tell, but she hoped she'd live long enough to learn the truth.

Schmidt called Richmond back into her office just as the trio exited.

Nikki cast a glance over her shoulder and watched Schmidt close the door. When she turned, midnight eyes were burning holes through her.

"I didn't need your help in there," he spat.

"You're welcome," she snapped back, her gaze locked with his.

Around them, the hall quieted as kids rushed into classrooms in the last seconds before the bell rang for third hour.

He clenched his teeth. "That wasn't a thank you."

She'd never actually seen anyone speak through gritted teeth before. It was fascinating. And if he was trying to intimidate her, the attempt failed miserably. His body radiated white hot, but Nikki found him more intriguing than terrifying. "Again, you're welcome."

Storms began to brew in that dark gaze, and she wasn't sure why she didn't find it scary. Blond spikes covered portions of his face, but though his teeth were clenched and his eyes had hardened to dark marbles, his lips remained soft. Maybe something only an artist would notice, but his full mouth was loose, no hint of tension. And that was even more interesting than his eyes.

He drew a long, slow breath, shoulders rising.

Nikki fought the urge to smile.

"I didn't need any backup in there, that's all I'm trying to say."

Get over yourself. "Oh, you didn't?"

He jerked his head forward. "No, I didn't."

"Well, I think you did. Schmidt was about to call the cops back and have them come and haul you away with Joey and the other guy, so whether you want to admit it or not — and from your know-it-all posture and self-serving attitude, I'm guessing not — I did you a favor. So you're welcome."

He loudly exhaled all the air he'd sucked into his lungs. "Fine."

"Fine," Nikki echoed, but found herself still fighting a goofy grin.

He must have noticed, because he cocked his head. "What now?"

"Sorry, it's just that you were so busy puffing out your man chest, I was afraid you might burst."

If it was possible, his eyes darkened even more and thinned to slits.

She swallowed.

Behind her, Dr. Richmond left the principal's office. He patted Nikki's shoulder as he walked by. "Don't worry. Everything is back to normal, now."

Normal? Not likely.

"Nikki, I want you to meet someone." Her dad stuck his head through the kitchen doorway and waved to her as she opened the front door.

She stepped in the house, dropped her backpack onto the couch, and ran a hand through a tangle of windblown hair. She pointed to the powder room — what her mom insisted on calling their downstairs bathroom. "Can I freshen up?"

Her dad shooed her. "Go on, but make it quick."

Before she reached the bathroom, a rumble of hearty laughter drifted to her. She paused, shrugged, and went to the mirror to inspect her wasp's nest of a mess. As she dragged a brush through the knots, laughter erupted from the kitchen again. As well as a deep male voice she didn't recognize. She cracked the door open and peered out. From her vantage point, the wall blocked all but a sliver of the dining room. Someone breezed past. Tall, dark hair, and jeans. A crisp white shirt, maybe expensive. And he called her mom Mary like he knew her — no, like he knew her really well.

Was this some distant cousin she'd never met? Not likely. The Youngbloods didn't have any family. The three musketeers. Or the three little pigs, depending on the day. Intrigue forced her to hurry and pull the brush one last time with such force, her head ached.

"There you are," her dad said.

She'd been right about the shirt. Linen, a material she recognized thanks to her mom corrupting her mind. Expensively cut and hugging his chest and shoulders. On closer inspection, his pants were what Krissy would call rock-star jeans: faded lines at the front pockets and calves, but dark everywhere else. He wore pointed leather shoes, or maybe boots, a kind she'd seen in Sax Fifth Avenue when her mom and dad took her shopping on a rare trip to New York. She kept thinking they might be called pixie boots, but what guy would wear something with the word *pixie* in it? Some kind of scaly animal-skin belt encircled his waist. He sported a deep tan, perfect brown-black hair, and a mega smile. And when she stepped up to meet him, sparkling black-diamond eyes locked on her. "So, this is Nikki."

Wow. Men like this lived in LA or New York or something. Not in the middle of nowhere Missouri. And there was something else about him, something that set her on edge, but his flashy smile, strong-but-yummy cologne, and the gold chain at his neck kept distracting her.

She reached her hand to shake his. "I'm at a disadvantage here," she said. "You know my name, but you haven't told me yours."

"Aren't you charming, Nicole? My name is Damon Vessler. I'm an old friend of your mom and dad. In fact, we work together."

Nikki frowned. Work together? Her mom and dad's deal was all their own.

"Sort of," her dad corrected. "Mr. Vessler purchases a lot of weapons from us. When we have surplus, he sails in and saves the day." He cleared his throat.

Nikki's gaze skated to her mom, who was struggling to portray absolute happiness about the unexpected company. "So, you sell antique weapons?" Nikki asked him.

Vessler smiled. "Some. But that's just one of my many interests. And I'm a hopeless romantic. I keep most of the weapons for myself. Once I fall in love with a piece, I'm incapable of turning it loose." Something protective flashed in the depths of his obsidian gaze, causing a tiny ripple across Nikki's stomach.

Her parents reacted too. She could feel their tension drifting on the lasagna-scented air. Nikki donned a perfect smile. "Are you staying for dinner?" Her eyes shifted from Vessler to her mom. Gotcha! Mom reacted just as Nikki thought—horror stricken. So, if her mom didn't like this guy, and her dad was visibly uncomfortable with this guy but trying so hard to be cheery and nice ... *Why is this guy in my house?*

"I'd love to stay for dinner, but unfortunately I'm headed to Nashville in a few hours. Some organization wants to honor me."

Humility was ugly when it was false. "Really, why?"

"It's for some humanitarian work I like to do."

Nikki nodded, waiting for more.

Vessler shrugged. "As I said, I have a lot of interests. I'm an inventor of sorts and apparently one of my pet projects has helped a magnitude of people in a third world country."

"What kinds of things do you invent?"

Again, she was being studied by eyes that said one thing but hinted at something far different. "Boring stuff, Nicole."

Her dad spoke up. "She might not find it boring. She's actually quite interested in science."

Vessler's eyes trailed to her dad and held for a few agonizing moments. "Your father is being far too kind. Trust me."

He headed for the front door with her dad in tow. Nikki stayed close on their heels. "It was nice to meet you, Mr. Vessler. I hope our paths cross again, as I'd like to know more about what you do." There was the slightest hint of a challenge in her words, and she wasn't even completely sure why. He'd been nice enough, but seemed too comfortable in a home not his own.

He turned and locked his gaze on her. "You'll be seeing more of me, I promise. Events of late have afforded me the opportunity to return to my first love."

The look in his eyes was searing, like he was branding her. "Your first love?" she uttered, and realized she'd taken a step back.

But all the tension disappeared with his captivating smile. "Yes, the beautiful Ozark Mountains. I do my best work right here."

And then he left.

She felt like she wanted to take a shower. But at the same time, he'd been so very attentive to her, treated her like an adult, an equal, and she couldn't help but like that about the guy. Her first impression was likely due to her suspicious nature. She really hoped she'd get another chance to talk to Damon Vessler again. He was a humanitarian, after all.

Mace sat down last at the dining room table. All three boys had dropped their backpacks by the front door and Vine was mumbling about homework. There'd be time for that later; right now they needed to get down to business. It was four thirty in the afternoon, and they had no guarantee Nikki was in for the night.

At least the heat was off him for a while. One day of school and Raven had landed in the principal's office. *You'd think Will would expect that by now.* Their guardian wasn't happy with his prodigal, and Mace had never been so happy to be ignored.

The massive table seemed to have shrunk, with Will taking up most of the space. Will was thick: thick muscles, thick arms, built to be a warrior and withstand the ages. Mace, Raven, and Vine were lean and sinewy like most Halflings. Mace didn't mind his slender form. He'd watched Will struggle with everything from finding clothes for his ginormous frame to fitting into cars. Through the years, Will had discovered the big and tall men's section of department stores. But for Mace, being leaner made it easier to pass for human. Something he planned to use to his advantage.

"I think Richmond's the target," Raven said, drawing Mace out of his thoughts.

"You think the three of you were sent here for Dr. Richmond rather than Nikki Youngblood?"

Mace's gaze narrowed on the darker Halfling sitting straight across from him. The motion wasn't lost on Raven, who countered with a scowl. Mace was often struck by how opposite they were: Raven was the contradiction of everything Mace believed in.

Raven's brow quirked.

Are you baiting me again? If he was trying to shift the focus of this journey from Nikki to Richmond just to play some stupid power game, Mace wouldn't fall for it.

Raven didn't like Nikki, Mace could tell, and that fact gave him a surprising bit of pleasure. He didn't want Raven to like Nikki. But he did want this supposed leader to do his job, and throwing out some ridiculous story about Richmond wasn't going to alter the plan. Not once a plan was formed, anyway.

Will spoke, directing his words to Raven, and redirecting the fireworks between the two boys. "The hounds were after Nikki."

Raven nodded a few times and actually seemed like he was thinking about the situation, the journey, the plan. "I don't think we're here about the girl. I think she's just one piece of the puzzle."

Mace stiffened. He didn't want Raven pulling their attention in another direction while Nikki was in mortal danger.

Vine pushed his long hair from his eyes. "Could it be about both of them?"

Everyone looked at him.

He rolled a gum wrapper between his fingers. "You know, could this journey have something to do with Nikki *and* Dr. Richmond? I saw them talking after school and, I don't know, they seemed pretty close."

"Your perception is solid." Will offered a nod of approval. "Good job, Vine. And good job as well, Raven. I'm surprised you picked up on a connection in the midst of such turmoil."

Raven didn't want a pat on the back, as was evidenced by his arms folding over his chest. He was frustrated at Will. And for once, Mace understood the frustration to some small degree. Will didn't offer much help in the way of handing the boys a map of each journey. What he knew stayed buried until they unearthed it for themselves or until heaven whispered for him to tell.

"Let's talk about what we know," Will said.

Raven tossed a hand into the air and let it crash against the table. "Why don't you start? After all, you're the one with the direct line. Straight communication. We're not allowed, remember?"

Will stood and planted massive hands flat on the table, only inches from where Raven's lay. His soft words contrasted the intimidating posture. "If you choose anger as your path, you will not hear the quiet voice. When heaven whispers, I hear. But I see through a dark glass. To utter the images and echoes that pass before my eyes would only muddy your path. Clarity is in faith. And despite your guise, faith is as attainable for you as the next breath."

Vine swallowed hard, choking on his gum. Will and Raven stared each other down as Vine coughed and hacked his gum into his hand.

Will didn't see everything, but a *hint* of a direction would be nice sometimes. Seeing through a dark glass was one thing. Stumbling in the dark was something else.

Raven didn't seem convinced. "Yeah, yeah, Master Yoda. Can we just move on?"

"Find your center, Raven. Sowing seeds of discord will neither move us closer to our goal nor help you become what you are destined to be in the age ahead," Will said.

"Destined to be in the age ahead? You know, sometimes I

get sick of living for the day ahead. Sometimes I just want to live for right now." Raven's words were clipped and filled with self loathing.

Enough so, Mace almost felt bad for him.

"As do all," Will agreed. "There is no crime in that. To feel that way is human. To act upon it is sin."

Raven's face twisted into a scowl, no doubt at being compared to humans.

"Do not despise your origin," Will said.

"Sorry, I'm an outcast of both the heavenly and the earthly realms, so it's a little difficult to *not* despise my origin. Oh, but you wouldn't know how that feels, would you?"

Mace's frustration grew. "Can we move past the narcissistic monologue and please get back on track? We were talking about Nikki and the importance of protecting her."

Raven's eyes slashed to him. "Ohhhhh. Somebody's crushing hard."

That was it. Mace jumped so fast his chair crashed to the floor. "What's the matter with you?" He moved across the table, jarring their cups and causing a thin vase to teeter on one edge.

Vine stared mouth agape, but when the vase tilted his hand shot out, lightning fast, and caught the top-heavy bouquet. When he removed his hand from the glass, a long string of gum kept him partially attached. "Eeeew!" Staring at his palm, he rose and headed toward the kitchen.

Will motioned for Mace to sit. "You seem to be full of energy, Mace. Why don't you tell us what's on your mind."

He pulled a breath and listened to the quiet ticking of the clock behind him. *I wish it didn't sound like it was ticking away the days of Nikki's life.* "I don't know, Will. She's no ordinary teenage girl. At least, I don't think she is."

"He's led a bit of a sheltered life," Raven said, cupping a hand around one side of his mouth and leaning toward Will.

Will gave him a warning glance.

Raven continued, unmoved. "She's definitely no normal teenage girl."

Vine returned to the table with an ice cube in his hand. "Why, Raven?" he asked, and his face slid into a deep, dimpled grin. "Because she didn't fall all over herself when you strutted into the school?"

Raven looked over at Vine with contempt, but Mace saw that, as always when it came to Vine, it was masked by just the tiniest hint of fondness. The kid was lucky Raven liked him.

"Honestly, Will. We know next to nothing about the girl." Mace cast a glance to Vine and frowned when a stream of water ran out of his hand. "Dude?"

Vine moved to show the melting ice in his palm. "I read today in *Woman's Home Journal* you could remove bits of gum with ice."

Raven chuckled. "Okay, there is so much wrong with that statement."

"I read it too," Will said. "The owners of the house left a stack of magazines in the pantry. That information was in one of them."

Will had rented the furnished home after finding it on the internet. Mace liked the variety of rooms and the tall ceilings in the two-story Victorian. Best of all, the living room was huge, big enough to leap from.

Mace rubbed his face with his hands.

Vine dropped into his seat. "It's not like I sat around all day at school reading women's magazines," he mumbled.

"Let's hope not," Raven interjected. "As if you don't stand out enough, you gotta draw attention to yourself."

"You should talk," Vine countered. "I saw you swagger down the hall trying to get all the girls to look at you."

"I don't have to try, little brother. They can't help themselves."

Mace's pulse pounded in his ears. "Can we please get back to the subject?"

"Yes," Will said, and the air changed. He sat for long moments while each of the boys waited. "Something is stirring."

The words put Mace's wings on alert. He dropped his hands from his face.

"Nikki Youngblood is at an art gallery."

"Is she in danger?" Mace stood, and both Vine and Raven were quick to follow his lead.

"Not yet, but she will be soon," Will confirmed. "I feel an ancient evil reaching out to her. In fact, I'm starting to wonder if the hounds weren't sent to kill her."

"What? That doesn't make any sense. Do you think they slipped through the midplane without instruction?" Mace asked.

"No. I think they were sent to torture her but not kill her."

Mace's gaze drifted from Will to Vine, then from Vine to Raven. The weight of Will's words cut a jagged line of harsh reality through the room, a menacing reminder what was on the line for the pretty brunette if they failed.

Even Raven's face drained of color. "There's only one thing I can think of that's worse than being killed by a pack of hell hounds."

"What?" Vine asked.

"Being left alive by a pack of hell hounds."

Chapter 8

Nikki's nerves jangled like too much change in a pocket while she listened to the gallery owner.

"Your trio of paintings are hanging in room number three. I call it the lavender room." While Nikki was wearing the outfit Krissy had picked out, she felt like a fashion victim next to Coleen Elgren, whose slick hair was scooped into a tight ponytail at her neck, perfectly complementing her smooth black pantsuit and matching stiletto heels. *How can the woman be dressed so simply, yet so elegantly, and why aren't her hands sweating like mine?*

Nikki jerked a quick nod and inconspicuously turned her palms outward, hoping to catch a breeze from the air conditioner.

Coleen placed a slender hand on her shoulder. "The first gallery showing is always the toughest. Don't worry. Your paintings are beautiful." She flashed a chemically whitened row of perfect teeth. "We may even get an offer to purchase one.

Earlier in the day, a very handsome, and — judging by his custom fit Italian suit, I'd say, very rich — man stood in the room staring at them for nearly an hour."

Several thoughts struck Nikki in quick succession. First, why would some wealthy Italian-suited guy stare at her paintings? Second, the color of lavender made her want to vomit. And third, there was nowhere to rub her hands! She couldn't even rake them down her thighs because she was afraid of leaving handprints on the new black dress.

Coleen meandered toward the front entrance, where a young man in a white tux held a tray of dainty glasses filled with some bubbly drink. A young woman to his left offered fancy cubed cheeses and delicate chocolate-dipped strawberries, each one a tiny work of art in its own right.

Where's Krissy? She was supposed to be here to hold my hand through this.

As if summoned by her wish, Krissy fluttered through the front door dressed in a forest-green wrap-around dress paired with a wide-wicked, cool silver bracelet Nikki'd never seen before.

She practically floated past the white tux guy and landed at Nikki's feet. Unable to contain her excitement, she bounced up and down — but oh, so gently — and squeezed Nikki's hands. "This is sooooo cool," she squealed. The smaller girl's curls bounced with each animated giggle.

Why couldn't Nikki just relax and enjoy the night? Why did she have to be a string of cord wound so tight it might burst from the pressure? Krissy's hand squeeze helped. She was right. It was cool.

"Neat bracelet," Nikki said.

"Thanks. My mom bought it from a street artist in San Francisco. I thought it was apropos since we're at an *art* gallery."

Nikki dropped her chin a degree. "Are you doing the 'take an obscure word to work' thing again?"

Krissy beamed and Nikki calmed. "Apropos is not an obscure word. It's utterly divine and I'm going to use it in conversation as much as humanly possible." Krissy's palms rubbed against Nikki's, drawing her attention to their hands. She must have noticed the sweat.

Nikki made her best "help me" face at her best friend.

"You're nervous?" Krissy asked.

Nikki nodded.

"How can you be nervous? You've fought in nationwide karate tournaments. This should be a piece of cake."

Krissy was right again. But karate tournaments were a completely different beast. Nikki blanched at the thought of suddenly raising her hands in a fighting stance and pounding her fists into midair while bouncing on her tiptoes. Uh, that probably wouldn't fly in art gallery central. Definitely not apropos. "This is completely different." She drew Krissy away from the crowd and along the wall beside a series of sculptures in bronze appropriately titled *A Series of Sculptures in Bronze.*

"How is it different?"

"First of all, at fighting tournaments, I get to … you know … fight. Fighting helps calm my nerves." *Oh dear, did I really just say that out loud?*

Krissy blinked.

How nice, her eyeballs match her dress. Nikki cocked her head. "You are the only friend I have who changes her eye color to match her clothes."

Krissy dropped her hands to her waist. "I'm the only friend you have period, and my eyes don't match my dress, they compliment it. See." She tilted her head into the can light illuminating one of the bronze statues. "The darker shade of the dress pulls the seafoam specks in my pupils, making them pop."

"The pupils are the black part. I think you mean the irises."

"Whatever."

"Technically, you mean the seafoam pigment in your contacts."

Krissy cast her eyes heavenward. "You make it sound so detached."

"Sorry."

"And you changed the subject. Why are you so nervous tonight? You love painting. It's a huge honor that the gallery wanted you."

Krissy didn't have to tell her what an honor it was. Artists sometimes waited their whole lives for such an invitation. But hanging her work on a wall for all to see and criticize was maybe the most difficult thing she'd ever done.

With Krissy's arrival, the tension had melted some. She guessed she'd have to add security blanket to her best friend's list of responsibilities. Nikki felt she could now consider entering the lavender room, or maybe even saunter over and snag a hunk of cheese.

But then Krissy's eyes turned to saucers and she drew a deep rib-shaking breath. Her pupils grew rounder and rounder until Nikki thought her eyes might pop right out of her head.

Nikki turned and glanced over her shoulder to see what had caused her friend to pale to ghost-white, then arc a rainbow of pink shades that could rival the blush section of the MAC counter.

"What are they doing here?" Krissy hissed.

The three tall, broad-shouldered guys strolled through the entrance, each one looking as comfortable in the art gallery as a butcher in a meat market. Even the young one with the long platinum hair oozed confidence, his light eyes scanning the walls of priceless treasures. In fact, all three sets of eyes were searching the surroundings. Nikki marveled at this, because they weren't inspecting the artwork, they were *probing the room*. The younger one scanned the right. Raven, hands sunk into his pockets, examined the left, and Mace searched right down the middle, his gaze landing here and there on different people as he went. And if she wasn't mistaken, they were *smelling* the room. It was subtle. If you weren't absorbing the whole scene, you wouldn't even notice. But now and then, one would tilt his nose and sniff.

Krissy had a death grip on Nikki's arm. "Oh, I want one," she said, and Nikki felt heat rise to her cheeks. In fact, the whole room was suddenly warmer. *I want one too.* The thought shocked her and the heat on her face rose to a scorch.

When Mace's cool ocean gaze landed on her, his forward momentum stopped.

She tried to swallow the ball of cotton in her throat, but it wouldn't go down. Nikki flushed. The prickly heat drained from her face, down her neck and shoulders, and onto her arms.

"Ouch," she heard from somewhere far off. It was Krissy. "Hey, you shocked me."

She knew she should answer or mumble an apology, but Nikki was lost in an ocean-blue world.

His eyes dropped contact for an instant while he nodded to the younger guy and said something to Raven. They walked away in opposite directions, leaving Mace to look at her.

Off to her right, Krissy followed the younger one deeper into the art gallery. Suddenly, in a room full of people, she and Mace were the only ones there. Such a warm, fuzzy feeling surrounded her in that moment, she couldn't remember what she'd been so nervous about.

His tongue darted out and moistened his lips as he strode to her.

Wham, wham, wham. Was that her heart or had someone tipped the series of bronze sculptures like dominos? *Don't just stare, dummy. Smile.*

Mercifully, he spoke. She wasn't able. "Hi."

She nodded and opened her mouth.

His lip curled in a devastating half grin. "I hope it's okay that we came tonight."

She nodded again, ever the brilliant conversationalist.

"Good. Who was the girl with you? Vine said he thought her name was Krissy."

"Yes." Finally a word. *Now, string a few more together and you won't be a complete dweeb.* "She's my best friend."

But Mace's concentration shifted to the front door where a handful of new people were coming in. He seemed to scan each one yet kept half his attention on her.

She frowned, weirded out by his strange behavior, his odd intensity. "Why exactly *did* you come tonight?"

He flashed an even row of pearly teeth. "We hardly know anyone in town, and since you and I met and sort of became friends..." He raised his open hands in a shrug.

Sort of became friends? "I called you a freak," she blurted, then clamped her hand over her mouth.

He reached to her wrist and removed her hand from her face.

She forced herself to move her eyes from his hand. "I'm sorry. I didn't mean that the other day. I'm grateful for what you did. You saved my life. Twice."

His mouth quirked and he released her hand. "Can we talk about something else?"

"Okay. This is my first art show and I'm really nervous. When I'm nervous I blurt things I shouldn't."

"Like right now?"

She bobbed her head.

"Where's your painting?"

She motioned with a limp hand behind her. "They are in the lavender room."

"They? More than one? That's really cool."

Her fingertips drummed the side of her dress. "Thanks."

"Are you happy with how they look? You know, placement in a gallery is extremely important."

"I haven't been in there yet."

"Are you kidding? Come on." He placed a hand at her waist and applied gentle pressure, coaxing her deeper into the gallery. The rush of remembrance surprised her, the electrifying hug in the barn revisited her flesh, and she was glad when she passed under an air vent offering a fractional amount of relief. He leaned closer as they passed through various rooms. "Don't take this personally, but the color lavender makes me want to puke."

She cast him a sideways glance. "I thought I was the only one." Once in the wretchedly painted room, she motioned to her paintings.

For several seconds he stared at them. "They're great," he said.

She had to admit, matted and framed in elegance and secured to the wall, they did look good. "I messed up on the last one and had to start over."

"I see your intention, though. The gate in the center, the

pots of flowers surrounding it. It's like an invitation. Really nice work, Nikki. You have a lot of talent."

Hmm. She hadn't thought of it as an invitation. She'd just been walking through town when she'd spotted the brightly colored flowers, and knew she couldn't fit the whole scene onto one canvas. "It's really not that special."

He turned to face her. "It is. It evokes emotion. It makes something happen inside when you look at it."

She swallowed hard. *He* evoked emotion. *He* made something happen inside when she looked at him. She really hoped her thoughts weren't as visible as they felt.

"Mace," someone said from the doorway. Raven nodded for him to come.

"Stay here," he said. "I'll be right back."

But his words had an authoritative ring to them, one she didn't appreciate. She sighed and turned to look at her pictures again. "Lavender's not so bad," she muttered.

Chapter 9

I found him," Vine said. "Dark-haired guy at the front door.
Where's Nikki?"

Mace's heart rate quickened. "She's in the back. There's no
way he could get to her." Mace scanned the guy, whose posture
seemed awfully calm for an attacker. "How do you know he's
after Nikki?"

"Gun," Vine said.

Mace drew a deep breath, and the ting of metal and gun-
powder filled his nose. "Good job, Vine. How long has he been
here?"

"A couple of minutes. He talked to the thin lady in the black
suit." Vine motioned back toward the door. "As you can see,
now he's looking for Nikki."

It was true. The thirtyish man's cold black eyes and fake
smile darted around the room.

But Mace, Raven, and Vine created an impenetrable wall

outside the lavender gallery. They could handle this easily, and hopefully the art patrons wouldn't have a clue.

"Nikki won't come out here, right?" Raven said, words teetering on panic.

"No, I told her to stay in the ba—" But even as he spoke, her scent entered his nose with such force, it kicked the whole operation into overdrive.

Nikki took Mace by the shoulder. "Hey, guys, Krissy wanted me to ask if you—"

He didn't look at her. His entire being was focused on the dark-haired guy, who began reaching inside his coat when Nikki entered the room. "He's going for his gun," Mace said. "Vine, go!"

The command was unnecessary; Vine was tackling the guy as Mace and Raven turned and tackled Nikki.

To their surprise, a black leather checkbook went sailing into the air as Vine dropped the guy to the floor.

Mace and Raven flew to their feet and hustled Nikki into the lavender room.

The next fifteen minutes passed in something of a blur. Coleen, with one sprig of hair rebelliously slashing her face, stood toe-to-toe with Nikki. In the flurry of words, there was something about "friend's childish pranks," "the man could press charges," "she didn't have a clue why he still wanted to buy Nikki's paintings," and so on. "Do you know the man they attacked?" Coleen snapped.

Nikki shook her head. "No. I didn't even see him."

Coleen smoothed her hair and straightened her posture. "I can't afford a lawsuit."

"I'm sorry. I'll make the boys leave. I don't really even know them that well. They're ... new at school."

Coleen's face softened. "When they arrived, I thought they were models. I even toyed with the idea of offering to sculpt one of them." She shook her head, an attempt to clear the runaway thought, no doubt. "I suggest you stay away from those boys. They are nothing but trouble."

Tell me about it, Nikki wanted to scream. "Did they happen to say why they tackled the guy?"

"They said he had a gun."

Cold swirled down Nikki's back. She thought she'd heard the younger one, Vine, say something about a gun.

Coleen hardened. "Don't even consider the thought they did the right thing. The man opened his coat wide and there was nothing there."

Nikki nodded. But she knew guns were most inconspicuous in the back of a belt.

She chewed on the incident for the next hour while people meandered in and out of the lavender room. She'd become its occupant, too mortified to leave. Krissy left for home hours ago, leaving just her, three paintings of a gate and flowers, a lavender room, and a string of art aficionados who tried to ignore her, but whose stares she felt nonetheless.

When the hair prickled on the back of her neck, she knew someone was close.

He breathed a hot puff of air along her spine, and she jumped.

Raven grinned. "Nice paintings."

Nikki threw a look to the doorway. "What are you doing here? I thought Coleen threw you out!"

94

His eyes drifted over her. "She did. I came in through the back."

Her nerves were all jittery. "Well, just slip right back out, because my art career is over if she catches you."

Raven was staring at her shoulder. He slipped his index finger along the dress strap and she felt the material unwind.

He flashed a beaming smile. "Sorry. You were twisted."

Her hands fisted at her sides. "You're the one who's twisted. Leave."

"No," he countered, and tiny dimples appeared on his cheeks.

Nikki's gaze drifted to the doorway. "Did that guy really have a gun?"

"Yup."

"Where is he now?"

"We watched him leave a few hours ago. Don't worry, Nikki, you're safe with me." He reached for her strap again.

She leaned away from his touch. "I highly doubt that." Did he have to stand so close? Touch so much?

He flashed a devastating look. "Maybe not *completely* safe."

"I've been warned about guys like you."

He moved closer, appearing to pull her exhale into his lungs. His eyes dilated for an instant and his body seemed to go limp. But a second later, he was back to normal. "You've never known a guy like me."

"Well, I don't think I've missed out on anything," she said, feeling a puff of pride.

"You are one cold female." His eyes left her and fell to her paintings. "I only came back to tell you what I think of your artwork."

"Can't wait. And after you tell me, promise you'll leave."

"I promise, even if you beg me to stay."

"That's highly improbable."

He gave the pictures a fleeting glance. "You didn't draw these because you liked the flowers or the gate."

"Oh, really?" She crossed her arms over her chest. *He's already blown it. That was exactly why I chose the subject matter.*

"Really." He pointed to the painting in the center. "It was the crack in the pot."

Nikki's smug smile disappeared.

His finger traced along the blemish. "Yeah, all that life, destined to drain into the pavement. Pretty and colorful on top, but broken and useless if moved." He angled to face her and Nikki found herself turning to face him as well. "You don't even see yourself as a real artist."

She dragged her lower lip into her mouth and bit down. It was true, she didn't.

"You think you're a fraud, just copying what someone else created." He exhaled right into her face.

Rather than feeling violated by the hot breath, she realized she was savoring it.

"I like your painting," he whispered. "I like things that show the reality of life. And death." Raven stepped away, and there seemed a cold void where he'd been.

"Wait!" she said, before she could stop herself.

Facing away from her, he paused, his shoulders dropping a degree with her words. His head turned slowly, giving her a view of his striking profile. "Can't. I have a promise to keep." He disappeared through the back door.

With a head shake, Nikki ran after him into the largest gallery room. He was gone.

"Botched. That's the only word to describe this stupid mission. Completely, utterly, absolutely botched." Vine collapsed into his seat.

Raven leaned back, balancing on two legs of the dining room chair. "That's four words."

Vine's hand raked through his long hair. "Man, I felt like a complete idiot."

"A complete, utter, absolute idiot?"

Vine glared at him across the table.

"Enough!" Will's abruptness caught them both off guard. "You jumped too quickly, that's all."

Mace had remained quiet, lost in a sea of his own battles. Did they jump too quickly? All three smelled the gun, but a gun didn't mean an attack. In Missouri a lot of people carried guns. But it was the smooth, cold, snakelike look on the man's face that even now caused Mace's blood to chill. Everything about that guy was wrong. He was too cool, too callous. And Mace would swear he smelled the spirit of murder around him. *How many times can we mess up?* How many mistakes until ... "Are we going to be pulled out of this journey, Will? Is the Throne going to look down and say, *Hey, losers, why I don't I send someone capable of not looking like a —* "

Raven dropped forward. "Like a complete, utter, absolute idiot?"

Will shot a warning look in Raven's direction, then turned to Mace while tension mounted around the table. "The Throne doesn't give you a mission, then jerk the rug out when you make a mistake. That's not the structure of the kingdom. We make mistakes. And we move on."

Raven's mouth jerked. "You should know."

Will's jaw remained set, but his eyes flashed sadness. "We all have things we'd like to change. But that cannot keep us from moving ahead."

Raven was sick of the fatherly advice — Mace could see it in his contemptuous glare. At least the three of them wouldn't be removed from the mission. Mace's mind raced; maybe he could repair the damage. "Nikki Youngblood won't ever want to speak to us again. That's going to make it kind of difficult to protect her."

Will nodded, thoughtful for a moment. "I believe you underestimate Miss Youngblood. You've lost some ground with her, but in Nikki's heart I think she knows she's in danger. And if what we think we know of her is true, she's a girl with an eye for survival. That could work to your advantage."

Mace wished the words soothed the barbed wire in his stomach.

Vine opened a bag and offered a piece of red licorice to Raven, who scowled and shoved it away.

Will spoke. "Raven, are you displeased with this journey?"

He laughed without humor. "So what if I am? Like it matters. Like I have a choice. I'm the product of two beings who were never created to be together and I've inherited the worst of both species. This journey is the least of my worries."

The bag slipped from Vine's fingers and fell to the table. "I think we've inherited the best of both species."

"You are a Halfling, as were your parents before you. A man who hates half of himself hates all of himself," Will warned.

"See, that's just the problem. I'm not a man. Exactly. But I'm not an angel either. Trapped halfway between, where do I fit? Oh, yeah. *Nowhere*."

Mace watched the exchange with pounding aggravation. He was tired of Raven's eternal "It's not fair" spiel. He'd rather focus on the girl. The look of shock and disappointment on her face after he and Raven tackled and sheltered her from the *dangerous checkbook*. Even if Nikki forgave them, she'd never trust them. She would be scared to come anywhere near them. But then a familiar scent — so faint he barely noticed — trickled into his nose. Will was right about Nikki. She truly was a girl with an eye for survival — she just wanted to approach it on her own terms.

"We're all in a war," Will said.

"Not the humans," Raven countered.

"Especially the humans. They're at a huge disadvantage, not being born with eyes to see the spiritual battle. Yet they still must choose a side. And it's their faith alone that equips them to make that choice."

"I hate humans," Raven mumbled. Not one being at the table believed that. What Raven hated was himself. Mace wouldn't be surprised if Raven didn't secretly wish he was human.

"You have a destiny, Raven. That's all one can ask. Man or angel." Will narrowed his gaze on him. "Or Halfling." As the tension drained from the room, the muscles in Will's giant shoulders relaxed.

The scent was intensified and with it Mace's heart rate. He wondered why the others hadn't clued in. Suddenly, Raven's eyes met his and held, and a thin smile appeared on Raven's face before he closed his eyes and drew on the scent, deeply dragging her smell into himself.

Irritation zinged through Mace.

"Now, let's talk about what we've learned. Who wants to start us off?"

"I do." The feminine voice came from the dining room doorway. Standing with her back straight and her fingers jittering nervously, stood Nikki, now clad in her typical jeans and T. Beyond her, the front door hung open.

Will's mouth dropped.

Vine pointed. "How'd she — ? How?"

They'd *all* underestimated Miss Youngblood. She was tenacious, Mace decided. Good. Tenacity he could use to keep her alive. Though she was gutsy, barging into their house like this. What was strange, only he and Raven sensed her. Perhaps Uncle Will had been too involved to notice, and Vine, well, was still a newbie.

Mace knew that few things ruffled Will's feathers. Literally. But this girl had Will's pinions on high alert. Recovering quickly from the surprise, Will donned a practiced smile. "Excuse me, dear. You must have the wrong house."

She pointed to the door behind her, long hair flowing as she gestured. "Oh, I'm sorry. I thought this was the house where *angels* live."

Will rose slowly. He maneuvered around the table and came to rest less than a foot from Nikki.

She visibly shrank, dwarfed by Will's giant stature and his intimidating stare. Her head tipped back to look up at him, and when she swallowed it was clear she'd begun to rethink her head-on strategy. She started to step back, but stopped herself. Or something stopped her. Fingernails clicked her apprehension.

"What is this talk of angels?" he asked, and threw a glance to the boys, his clear-blue eyes lingering on Mace and Raven.

"That's what you are," she said, voice weak. "If I've figured right. You're guardian angels."

Raven snickered.

Vine frowned.

"They saved my life when those wolf things chased me, and he called me a daughter of man," she said, pointing to Mace.

Will gave him an accusatory look.

Now, telling her that seemed a silly, melodramatic thing to do. But she was so beautiful lying there on a blanket of forest-green grass. His heart had bumped strangely, even then. In the moments he first looked at her, he knew he felt something for Nikki. In fact, his first words to her, *daughter of man*, were a warning to himself, emphasizing who she was and all he couldn't have. He offered Will a sheepish shrug.

"I'm not an idiot," she continued. Raising a finger, she poked Will in the chest.

He scowled.

She poked harder. Then again.

Vine laughed aloud but was quickly quelled by the turn of Will's head.

Another poke.

"What are you doing?" Will asked her.

"Seems like angels would be made of mist or something. You know, I didn't think I could feel you … Of course, that doesn't make sense, because I certainly felt Mace in the woods and again on the back of my bike. Oh, and again when I was body slammed in the art gallery. I guess my brain is having a difficult time marrying all the pieces of this monumental puzzle." Her open hand patted his chest. "You certainly seem real enough."

"Do you know a lot about angels?" Will asked, now calm and cool.

"Not really." Her head tilted back and forth. "I guess as

much as the next person. There are cherubs, those cute little flying babies with wings that don't seem big enough to carry them, and—"

Raven's laughter from the table stopped her. Mace rubbed an open hand over his face.

"What?" she asked.

"Cherubs? Do you know anything about spiritual matters, young lady? Have you even read the Bible?" Will's tone lowered to condescension.

Her eyes widened. "The whole thing? Isn't it two-thousand pages long?"

"Have you read *any* of it?"

"No. I'm a realist."

Will threw his head back and laughed. "Of course you are. And that's the reason you barged into my home to announce angels live here."

She frowned, obviously offended by the remark. But the giant stared her down.

After a long time she shrugged. "Okay, I'll admit I don't really know much about the Bible."

Will gestured to Vine, who stood from the table and retrieved the giant black leather book from the fireplace mantle.

Nikki followed Will to the table, where he thumbed through soft pages and then pointed down.

She read. "Oh, I guess cherubs aren't babies after all."

"No, miss. In fact, Lucifer himself was known in the courts of heaven as the anointed cherub."

Mace watched the blood drain from Nikki's face. She sucked a breath. "You're Lucifer."

A storm swirled in his gaze. "I. Am. Not. Lucifer." His heated voice matched his glare. "And you will *not* utter that again."

"Yes, sir." She looked at Mace for support.

He couldn't help but wonder what she must be thinking right now. Her arrival either jeopardized the mission or was just the break they needed. Nikki was a fighter. If someone — or something — wanted her dead, she'd be smart. She'd accept the fact that half angel beings had her back.

As the two of them gazed at one another, her features softened. "You're all *angels*, though. God's messengers ... right?"

"Mace is no angel. Though angels do exist," Will said.

Thanks, Will!

Her eyes narrowed. "I would assume one of *God's* angels couldn't lie?"

"An angel would not lie," Will said.

"Good," she said. "Then tell me what a Halfling is."

Chapter
10

Mace placed a hand at the small of Nikki's back. Through her T-shirt she felt heat radiating where he touched her. Once on the back porch he gestured in an arc toward a variety of seating possibilities. She chose the porch swing in the hopes that he'd sit beside her.

He did.

"Are the others coming out?" she asked.

"No." He set the swing into motion while the inhabitants of the backyard — squirrels, birds, and different types of bugs — began their evening rituals of sight and sound while a million questions bombarded her mind that all seemed wrapped in one horrific truth.

Something terrible awaited her. Though the three guys and that monster of a man she met inside the house were strange to say the least, there was a bizarre sense of security, an over-whelming feeling of shelter around them. Even Raven, though he was far from safe. In contrast to his ice-cold persona at school, he'd stood white hot at the gallery — in what she was beginning to see as true Raven fashion — too close, too bold, and way too potent. Stealing the air she breathed and touching her bare shoulders without invitation — there was no sense of boundaries with him. That alone was a dangerous thing.

When her thoughts returned to Mace, the warm angel beside her, she sighed.

The sun hung low, pressing against a hillside across the valley. Its softening light cast muted colors along the wide expanse of Missouri sky. Pastel shades shifted from pinks and oranges to more dramatic purples and blues, melting together like some great, living, giant piece of artwork.

"It is," Mace said.

Her head snapped to him. "I didn't say anything." She inched away. "Do you read minds?" *Oh, that could be very bad.*

"No." He cast a faint smile at her. "Not really. But once in a great while, if I really tune in, I can pick up a thought or two."

"So" — she stretched out the word — "you were tuned in to me?"

He angled to look at her fully. His gaze trailed her face, setting the skin on fire.

Such intensity hovered in those blue-green oceans, she fought the urge to look away. No wonder he was so perfect. No wonder his skin radiated like sunbeams trapped in flesh. No wonder she was so … so deliciously drawn to him. He was an *angel*. But she wasn't drawn to Vine. And she certainly wasn't drawn to Raven. Okay, there was a tiny part of her, and she wasn't sure how powerful that part was, that was irrationally drawn to the bad boy.

"Yes," he whispered, and she realized he'd been studying her face as well. "I tuned in to you."

She pulled in her bottom lip and bit down.

His eyes dropped to her mouth and lingered. "I'm really sorry about all the trouble we've caused you. We're only here to help. I hope you believe that. If you listen with your heart, you'll know we don't mean you harm."

"Listen with my heart?" she echoed.

His brows drew together for an instant. "Yes. Listen with your heart."

Her fingers threaded together on her lap. She wasn't a girl who ran around going after every whim of her heart. In fact, she'd trained herself not to follow that unreliable path and instead listen to her *mind*. Always. Even when drawing, she studied the subject, then meticulously brought it to life on the canvas. And her paintings were nearly photo-quality images of what she saw. What she saw with her *mind*. If she got her heart involved, who knew, the artwork could end up looking like Picasso. *No, thanks.*

She couldn't contain the words anymore. "I know you're an angel," she sputtered.

The muscles in his face hardened like she'd smacked him. "No, Nikki. I'm not."

She rolled her eyes on the exhale. "Stop trying to dissuade me."

A tight muscle flexed and released as he clenched his jaw, casting a shadow along his smooth neck.

She ran a hand through her hair. "You guys are beautiful. Look, I'm an artist, so I study people. I've never seen more aesthetic faces."

"You're an artist," he said and his mind seemed to trail somewhere far away.

"Yes. You already knew that. Remember? Art gallery?" She pointed to the silver dollar–sized spot on her forearm.

He grabbed her arm. "What happened?"

"Nothing." But inside her nerves jumped at his sudden interest. "It's just a rug burn from hitting the carpet. My arm sort of got sandwiched between you and the floor."

He carefully placed her arm across his lap and gently rubbed his fingertips around the wound. "I hurt you. I'm so sorry."

She should say something, but the velvet feel of his hands trickling over her skin stopped the words.

His head bent, and he lifted her arm to his lips and dropped a kiss beside the wound.

Well now.

Nikki faced forward as he released her. She tried to give her attention to the surroundings, but everything around dulled to black and white and Mace was the only color. Too much color! Too much that didn't make sense about all of this . . .

Listen to your mind, not your heart. "This can't be real."

He offered a noncommittal lift of his brow.

"I mean, I know it's real. I know we're sitting here. But I grew up believing in the things that were scientific, concrete." Still nothing from Mace: she was pretty sure he was giving her time to wrap her mind around it. "So, it just has to make sense scientifically, that's all," she said, half statement, half question. Nikki tapped her cheek while she scanned her memory for anything able to help connect the dots. "Okay, let's think about the rainforest. Scientists are always finding new species of insect in the rainforest, right?"

"Uh, if you say so."

She gave him a fleeting glance and wondered if he was holding back a smile. "They are always finding new bugs. So, that's it."

"Are you suggesting I'm an insect you've discovered?"

She fought the eye roll. "No. But those bugs didn't just

107

appear one day — they'd been there a long time, but no one had discovered them. You've been here all along, but you just hadn't been discovered yet. And now that I've discovered you … well, it makes all this make sense."

His eyes twinkled with amusement. "That really makes you feel better?"

No, it didn't.

"Let me get this straight. You've discovered a new species of insect." He leaned slightly closer. "That would be me. And you're gonna name it what? I'd go with *Angelicus Protecti*."

"I can handle it if it's supported by science."

"What about having faith, believing in something you can't see or label or name?"

"I believe in science." She'd never known how final, how closed those words sounded. Science was all about discovery, ideas, hunches. Yet, right now it was both her crutch and her lifeline. "Sorry if you don't like it. That's just how I am."

"Nikki, were you drawing before we found you in the woods?"

The total subject change surprised her, and it took a moment for her mind to catch up. She'd expected him to argue and try to sway her, not change gears. She found herself a little disappointed. "Um, in the woods, yes," she said. What else could she say? *I was drawing, and, by the way, your presence in my life is making me question everything I've ever known. Beautiful sunset, isn't it?*

He set the swing into motion. "Maybe you're a Seer."

"A what?"

"Someone who sees things." His brow furrowed in thought. "A Seer sees into the realm of the supernatural. It's kind of like being able to look through walls, only the walls are the dividing lines between realms."

Well, that makes it clear as mud.

"For instance, a person can't see an angel's wings unless they are able to look at them in the Spirit — unless they are able to look at them through the heavenly realm. If you're a Seer," he went on, "you might not be in as much danger as we first thought. Maybe Raven was right. You aren't who we're here to protect."

"If I was a Seer, wouldn't I know it?"

"Not until you embrace it."

"Whoa, whoa." She made the time-out sign with her hands and forearm. "Did you say angel *wings*?" Of course angels would have wings. That made sense. But Mace, Raven, and Vine didn't have them … Her head hurt.

He gave her a cautious look, as if he were afraid she'd lose her mind soon. "As I was saying, maybe we're not here to protect you. Maybe you just keep stumbling into the line of fire. In fact, I hope that's the case."

That rush of cold again, like tiny claws scraping from her scalp down her neck and back. "Why?"

"Because if you're the one we were sent to protect, the enemy has targeted you."

What's a girl to say to that? She tried to take it in. "So, it's good to be a Seer?" *Please, please give me some glimmer of hope. I'm drowning here.* Then she remembered his earlier words. "Wait, did you say I see the supernatural realm?"

He gestured, encompassing everything. "Around us, around this natural earth, another realm exists. Not only does it exist, but it's in constant motion. Things that happen here are affected there. It is written that 'Whatever you bind on earth will be bound in heaven, and whatever you loose on earth will be loosed in heaven.' It's not talking about the *place* of heaven.

It's talking about the heavenly realm. The supernatural realm. We call it the midplane."

"Uh huh."

Frustration furrowed his smooth brow. "You believe a house full of angels live here, but you don't believe there is a realm from which they come?"

She pressed her hands to her eyes. "Okay, sorry. I just ... This all weirds me out a little."

"Nikki, this is the real world. You can pretend it doesn't exist — most people do — but it doesn't alter the truth. You saw the hell hounds in the forest."

Her eyes widened. "Hell hounds? That's what those things were? *Hell* hounds?"

He nodded.

Nikki ran her fingers through her hair as she shook her head. "No, that's what *you* think they are. I didn't grow up believing in stories about hell hounds and some misty realm we can't see."

"Mist? The same mist you thought angels were made of?" he asked.

She released a tiny smile. "I see your point. But somehow this conversation turned to me, and I want to know about you. Mace, you're an angel. Just admit it."

An unexpected veil of sadness hooded his features. "There are two classes of angels: heavenly and fallen. The fallen are one-third of the angels, those who were cast from heaven with Lucifer."

"So, you're a *heavenly* angel?" she asked.

"No."

She swallowed, and a big part of her wanted to clamp her hands over her ears and beg him to stop. Instead, she pulled a deep, calming breath.

"Heaven's angels are mighty warriors who battle evil continually, not guys like me who end up attending high school. They're massive in stature, precise in purpose, and driven beyond human understanding. They're perfectly fashioned weapons who don't know defeat. A heavenly angel can never retreat and carries the scars of many battles." He looked away. "I'm no angel. I have no right to enter the great hall of the chosen, where the martyrs rest beside warriors. I've no place in that kingdom."

Her internal alarm began ringing. Two classes of angels. And he wasn't in the first class, which left the fallen class. Whether she believed in all this stuff or not, having a house full of fallen angels trailing her couldn't possibly be a good thing. As she was about to confront him head on, however, she looked into his eyes and saw ... purity. And that purity just didn't fit with the whole follower-of-Lucifer thing. "I can't believe you're a fallen angel. I *don't* believe it."

"I'm not." He laughed, but there was no humor in it. "I don't fit there either. That's why we call ourselves Lost Boys."

"When I walked in, I heard Will say *Halflings*."

"Both terms mean the same thing. We're the offspring of fallen angels and human women. Our ancestors were of the fallen."

She shook her head, relieved. "But that's not bad. So angels fell in love with humans. Is that so wrong?"

Mace went rigid. "They didn't fall in love. They were sent for an evil purpose. Yes, they saw that the daughters of men were beautiful, but there was no love involved. Lucifer planned to mar the bloodline — if fallen angelic blood mixed throughout the entire world's population, there would be no way for God to fulfill his promise through a purely human vessel."

"So, Lucifer tried to *trick God*?"

"Yes," Mace said.

Nikki stared at the appearing stars — at whatever was supposedly up there. "This is a lot to absorb."

"It's too much to absorb, actually. Come on," he said, and gently began to tug her to her feet. "You've learned enough for tonight."

She wouldn't budge that easily. Nikki dug her heels into the porch floor. "I want to know more."

"And I said, you know enough for tonight."

She pulled from his grasp and crossed her arms defiantly. "I'm not leaving."

"It's gonna get lonely out here."

Nikki huffed and decided to try a new approach. She gazed up at him. "Pleeeeease?" She batted her eyes as insurance.

Mace's resolve crumbled and he sank onto the swing. "One more question, then we're done."

"Why would the enemy — whoever that is — have me as a target? And how did you get here? And what about your parents? Are they like you?" she asked.

"That's way more than one question, though I can actually answer the last two. My parents are both Halflings. But I don't know them."

"What?" There was no hiding the sadness in her tone.

"Nikki, try to understand. I belong *nowhere*. Halflings can't stay with their parents because it's too dangerous, so we're snatched at birth for our own protection. I'm bound to earth, yet an outsider to it. I'm the universe's orphan."

"So that's why you're called Lost Boys?" Her eyes turned to liquid as she recalled Peter Pan and the tale of boys with no homes, no families. Her least-favorite part of the book had always been when Peter returned to his house and found the window locked. "What will happen to you?"

His muscles tensed. "I try to not think about it."

But she'd think about it. Probably for the rest of her life. It seemed as if an unkind world — much larger than the one she knew — swallowed her. A place of pain where innocent boys were snatched from their parents and paid penance for sins not of their own making. "Mace, I want to help you," Nikki said, finally beginning to understand the storm of emotion that continually churned in his gaze. This wasn't "Will I make the football team?" drama.

"You can help by cooperating. If we've been sent to protect you, it means the Throne has plans for you."

"The Throne?"

He nodded. "The One we serve. The Creator of all things."

Everything in her sphere of vision started to darken from the outer edges, working in. "And he has plans for me?"

A hint of a smile touched Mace's face. "He has plans for all those he created. But many never choose to walk the path laid before them."

"Well, I don't choose it. Last week I was a normal teenager. And suddenly I'm being hunted by dogs from one realm and angels from another and supposed to *embrace* it? No." Her voice rose. "No, I don't want to be in the middle of your war."

Mace's posture softened. "Everyone is in the middle of this war, Nikki. Humans, Halflings, and angels — both fallen and heavenly. You've ignored the battle for seventeen years, but something on the inside of you knows my words are true. You're in a war and it's time to choose a side. If you don't, a side is chosen for you."

All the air left her lungs. She slumped against the support of the porch swing, letting the slats press into her back. So much for solid ground. So much for firm foundations and photo-quality paintings. "Welcome to hell," she muttered.

"Uh, actually, hell is way, *way* worse than anything this realm can offer."

Her mouth dropped open and she cast a long look at him. "Please refrain from any more details."

"I tried to tell you you'd learned enough for one night." Mace scooted closer so that her arm and his were touching.

The contact created a slow river of calm that slid through her as if the weight of several worlds hadn't been dumped on her narrow shoulders. The sky was nearly dark now, so she tried to make out the hillside across the meadow from where they sat. Instead of helping ease her mind, the darkness made the world feel both larger and smaller to her. When a breeze drifted by, she shivered.

Mace pressed closer, creating more contact between their sides. His thigh shifted to touch hers. How could she feel so chaotic and yet so peaceful? Sitting on the porch swing, gently sliding forward and back with the most unusual being she'd ever met, Nikki made a decision. "If I'm in a war, then I want to help you. You, Mace. How can I help you feel like you belong somewhere?"

He'd tilted his head to look at her, and the look he gave — one of such appreciation and admiration — nearly destroyed her. Her hand was warm. She glanced down and realized their fingers had intertwined. A heartbeat thundered in her head when Mace's eyes dropped to her mouth. Was he going to kiss her?

But an instant later, he pulled away. "You can't help me. I'm beyond redemption." His words dropped like lead weights onto glass, shattering the moment.

This was eternity drama. "But if there's no redemption for you, that means you're fighting a war for someone who rejects you."

"I fight for what's right, Nikki. The enemy we battle has an insatiable appetite and, unfortunately, he loves to feed on humans. Let me give you an example. Do you know much about the Holocaust or about Hitler?"

"Not much." She called on memories from history class. "Hitler was trying to create a race of super humans, an Aryan nation. Blond hair." She gasped. "Blue eyes." Like Mace, Raven, and Vine. Though Mace's and Raven's could be considered almost brown. Still, they fit the Hitler specifications.

"Not create, exactly. Hitler was searching for Halflings. He wanted to build an unstoppable army of half humans, and even used genetic testing. To this day Halflings are hunted by demons and men willfully given over to the enemy."

"That's why you aren't left with your parents?"

"Each of us must be accounted for. A caretaker looks after us, usually in groups of three Lost Boys. The caretaker can protect us better than our parents would."

"Why can't your parents protect you if they are both half angels?"

"It's hard to explain, but they would be mercilessly hunted if a child were left with them. Whereas Will has a direct line to heavenly communication — something Halflings don't have — and he's battled the enemy for Millennia."

"Why?" Her gaze flittered to the back door. "What *is* Will?"

Mace's gaze darted back to the house, then to the ground before returning to her eyes. "A heavenly angel. Though caring for us isn't a glamorous assignment."

"What do you mean?" she said, still trying to unify words like *half angel* and *the Holocaust*.

"I'll explain, but he can't know I told you. Will once held a high position in heaven's army. He was a general with a multitude of angelic warriors beneath him. But … he was demoted."

"What did he do?"

There was a moment's pause before Mace answered. "He murdered a human."

Nikki popped up from the seat, body tensing. "On purpose?"

"Uh, yeah, I think that's why they call it murder." She stared down at him. *There's a human-killing angel warrior inside, who isn't exactly fond of me at the moment, and that's all you can say?* Mace's mouth quirked a little. "Maybe you can ask him about it sometime."

She pulled a breath. Then another. And a third. "Okay, okay, so three Lost Boys to one caretaker and you fight for what's … *right*. Where do the assignments come from? Are you a prisoner or do you freely choose?"

"Each of us must choose on which side he'll fight."

"Are there Halflings fighting on the enemy's side?" Nikki asked.

"None that I know of. From birth we're told what we are. Our place in the universe, or lack thereof."

She shook her head. "I'm sorry, Mace. But God doesn't sound very nice. This sounds like a really crappy deal."

His body became rigid. "We aren't his seed. But he allows us the privilege to war on his behalf. There is no greater honor in heaven or earth. Our journeys, or assignments, come directly from the Throne. And we're exceedingly glad he's taken us in."

"You *want* to fight?" she whispered.

"I'm a warrior, Nikki. This is my purpose. So don't feel bad for me."

"Sorry," she muttered. *Note to self: Don't bash God.* In fact, she needed to be careful about bashing this whole unfair situation. It seemed as though Mace had every obstacle thrown at him, and likely no reward at the end of his journey, he served the Throne faithfully and apparently worked hard to protect humans. No wonder he was so serious: in his line of work, people's lives were on the line. A thought occurred to her. "You all have different shades of blue eyes."

He nodded.

"Are all Halflings like that?"

"All that I've seen. But I've never seen a female. It's possible their eyes are different."

"Are there no female Halflings?" She caught herself. "Wait, that's a stupid question. You said both your parents were Halflings."

He smiled. "There are a few females, but since the male determines the sex of the child, and our male ancestors were angels, and all angels are male, we're less likely to encounter females."

All angels are male? Okaaaay. That truth killed another of her assumptions. No flying baby cherubs and no females. *Check.* Her eyes blinked back a strange static sensation while unearthly particles seemed to gather, dragging her attention back to the sky. The air surrounding the porch became electric, causing her exposed skin to crawl as if a thousand ants scurried beneath the surface. Her heart rate increased to — what felt like, at least — an unhealthy level. Just how many times could it do that before bursting through her chest? "What's happening?" She stopped breathing, not wanting to draw any of that weird electric air into her lungs.

Mace stood and started to lead her back into the house. At the door, he paused, and slowly, so slowly, a smile spread across his face. "Breeeeeathe," he whispered, and the words feathered across her face.

Something internal shuddered and her mind whirled to catch up, to process that an angel's breath had just assailed her and set her on fire. In that moment, the electricity in the air disappeared. All that remained was her, Mace, and his breath that completely and thoroughly tore her world away.

Chapter
11

Mace led her into the house, passing through the kitchen and into the living room, where Raven and Vine sat on the couch and Will stood stoic in the center of the room, his massive back to them.

Mace spoke first. "What's going —"

A wide hand slashed the air, stopping firm at shoulder height. "Quiet," Will said. "Heaven whispers."

All movement ceased as Nikki drew a sudden intake of air; even Raven had become focused on Will like a curious child. The moment stretched. She wondered how long she could hold her breath before passing out. Tracers of light shot past her vision.

Mace placed a hand on her arm. "You can breathe," he whispered, a tiny smile tugging at his mouth. "I thought we covered this outside."

She exhaled, blood rushing to her brain. "What's happening?" she hissed just loud enough for Mace's ears.

He leaned closer, their arms dusting one another. That was nice — her arm felt lonely since leaving the porch swing.

Mace whispered, "Will's receiving a message from ..." His words trailed off when the giant angel turned to face them.

"You must go quickly, Mace." Will's finger pointed to them as if it were a knife pinning them to the wall. "There's a laboratory about an hour away. Within its walls are the answers to our journey. But you must hurry." His gaze slashed to Nikki, sending chills down her spine. "Take the Seer with you."

Raven and Vine both stood. "Seer," Raven mumbled. "We should have known." His accusatory glance drifted to Will. "You could have told us."

"Raven and Vine will remain here," Will's voice thundered.

Mace grabbed Nikki's hand and tugged her toward the front door, stopping to grab a notebook and pencil from the foyer table.

He paused when she hesitated. Why her? Raven and Vine were ready to go. Why did Will instruct Mace to drag her along?

"Nikki, the answers are waiting for us. Aren't you curious?"

Curious, yes. Ready to jump headlong into a battle between two worlds? Not so much. But what else could she do — go home and hide under the covers? No. She wasn't geared to run and hide. The faintest of smiles pulled at her lips. "Let's go."

They ran to Mace's black Camaro. He pulled the passenger door open and threw her inside, then shoved the notebook and pencil into her hand before slamming her door. "Draw," he said as he dropped behind the wheel.

She held the writing utensil as if a foreign object. If he didn't look so serious she would have laughed. "Draw what?"

"What you see," he said with a shrug, and tossed gravel as he pulled out of the driveway.

"You don't understand ... I can't just — "

He tapped the paper with his index finger. "Draw what you see with the eyes of your spirit."

She shook her head, heaved a breath, and lay pencil to paper. Compared to everything else she'd seen and learned in the past few hours, this instruction seemed simple. And in a way it made a lot of sense. The first lesson she'd ever received was *Don't draw what you see, draw what you don't see.* The negative space. The half oval that makes the hole in the handle of a coffee mug. The shapes around a chair's legs. The curves behind a flower petal. Within a few minutes, lines and shapes became the outline of a building: tall, at least four stories, surrounded by a wide parking lot and landscaped trees and shrubs to soften the harsh structure. A row of windows anchored the first floor. "Hey," she said, glancing over at him. "It's working." Her focus returned to the page as the amazing process continued. But strange, curved angles jutted from the top of the building, pointing to the sky with disturbing ferocity.

"Is the building shaped strangely?" Nikki asked.

Mace's attention left the road for a moment. "I don't know. I've never been there. Why?"

She tapped her pencil against the drawing.

Mace's eyes scanned the page. He pressed his foot into the gas pedal.

She looked down at the picture of the building with the weird, jagged roofline and wondered why it had caused such a severe reaction for Mace. "What? What did you see?"

"It's on fire."

"What are we supposed to learn in a burning building?" she demanded, close to panic. From a quarter of a mile down the road they could see white, billowy clouds with dark-gray linings crowning the roof. Golden and red flames gave the center a campfire hue. Already the smell of smoke entered the car.

"Keep drawing," Mace ordered as he pulled the car to a stop. "It may be our only way to discover what we're doing here."

Nikki's hand moved anxiously across the page, shading, outlining. Suddenly a room took shape, now filled with smoke drawn by her own hand and flames that danced on the door and across the wall.

Mace snatched the paper, angled it left then right. "This way." He dashed from the vehicle and Nikki rushed to catch up.

The front opening to the building bulged with an orange inferno that glowed sadistically inside the glass doors. "Wait," Nikki said, pencil to paper again. She drew feverishly fast, still amazed by the ability to channel images. "There's a window with no fire!"

Mace consulted the paper as he took her hand and ran to the side of the building. "This one." He paused before a row of shrubs that fringed the window. She was getting ready to sketch another entry point as Mace stepped into the brush and slammed his elbow into the glass.

Nikki screamed.

He turned and took her by the shoulders. "Do *not* enter this building." His eyes burned and the fire flashed in them, solidifying his words. "Do you hear me, Nikki? No matter what happens, promise me you won't."

"You need my help." The smoke stung her eyes. She tried to blink away the searing sensation. "You don't even know what you're looking for."

His grip tightened on her upper arms, and his hands hardened to steel. "Promise me you'll stay here. As for me, I'll know when I find it."

Reluctantly, she nodded.

With that, he disappeared inside.

Minutes ticked past. *I should have drawn faster. If I had, maybe he'd be out by now.* She paced, crunching blades of grass beneath her feet. When her hand began to ache, she looked down at it. She'd squeezed the pencil so hard it broke. Open palmed, she stared at the two pieces of cedar and graphite. A flash of movement came from the building, and she turned toward it with a sigh of relief. *Mace.*

"I'm not finished—there's more." He dropped a laptop into her hands. On reflex, she dumped the charred, blistering machine into the brush while Mace vanished into the orange glow.

Chewing her lip, she grabbed the paper and broken pencil. If she couldn't get into the building, at least she could try to find out what was happening. As she sketched, a form took shape. When the pencil shaded the features of a face, she blanched. "Oh no. No." Life and death decisions shouldn't be made in haste, but there was no time to consider the pros and cons. Someone was in there lying on the floor. Someone was going to die if she couldn't get them out. Climbing through the window, she coughed then sucked air that filled her lungs with more noxious fumes. Her cheeks felt on fire as she stumbled through the heated rubble inside, and for an instant she wondered if this was what hell was like. Cupping her hand over her mouth, she took tiny gasps until she'd entered the right office.

Sprawled on the floor behind the desk was the body she'd seen in the picture. She returned to the doorway and screamed for Mace, but only gravelly screeches emitted from her strained vocal chords. Grabbing a metal file drawer, she systematically banged it against the doorframe, hoping to draw Mace's attention or rouse the person on the floor.

Above her a beam cracked then collapsed. She leapt into the room in time to avoid its fall. Amber sparks rose in a rush like sinister laughter.

Through the flames at the doorway, her hero appeared, his lean form framed by the firelight behind him. And for a devastating instant, she thought, *Dragon Slayer, fighting from inside the very belly of the beast.* He burst through the door and hurdled over the burning beam. Before she could protest, he scooped her into his arms.

"Wait," she said in a scratchy whisper.

"I gotta get you out of here," Mace said and began to move toward the exit.

"Over there." She grabbed his chin and pointed to the desk.

His eyes widened and he carried her to the body then set her on her feet. "Can you walk?"

Her hands slid from his muscled arms, now thick and bulging with adrenaline. "Yes."

Again, Mace used his elbow to bust the office window, and together they lifted the form in the white coat through the opening. The man's jacket snagged on the spikes of glass that cut his flesh as well. Like a ragdoll, he flopped onto the ground, brush breaking much of his fall.

Mace lifted her through, careful of the now-bloody shards. He leapt through after her with the grace of a panther.

After shaking her gaze from Mace, Nikki dropped to the scientist's side, loosening his tie and attempting to shake him awake. The sixtyish man wouldn't stir. A rounded, smooth face remained motionless while fat tears formed in Nikki's eyes. "Don't die," she pleaded. "Please." She shook harder. This was someone's dad. Grandpa, maybe. People expected to see him later, laughing and joking. In a feeble attempt to rouse him, she pounded his chest.

Nothing.

Tears blurred her vision, but her eyes drifted up to Mace, who stood above both of them.

"Nikki," Mace spoke softly. "If it's his time, there's nothing we can do to alter that."

She frowned, anger blending with her despair. "That's it? You aren't even going to try to help him? What kind of a monster are you?" Loosening the man's tie even more, she dropped her head to his chest, listening for a heartbeat. *Angel Boy might give up, but I'm not. Now* breathe!

Mace placed a hand on her shoulder. "We retrieved what we came here to get, now we have to leave. In another ten minutes this place will be swarming with police and firemen. We can't risk being caught. I've found they're not so understanding when it comes to missions from God."

She pulled from him and began to give the man CPR. "Do what you want, Mace, but I'm not leaving until I know there's absolutely nothing I can do. If you were human, you'd understand."

Silence stretched. "Then it's a good thing I'm not." He grabbed her arm, but she jerked from him, her grip tightening on the still man.

Mace sighed and scanned the area. "Where's the computer?"

She nodded toward the bushes where she'd dropped it.

"I'm taking it to the car. I'll be right back. That computer is our only link and I can't risk the police confiscating it. Just — Don't leave."

She shot him a look that said *You're the one who wanted to run away.* Maybe he'd be able to channel that thought.

Mace sensed something wasn't right. Pausing at the trunk, he lifted his nose into the air and sniffed. Hard to smell anything over the smoke, but hate drifted on the currents surrounding him. The hairs rose on the back of his neck, causing a shiver down his spine and a tingle through his wings. *What would Nikki think of my wings if she saw them? Will she ever look at me with the eyes of her spirit?*

The wind shifted with his thoughts, and his gaze shot west to a parking lot where a Hummer perched at the corner and faced the burning building. He scanned the vehicle with eagle's eyes. No one. Then he saw a flash of light glinting off metal above the vehicle's bumper. Honing his eyes, concentrating, a man took shape. And a gun.

Tears flooded Nikki as she looked down at the now-alive scientist. "You're okay," she said through choked sobs. *And Mace said the CPR was pointless.*

His eyes slowly focused on her own. "You came back," he mumbled almost incoherently. Raising a trembling hand to her cheek, he brushed her face tenderly.

She placed her hand over his.

"You look so beautiful," he said, voice cracking and rough from the smoke he'd inhaled. "Are you my angel?"

"I'm no angel." She laughed and considered the irony of the comment. "But we did save you."

His head tilted toward the building, neck straining. "It's all gone, isn't it?"

"I'm sorry," she said.

"My life's work. But you ... Look at you. So beautiful, so alive. You saved me."

He took a hold of her hand. "Thank you for coming back."

Chapter
12

He'd have to outrun the bullet to get to her in time. The crack of the gun splintered the air, but Mace closed in on his target. When he got to Nikki, he saw the blood.

Mace gathered her into his arms before casting a final look down to the scientist, now dead in the very dirt Nikki had revived him in.

She was wailing. Off to one side, he heard the motor of the Hummer come to life, then saw the truck barrel out of the adjacent parking lot. Rather than risk a leap into the midplane with her in his arms, Mace ran to his car and gently placed her inside. *Why did I let Vine talk me into this car? I might as well write "follow me" on every surface.* He flew over the hood and dropped into the driver's seat. In less than a heartbeat, he peeled away from the fire.

"Too fast," she mumbled, trying to wipe the drying blood from her hands.

Mace took the first side road, leaving the building just in

time to miss a police car sailing past on the main road and headed for the fire.

"You're going too fast."

Flashes of headlights illuminated the trees as he sped up. He needed to put as much distance as possible between them and the fire, and, even more urgently, between them and the Hummer. "No, Nikki. It's all right. Halfling reflexes are way faster than a human's. Trust me." *Just not amazing enough to get to her before the gunman's bullet.* He attempted to shove the thought from his head. She could be dead. *Good job, Halfling.* Mace prided himself on his awareness of things. Everything. He considered himself a watchman, not only over his assignments, a watchman over all. That's why he'd keep an eye on Vine. And though he was conflicted about Raven, he'd resolved to watch out for him too, offering a hand of rescue to pull Raven out if he ever swam too far into the deep end. But tonight had taught him one valuable lesson.

Where Nikki Youngblood was concerned, awareness was a dangerous thing.

Mace glanced at the speedometer, then her as she scrubbed in an attempt to remove the blood. He knew the signs of slipping into panic. Shock would soon follow as her brain caught up to what had just transpired.

He turned down another side street. "I'm going to get you somewhere safe. Somewhere you can clean up." One more turn landed them on Lake Road 182 in time to hear the siren of a second police car speeding past on the main route.

Rocks crunched beneath the tires, almost soothingly, as they bounced and jostled down the road's rocky decline. Beside him Nikki moaned, lips white from fear. He placed a reassuring hand on top of hers, now clasped in her lap. Wild eyes shot to him enhanced by the green shine of the dashboard lighting. The unnatural glow made her appear crazed, feral.

He scanned ahead with keen eyes and locked on water. "There's a lake at the end of this road. We'll stop. You can clean up there, okay?"

But she didn't answer. She stared at him, unmoving.

He'd let her down. Never, ever had he messed up an assignment so badly, yet on this one he seemed incapable of doing anything right. Nikki could have died. The thought shot through him with such force, he nearly broke the steering wheel in his hands, stopping only when he heard it creak and pop. He loosened his grip.

"Mace, that man died in my arms."

"I know. I'm sorry." But it was his fault — he should never have left her there. He squeezed her hands lightly and she yelped.

He withdrew his touch. "What's wrong?"

"My palms." She searched them. "I think they're burnt."

Beneath the dried blood, he could see puffy skin and small white blisters separated by streaks, as if she'd pressed her hands to a barbeque grill. Horror registered in his brain as his glances shifted from her face to her hands and back. *And I was so worried about getting her cleaned up.*

"It's all right." She tried to smile. "I'm fine."

But the bewildered look told him otherwise. "Of course you are." And for a quick moment his heart turned to gelatin. Duty, responsibility, right, and wrong were all blending into a mixture he had little hope of understanding. And no hope of controlling.

Her attempt at bravery didn't help. It only heightened his awareness of her, and in turn the heightened awareness seemed to slow his reflexes and shatter his equilibrium. A complication he didn't need.

"Wha-what about you? You were in the lab longer than me." She grabbed his arm, winced, and inspected his elbow. "I watched you break glass twice."

"One of the perks of being a Lost Boy."

"You can't be wounded?"

"Oh." He rolled his eyes. "Believe me, I can. But it takes quite a bit."

He pulled the car to a stop when they entered a clearing. After opening her door and helping her out, they paused at the front of his vehicle, both halted by the shadowed strip of lake before them. Glistening black diamonds danced across the water beneath a full moon. Nikki stood perfectly still, and Mace followed her example, saturating himself in the land-scape's tranquility. A star-twinkling sky drifted peacefully above as if no horrors had tarnished its beauty. No burning laboratories, no dead scientists, no charred hands.

Taking her by the wrist, careful not to touch the burns, he drew her down a path leading to the water's edge.

"I'm a little dizzy. Need to sit down," she said as her knees buckled.

Mace absorbed her fall against his body then lowered her to the ground, where she leaned her weight against a rock. *What to do?*

Pulling off his shirt, he walked to the water. Cold wetness absorbed through the toes of his shoes as he sank his shirt, dousing it up and down until saturated. A few feet away she sat like a wounded bird, so helpless, and so in need of rescue. *My specialty.* He'd wrap the garment around her burned hands — and try not to wrap Nikki Youngblood around his heart.

His silhouette at the water made her heart thunder. She watched, now convinced there was a soft soul inside that shell of protection: he'd wanted to leave the scientist, yes, but only to keep her safe. And she did feel safe. Even though a bullet missed her by mere inches.

He returned to her with the dripping fabric. Before laying it on her bloody hands, he knelt down on one knee. "Okay?"

She nodded agreement, but winced when the material met her skin. She trailed each muscle with her eyes as he moved, gently swiping her hands. The pain lessened and his touch stopped her need to process what had happened. There was only him and her at the water's edge. His full attention was on his task. Her full attention was on him, causing a soothing rain of calm to pour down.

His collarbone shifted in tandem with his shoulders. His skin was such a strange color, now that she could see more of it. Pale but with a subtle warmth, as if he'd been brushed with purest gold. A jewel on a gold chain hung at his neck.

He *was* perfection, more so than any bronze statue she'd ever seen. "Can I draw you sometime?" she said, voice a distant whisper, as if it belonged to someone else.

All of Mace's movement stopped. His eyes searched hers as if reading much into her words. There was much implied. Did he feel it?

She noticed a bead of sweat above his brow ready to slip down his cheek. His forehead, interrupted by spikes of dark blond hair, tilted into a light frown.

She slid her hand from under the dripping T-shirt and reached to his forehead. Something in her caused a spike of boldness. Her index finger pressed against the sweat bead. As she did so, water from the shirt ran the length of her arm to her elbow.

When her finger began to move, his eyes drifted shut.

His reaction surprised her. She heaved a ragged breath while her fingertip traced the planes of his face. Brow, temple, cheekbone, jaw, throat. A scar marred his collarbone and for a moment she lingered there, wondering how many scars he carried. Then, she trailed its length, stopping at the base of his throat where the amulet dangled. His eyes remained closed. *Such trust.* Nikki pivoted closer and opened her hand until it was flat against his chest. "There's not a hair on your chest," she said with a soft laugh.

His eyes popped open and he glanced down. "No, guess not."

"Another perk?" she asked.

"If you want to call it that," Mace said, but his voice sounded uncertain. Something else — yearning? — measured into his words. She wasn't sure, but her heart opened a little more. How could it not? He was allowing her to glimpse his vulnerabilities.

She should stop. If her sanity caught up to her ... well, she'd likely die of embarrassment. She wasn't like this, and she certainly didn't just open her heart to people she barely knew. Nikki swallowed hard and tension started to drift into her muscles.

He must have sensed it. Mace dropped his other knee to the ground, closing some of the distance between them. His eyes were fire, and in them she read the words, *please don't stop.*

Uh-oh. Though Nikki knew this was her chance to escape, to stop, to bring some shred of common sense into this moment, she waited while the opportunity passed by. Instead of jumping to her feet and running the other direction — like her mind was telling her — she pressed her fingers into his pectoral muscle, ignoring the pain from the burns on her skin. "Please?"

"Please, what?" he said, and she realized he'd gone somewhere else in his mind. Maybe it was a place where no one was in danger and young people could enjoy a moment instead of thinking about where the next attack might come from. Her mind had strayed as well. But the softness of his tone drew her back. That drowsy, low tone she could drown in.

"I want to draw you. Will you let me?" Her fingers itched to roam over his skin, but she would never do that ... at least, not any more than she already had. "Can I sketch you?"

He swallowed. She could sense he was awkward with his trust, but also ready to meet her fearlessness with a dose of his own. His warm breath came faster against her cheek. Maybe he was preparing to tell her no. But instead, she heard him whisper.

"Yes. If you'll draw me as I really am."

As Nikki began to angle herself toward the car, where her sketch pad and pencils lay, Mace's face fell, and he pointed to her pocket. "Your phone's ringing."

Chapter 13

Nikki wasn't sure whether to thank or curse her parents for calling. *If they knew where I am …*

"Mom, I'm fine. I meant to call, but, well, I was busy. I'm sorry."

"That's okay, dear. I just wanted to make sure you're safe."

"I'm with a friend, Mom. Trust me, I'm well protected." *I'm safe … now.* As her mom went on, she overheard a voice she vaguely remembered coming from the background of the call. Vessler.

"Whose voice is that?" Nikki had always been a girl for hitting things head on.

There was a pause. "Your father."

No. It wasn't. "Who's he talking to?"

Another stretch of uncomfortable silence. "Oh, you must be hearing the TV." Her mom was a lousy liar.

The voices in the background dropped.

"It sounded like that guy who was at the house the other day. Damon Vessler."

"That's silly." A nervous little laugh. "What would he be doing here?"

"Why wouldn't he be there?" Nikki countered. "You guys are all *such* good friends. Besides, he collects antique weapons. You're at a weapon's show, right?"

"Of course, he *could* be here somewhere. I'll be sure to ask your father if he's seen him. Well, better go, honey. Glad you're all right."

"Mom, is everything okay?"

A long sigh drifted over the phone line. "There were a few unexpected twists at the auction, but everything is fine. At least, it will be soon."

Nikki glanced over at Mace, who was trying to look aloof but failing. "I'll head home soon, I promise. Bye, Mom."

"Bye, honey. We'll … we'll see you tomorrow." With that, her mom hung up.

Nikki pulled the phone from her ear and stared at it.

"You okay?" Mace said.

"Have you ever known you were being lied to, but you had a hard time minding because you suspected the person lying was just trying to protect you?"

Mace's lips quirked. "Uh, yeah. I think I know what that feels like."

"My parents are acting weird. And I'm pretty sure they weren't alone. I heard a voice in the background get mad and say something like, 'How'd they get there? You didn't follow them?'" She shrugged. "Seems strange is all."

"Let me get this straight. Your folks are with some man who was yelling at them about following someone?"

"No. I think he was on the phone with someone else while my mom was talking to me. I heard a cell phone ring."

"What do you think it means?"

"I don't know. But as soon as I heard that voice uneasiness sort of crawled all over me."

"And you think you know this guy?"

"Just met him. It's probably nothing. I'm just looking for demons around every corner."

Mace rubbed a hand over his face and mumbled. "That's because there are demons around every corner."

Clasping her by the wrists, he pulled her from the lake's edge, where they'd sat for nearly an hour. "Feel better?"

Nikki wiggled her fingers at him, but had to cringe. "A little. At least my mom and dad won't be sending out a search party for me. I didn't even feel my phone vibrating in my pocket. How'd you know—"

"Good hearing," he said pointing to the side of his head. "You sounded very controlled speaking to them."

"Thanks. My mom was totally panicked because I usually check in at this time of night. I think she would have questioned me a lot more if I hadn't turned the focus of the conversation back to her." Nikki tipped her head back and stared up at the sky. "How do I explain this night to them? They'd never understand."

"They will. They love you, Nikki."

Something about how he'd uttered those words made her sad. "Yeah. They've always given me a lot of freedom. Probably too much, but when they're out of town my mom freaks like the whole world is gonna end." She risked a glance into his blue-green eyes, now opaque and glistening in the moonlight. She should have stayed focused on the sky or the water or anything else. With his gaze so intent on her, she dissolved.

"Isn't that what moms do?" Something fringed his tone, some longing for things untouchable.

"I guess so," she whispered, and actually felt guilty for having a mother. She wiggled her fingers again, creating a bit of space and air between them. "You got most of the blood off."

"How bad do they hurt?"

"Hardly at all," she lied.

He slid his hand over her upturned palm, then stroked a finger from her thumb to her wrist.

"Ouch," she said, flinching.

"I, um ..." He fidgeted and looked at the moon, the water, his car. "I could help."

He'd already helped. And she'd helped herself to too many thoughts about *what if* scenarios that she'd never allow under normal circumstances. "How?"

He dragged a hand through his dark blond hair. "I have a bit of ..." He cleared his throat. "Well —"

"Mace, are you blushing?" she teased. In response, a soft pink hue flushed across his luminous skin.

"Let me just show you, okay?" Gently and slowly he lifted her palm toward his mouth. Just before making contact with her scorched index finger, he moistened his lips. Cerulean eyes flashed to hers as he pressed his mouth to her finger.

She was still. Warm, wet lips brushed her hand again and again, making the softest of all kissing sounds. She liquefied into a puddle, becoming a heap of dizzy, drowsy mush. "Wow." She studied the spot and wiggled the finger; no burning, no stinging, just fresh, pink skin. "What was that?"

"Another perk." He laughed. "Misleading, though. I can't do anything when it's life threatening."

"Amazing." She examined the digit. Angel kisses. He'd just dusted her skin with angel kisses. How many girls on the planet could say that? "Do you think this is where the term 'Kiss it and make it better' comes from?"

He smiled. "Maybe."

She cocked a brow. "My other hand hurts."

His tongue slipped out to moisten his lips again, a half smile on his face. "Is that so?"

"Pretty painful," she confirmed.

Mace's smirk spread to a full smile, his white, even teeth shining in the evening light. "I guess I have my work cut out for me."

He drew her hand to his mouth and Nikki sighed.

This night had been nothing like Mace had anticipated. And now that Nikki was safe and healed, he wasn't quite sure how to end it. "Are you ready to go home? I can drop you off. We'll get your bike from my house in the morning. Or I can have Vine and Raven bring it now."

"Um," she responded, and stared at the glove compartment.

All evening she'd rolled with the punches, but now fresh panic straightened her mouth into a tight line. He watched as she realized her world had completely changed. "You'll be all right tonight, Nikki. We'll guard your house." He played with the radio tuner, hoping to fill the silence, and a song called "Johnny Angel" filled the car.

She pivoted in the seat, turned off the stereo, and watched him drive. "Who will protect me? You, Raven, and Vine? Will?" She pressed her hands to her head. "Do you know how crazy this sounds? Do you understand what's happened to me?"

"I know. I wish I could change it." And he did, but there was a tiny part of him that was glad. If Nikki hadn't been in danger, he'd never have met her. He hated himself for the self-serving thought. Everything about it was wrong. Yes, he was half angel, but his fallen nature always sought to rise. He'd quelled it for all the years of his life, until now. Until her. "I wish I could erase it for you."

She shook her head hopelessly. "But you can't, can you? This is it. The real world. Angels and demons and hell hounds and madmen who murder scientists."

"It's not all bad, you know." *Don't say it. Don't go there.*

"Really? What part of it's good?"

The vehicle was designed to minimize road noise, but Mace would have been glad for a rumble of engine, a whoosh of wind against the car, anything. His feelings were a jagged wreck, and had been since he first saw Nikki. Inside, his heart burned to be closer. But deeper, he knew that could never be. He had one shot at an afterlife that didn't involve eternal torment — no matter how she made him feel, nothing was worth risking that. Not even Nikki Youngblood.

"Excuse me, but you didn't answer. What part of it is good?" she pressed.

"I found you," he said, before he could stop himself. Biting down on his own tongue, he tasted blood. Bitter blood. The wound healed before he could turn the radio back on and drown the silence.

"There are no accidents," Nikki heard Mace grumble as he crept the car into the parking lot.

The left back tire had blown, and the sound still rang in her ears as the car bounced into the only drive on the long stretch of road.

An ancient Catholic church of brick and stone hovered over them with a solitary light illuminating the sanctuary. Mace patted her knee, then pulled back and cleared his throat. "I'll see if anyone's inside. Let them know we're borrowing their parking lot. Wait here," he said and stepped from the vehicle.

Her door slammed before his had a chance. He glanced over the car at her.

"No way." She shook her head. "Call me chicken, but I'm not letting you out of my sight."

He smiled. "Come on, chicken."

They entered. The sanctuary doors slid quietly, then clamped shut behind them. Nikki jumped. Mace chuckled. She sank a punch into his upper arm. "You could show a bit of grace. I've sort of been through a lot tonight."

The smile dissipated into intensity, and she felt as if his eyes dipped into her soul. "I know," he whispered, and she decided she preferred the playful banter of a few moments ago. He slipped his hands into hers. "I'll never let you down again, Nikki. I promise."

She swallowed. "You didn't."

"I did. That gunman should never have been able to get that close to harming you." He glanced above, where arched beams anchored the walls and stabilized the building. "It's my job to be your shelter."

"Like you were on my bike?" Even in whispers, their voices reverberated off the soaring walls.

"Yes," Mace said.

Nikki's attention flittered around the room. "This sort of reminds me of the barn."

His smile deepened. "You were scared of me."

She set her chin. "*You* were scared of *me*." But was she scared then, or now? Feelings pinged through her that she hadn't experienced and didn't know what to do with. Krissy always badgered her about being so unaware of the opposite sex. Had she saved up all her attention, all that energy, for this one guy? It was as if all her awareness had rushed to her nerve endings in one blazing trail. Looking up into his eyes, she knew he felt it too. *Is he my dragon slayer?*

His hands left hers and fisted at his sides.

"I've never met anyone like you," he said, and she could see determination settle on him like a protective armor. Protecting him from what? Her?

No. No, she thought. *Don't slip away. I need you right now.* "I've never met anyone like you," she echoed. "And I'm not scared anymore."

He pulled her toward him and rested his chin on top of her head. "I still am, Nikki. For more reasons than you can imagine."

Coming to rest in the front pew, Mace slipped an arm around her and gave a light squeeze. "You'll be safe here while I change the tire."

She didn't want him to go. When he rose, she grabbed his arm but felt silly, so she loosened her grip. "Why do you want me to stay in here? As strong as you are, it will take you about four seconds to change the tire."

"I thought you could use a" — his gaze fanned the ornate cavern — "sanctuary."

After he left, she closed her eyes.

The space offered a peculiar serenity. Quiet had a rhythm all its own here, and, tipping her head back, she drank it in. In return she felt a peace that was clean and pure.

A sound to the right grabbed her attention. She jolted, muscles springing.

"I'm sorry, child," the robed gentleman said as he stepped toward her from the shadows. A kind smile touched his face. "I didn't mean to frighten you."

She placed a hand to her heart and exhaled the air she'd sucked in. "Oh, it's okay." She pointed behind her. "I, um … we … the door wasn't locked."

He raised his hands in surrender. "No need to explain. We're like the Seven-Eleven. Always open."

She laughed, sound bouncing off the walls.

"May I?" He gestured beside her.

She nodded, and the man sat. "This is one of my favorite times of the day to come here."

"Really?"

"Yes." Tilting his head back, his eyes closed, mimicking what she'd done moments before. "So quiet. Don't get me wrong. I love it when the cathedral is full of souls."

"Excuse me? I don't know how to ask you this, but do you mean souls like …" Finding no way to describe her question, Nikki fell silent.

He frowned. "People."

She sighed with relief. "Oh, that's good."

Moments passed. The crucifixion was suspended above them, and her eyes sought those of Jesus.

"You seem a bit troubled, my dear. I'd be glad to help if I can. Folks say I'm easy to talk to."

She tucked her hair back with an index finger. "Okay, well … Um, I don't know what to call you."

"You can call me Father if you like. Or Tom."

"Father sounds more official."

His eyes twinkled. "Are you here on official business?"

Her fingers toyed with the hem of her shirt. "Father, have you ever thought that the whole world is falling apart around you?" She bent her knee and pivoted on the pew to view him fully. "I mean, like everything you've been living for doesn't really even matter anymore?"

His eyes fell to the leg of her jeans, where splotches of dark stained the cloth. "If you're in any kind of trouble, my dear, I promise you're safe here." His eyes sought the spot again. "Did someone hurt you? Were you harmed?"

Her gaze followed his. "Oh, no." She brushed at the cloth. "Actually, we saved someone. Sort of."

He folded his hands in his lap in what she figured was a very Father-Tom way. "As humans, we all feel like that sometimes. Then the paradigm shifts."

She held up a finger. "What's a paradigm?"

He squinted. "A standard, a model for how we live our lives. Our prototype. You see, sometimes we get glorious glimpses into the realm our natural, finite minds have difficulty comprehending."

"You mean, sometimes we glimpse the bigger picture?"

He nodded. "Exactly. It is in those moments our character is defined. What do we do with what we've seen? Who do we become when we realize our path encompasses so much more than we imagined?"

A movement from behind caused them to turn.

Father Tom stood slowly and took his time examining Mace. "Son," he said, smiling and reaching out his hand.

"Father," Mace said, slipping his hand into the man's.

A recollection seemed to pass between the two that puzzled Nikki. Maybe they'd met before. Father Tom turned to her, a fresh expectancy driving his words. "You have an exciting journey ahead of you, my dear. Keep the faith. Go with God."

Mace certainly had a strange effect on people. As they left the building, she questioned him. "Did you know him?"

"After the spirit," he said.

She stopped cold at the car door. "What does that mean?"

"He recognized me."

"So, you *knew* him," Nikki said.

"No, he recognized the essence of who I am."

She crossed her arms. "Like when you get introduced to someone and you know they're bad?"

"Yes." He nodded toward the church. "He's a xian."

"Z-i-a-n?" Nikki asked.

"No, it's spelled x-i-a-n, but pronounced zy-an."

"It could be spelled a-b-c-d and it wouldn't help me. I have no idea what that is."

"They're people who embrace the fact that there is a spirit realm around us. They help us. Frequently." Mace reached for the door handle.

"All right. I guess I can live with that answer." She gestured to his car. "I've been dying to ask. Why a brand-new Camaro? Seems like you'd want to be more inconspicuous, blend in with all the other lean, golden-skinned, practically perfect teenage boys."

"Perfect, huh?" he said, and leaned on the car top.

"*Practically.*"

"We fight both unearthly and earthly foes. If a chase ensues and we can't ... use other means of transportation ... we need the best, fastest vehicles available. But they also must be dependable, easy to work on, easy to get parts for." He nodded to the sports car. "Vine talked me into taking this one. We have a lot of cars at our disposal."

"But you don't really own it?"

"We don't own anything, Nikki. Not much point."

"Oh." How sad. She shifted her attention to what he'd said before about *when they can't use other means of transportation.* But she decided not to ask. Her mind kept imagining angel wings. "I figured it was because you're all guys and most guys are gearheads who like fast cars."

He burst into a mega smile. "That too."

She tapped her fingers on the window. "How about if you let me drive?"

"No way."

"Why? Would Will kill you?" Nikki asked.

"No, but you might. Remember, I rode with you once before."

"I thought you didn't have a cell phone," she said as Mace sped them toward the house.

"Yeah, we got these today. At Viennesse, there's no reception."

"Where?"

"Viennesse. That's our home in Europe. Not just us though — other Halflings and their caregivers stay there between journeys as well. That is, when we aren't in the midplane."

"What do you do when you aren't on a journey?" Nikki lifted then dropped her shoulders, which had become stiff from the night's adventure.

"We train, study, practice our skills." He rolled his eyes. "Sometimes there are twenty Halflings there, so mostly we get into trouble. There's this creepy old guy — a xian who lives there and takes care of the place. We constantly give him grief. You can imagine."

Not in the way you think. Twenty perfect teenage boys would be any artist's dream. Any girl's dream, for that matter. She shook her head to clear her thoughts.

"Listen, do you think you're up for one more stop?" Mace asked.

"Is it going to involve burning buildings, gunmen, or any weird stuff from the …"

"The supernatural realm?" he finished for her.

"Yes."

"No, nothing bizarre." He thought a moment. "Well, nothing dangerous and bizarre."

"Great," she muttered, pulling the lever to recline in her seat. "Can't wait."

Mace dialed home while Nikki snoozed in the seat beside him. "Will, sorry I didn't call sooner."

"This is your journey, Mace. I'm merely an observer."

Mace chuckled. "For being an observer, you sure boss us around a lot."

Will's laughter bubbled through the phone line. "I guess that was an unfair euphemism." He lowered his voice. "I know about the fire at the lab."

"Heaven?" Mace asked.

"No, television."

"Ah, I told you the TV was a good idea," Mace said.

"There was no argument. How else could I watch my sitcoms?" Will asked.

"What did they say about the scientists?"

"They suspect that six perished in the flames."

"What about the one that was murdered?" Mace looked over at Nikki. Still asleep. "More important, why didn't any of them escape? There was no one outside when we arrived. Whoever was in the building when the fire erupted perished in the building, except for the scientist we dragged out."

"Where is he, Mace?"

"He's dead. Shot while Nikki held him."

Will sighed.

"Yeah, I know. Look, I retrieved a computer. Thought I could drop it off with Zero. Would that be allowed?" Mace said.

"Nikki's still with you?"

"Yes."

"How is she?" Worry hung in Will's words.

Another glance. "She's good." Her hair lay in long waves around her face. Dark lashes hooded her eyes, like black-velvet half moons. He couldn't help but smile. "Can keep up with the best of them. Resilient, you know ... for a human."

"Go. It's almost nine now. Seek Zero. He can help."

"I won't compromise him?" Mace asked.

Long moments passed before Will spoke. "No. Cover Nikki's eyes so she doesn't know the way."

"That won't be necessary. She's sound asleep."

"You've got to be kidding me." Raven said, flicking a toothpick from the car window. He didn't want to be here. He didn't want to watch Vine eat another piece of candy, and he didn't want to hear the younger boy's excitement at all his first-time adventures. He wanted ...

He wanted to be with Nikki.

Raven tried to swallow the thought along with a toxic gulp of reality. He *never* went for girls like Nikki. The redheaded shark was more to his liking. Nikki was a parasite burrowing under his skin, causing it to itch and inflame. *That*, he didn't need.

"Hey," Vine said. "A bowling alley. I've never been bowling before."

Raven pivoted in the car seat. "We're not here to socialize, Vine. You aren't some teenager looking for a girlfriend, okay?" *None of us should be. And we really shouldn't linger on what a relationship could be like.*

He'd become vaguely aware of Nikki in the principal's office. She didn't like the mistreatment he'd suffered and was quick to come to his aid. And that was ... interesting ... but that's all it was. Then, the painting. The splash of color and life draining from a broken pot had shifted something in him. But it was his assessment of the painting, and the fact she'd painted it without knowing why, that pushed him over the edge. He'd seen the flash of acknowledgment in her eyes, and something deep inside him rumbled to life. Something he'd thought dead. For a speck of a moment, Raven felt ... clean.

He forced the sensation from his being. "Look, Vine, we're from a different world. Nothing and no one can change that."

Vine's head dropped forward. He chewed his cheek.

Raven unfastened his seat belt. "And the sooner you realize that, the better off you'll be."

"Yeah, but I'm *here*," Vine countered, tucking a mass of hair behind his ear. "I might as well enjoy it."

"For a purpose. Not to act like some lesser being," Raven spat.

Vine looked over. "Is that what you think of humans?"

He shrugged and hoped the long spikes of bangs shrouded his face. "So what if it is?"

Vine shook his head hard and had to push back the hair that landed in his eyes. "It's just wrong. Humans are the seed of the incorruptible." His voice dropped. "You shouldn't even utter such words."

Raven threw a hand toward a group of teens entering the building. "Look at them. They're oblivious to the other realm. It's within their power to see it, but they just bumble along like the only thing that matters is where they buy their clothes."

"I wish I were human," Vine muttered.

Raven scowled. "Don't even say that, Vine. They're ordinary and average."

"Ordinary isn't so bad."

"It's worse than bad. Mediocrity breeds weakness. And weakness is death." Nikki Youngblood, with her flowers and broken pots and innocent charm, was weakness. Especially for him. And weakness he couldn't afford.

Vine wadded up the wrapper from the candy bar he'd devoured. "I thought this saving-the-world stuff would be more exciting and rock-star cool." He reached for a sack from the convenience store, which bulged with four different types of sour candy.

Raven sent him a twisted smile. "Yeah, real cool. Babysit a science teacher while he's bowling."

"You're the one who said Dr. Richmond was the target." Vine chewed the inside of his mouth while selecting candy. "Mmm, sour gummies."

Raven grimaced. "You're gonna rot your teeth."

Vine popped a handful into his mouth. "Can't help it," he

said, speaking around the mound of brightly colored worms. "Want some?"

Raven shook his head. He nodded toward the parking lot, eyes narrow. "Maybe Richmond's a pervert."

Vine paled. "Ew." They watched while Dr. Richmond exited his car, grabbed a bowling bag from the trunk, and entered the building. "I mean *ew*, really?" He searched Raven's face. "Is that what you think?"

"Sure," Raven said, but had to turn away to hide the smirk. "Come on."

"No *way*," Raven heard Krissy Cunningham mutter as the two boys approached the bowling alley's glass doors. Her hand smacked repeatedly against Suzy Carmichael's arm, jostling the girl. Krissy had been on Raven's radar until he realized he liked Nikki. Best friends equals bad medicine.

"Watch it!" Suzie mouthed to her friend when her drink sloshed. She moved her Coke cup to the other hand.

The boys strode effortlessly toward the door, both over six feet of lean muscle. Raven did a head toss for emphasis. As if on cue, the wind caught Vine's white-blond hair, sending it into a perfect half-circle over his right shoulder. Girls were nuts for Vine's hair. Too bad all that advantage was lost on a kid too young to use it.

The girls grinned at each other. Raven ate it up.

"Why are they staring at us?" Vine asked, and Raven glanced over to see the panic in his blue-gray eyes.

"Feel like a piece of meat?"

"No," Vine countered, like any little brother accused of something he was guilty of.

151

"It's because we look like a living, breathing Abercrombie commercial." Raven sauntered along with an air of defiance he'd taken years to perfect, but his gaze remained alert processing every tidbit of information around him with vivid clarity.

Vine tried to ignore the spectators and tossed a piece of candy into the air then caught it in his mouth.

"Yummy," Suzy mouthed from behind the glass. Apparently, she was a gummy candy fan too.

Krissy sucked the last of her Coke until the straw rumbled against ice. Raven had to wonder if their approach had warmed up the temperature in the concession stand.

"Maybe that girl Suzy likes me," Vine announced, nodding toward the window and the girls on the other side.

Raven stopped dead and slammed a hand into Vine's chest so hard he choked on a gummy worm. "Stay away from earth girls."

Vine set his jaw. "Why? You always date on journeys and don't say you don't 'cause I've seen you."

Raven grabbed him by the T-shirt and pulled him to his face. "I can handle it, Vine. You can't."

But Vine wouldn't back down. "How do you know?"

Raven shoved him away. "Because you're soft."

"Guess you don't remember our fight. I held my own with you when I hadn't tapped into my angelic ability. You know I can beat you. So, if I'm soft, what does that make you?"

Raven clenched his jaws tightly. This wasn't the time to put Little Brother in his place. "You heard me, Vine. Keep your distance."

"Good morning, sunshine," Mace said and smiled over at Nikki.

She rubbed her eyes with the backs of her hands and yawned. "It's not really morning, right?" She searched the horizon for the arrival of the sun.

"No, Sleeping Beauty. It's only nine-fifteen. You dozed the last twenty minutes or so. We're almost there."

She popped the passenger visor down and studied her reflection while they bumped along yet another gravel road. "Red, puffy eyes, hair in clumps. Oh, yeah, I'm just like Sleeping Beauty," she mumbled, pressing fingertips to the inside corner of her eyes. *Yeah, like that's going to fix it.* Giving up, she snapped the visor closed. "Where are we?"

"About an hour from home. We're going to drop the computer with a friend."

"Is he a zy, uh, xian?"

"No, a Halfling." He concentrated on the road. "But, Zero is … well, he's different."

"Different?" She pulled her hair into a ponytail and searched the floorboard of the car for something to secure it. "Different how?" Finding two pencils, she slid one into each hand. At the base of her neck, she twisted and tucked until her long hair was clustered into an updo.

"That was cool," he said and nodded to her hair. She quirked an eyebrow in response.

"So, tell me about Zero. You said he's different. Does he have some hideous black wings sprouting from his spine or something?"

Mace's jaw clenched. "No," he answered sadly. "You won't see anything like that." Heavy silence floated on the conditioned air and filled the car.

"What is this place?" she asked as Mace pulled open a thick metal door. A forever stretch of stairs spiraled down into the abyss. If this was some weird portal into the great beyond, she'd rather stay in the car.

"Miles of connected underground walkways and tunnels that were once used by the city. But after a small earthquake, they deemed this area unstable." He stopped at the first landing. "Oops, you probably need light, don't you?"

Her eyes had adjusted, but light would lessen the creep factor. "Yeah," she said, irritated that she didn't want to brave the tunnel without it. In the last bit of the car ride, Nikki'd become agitated about a number of things. The situation as a whole topped the list, but she was also mad at the scientist for dying, and most of all angry at herself and the pathetic way she responded to Mace. Helpless little victim just wasn't her style.

The problem was Mace made her want to drop her defenses and actually let someone else fight the battles. That equated to weakness, a commodity she couldn't abide.

He reached to the low ceiling and pulled a chain. Rows of can lights sprang to life, winding down and illuminating the stairs. He gave a half-hearted motion with his hand. "Head toward the light."

She cocked a brow. "Thanks, but I'm not quite ready to cross over to the other side yet."

"It was just a joke," he said.

Metal echoed with each step as they descended. On the next landing, she paused. In the dense quiet, her mind worked overtime like a multicogged machine designed to churn out a variety of emotions. It suddenly became important to determine her role in this train wreck. "Mace, what do I have to do with all this?" she asked simply, hoping the very tone would generate a simple answer. When none came she rested a hand against the round banister. The shocking cold sent a chill up her arm and down the length of her body. "You and Will said I'm a Seer, and that I'm not in as much danger, but I still don't understand."

He paused beside her. "When we're sent on a journey, sometimes we're in contact with a Seer and that connection helps us along the way. Seers can even get glimpses of the enemy's plan. When we first arrived, you'd seen into the other realm and kind of became a doorway for the hell hounds."

"They crossed into this realm because of me?" No more drawing in the woods.

"To destroy you. A hound can kill you quickly or —"

"Or what? What else could they have done to me?" *And am I really expected to live with these massive swings of emotion? First angel kisses by the lake, then the knowledge that hell hounds want to kill me?* Nikki fought panic.

"They might have tormented you until you went mad," Mace said.

She cringed.

"They tend to prefer torment, especially when they're running in packs."

She raised a hand to silence him. "Okay, I get it. Nice tidbit of info there, golden boy. Next time, when I ask, just tell me I don't want to know."

"I've tried that approach on several occasions. It hasn't seemed to work yet."

She stared at him for a moment, then continued down the stairs, feet clanging out her agitation.

"You're handling this amazingly well."

"Thanks," she quipped. Handling it well? No, she was a firecracker ready to explode.

He stopped at the next landing and turned her to face him. "Nikki, we're on the winning side. Hold that truth in your heart. It'll comfort you."

She shook her head and felt several fallen strands of hair tickle her neck. "I'm sorry, Mace. But I don't think anything will ever comfort me again." She pulled away from him and continued down.

"There's one more thing," he hollered to her.

She paused, heaved a sigh, and stomped back up the steps to him. "Fine. Fill me in. If I pass out from fear, just leave me here, okay?"

"You won't pass out." His voice had softened and she wanted to get lost in the words. How could she go from *so* cold to *so* warm that fast?

"Nikki, I swear I'll see this through to the end."

The words stopped her. It was an oath, a promise that he'd not leave her. But it also meant *she'd* have to see it through, when all she really wanted was to crawl into her bed and forget. "You might, but I'm not making any promises. Don't be surprised if I run away."

He spun a dangling strand of her hair around his finger. "You won't. You're a fighter."

Something within her gut clenched, acknowledged the term and accepted it, even embraced it. She shook her head, slowly. "I'm just an art freak who likes karate."

"No." His hands found their way to her upper arms. It was a motion against his better judgment, she could tell. "You're so much more. There's destiny in your eyes. Your heart thumps with a warrior's beat. Now that you know the battle, you'll never run from it."

"Don't be too sure." Her voice cracked.

"Never. It's what you were created for."

Chapter
14

A guy she assumed was Zero tugged the metal door open and offered a tight smile.

Mace reached to hug him. "Bro."

Zero fidgeted at the embrace. Tall and thin, pale and wiry, Nikki could see why he lived down here. Like a worm seeks refuge in the ground, Zero seemed perfectly acclimated to his subterranean surroundings. His hair and skin were lighter than anyone she'd met. *He's a Halfling? Maybe he's ill.*

She followed Mace into a metal room where computer equipment decorated each wall. Lights flashed and blinked and threw flickering shadows throughout the space. In one corner, a rumpled futon sagged.

Mace reached to the low ceiling and tugged the chain on a hanging light illuminating the dimly lit room.

Nikki gasped when the light caught Zero's gaze. His eyes sparked with colorless flashes of brilliance, reminding her of sunlight shining through icicles. Barely a drop of blue amidst the silver.

"Have you been outside?" Mace asked.

Zero turned away. "About a month ago."

"Dude, that's not healthy." Mace strolled to a fridge in the opposite corner of the room. The freezer bulged with frozen dinners. Mace pulled one out and shook it at him. "Not real food."

Zero shrugged. "Sorry Mom. I got Pop-Tarts."

"They're not food either. I thought Trinity was checking on you." Mace pointed to the trashcan overflowing with juice boxes.

"I don't need no angel babysitter. Vegan brings me food now."

"Vegan?"

"Yeah, she's a Halfling."

Mace's eyes lit up. "A female? Zero, what's she like?"

A hot, thick stream slid through Nikki's system, and her cheeks felt on fire. She blinked in surprise. Was this *jealously* over Mace's sudden interest in females?

"What do you care?" Zero pointed. "I see you've found your own."

Mace laughed. "Who, Nikki?" He shook his head. "No, she's no Halfling. A human, a Seer."

Before she could protest, Zero snagged her by the chin. Cold, bony fingers tipped her head back while he reached for a swinging light. He angled the brass half circle until its glare stung her eyes.

That strange silver-blue gaze examined her from no more than three inches away. Finally, he tilted her head down slowly and stared at her face-to-face. His thumb and forefinger dug into her chin. "Why'd you bring her here?" Other questions in his eyes, and his focus made her want to wrench from him. But she didn't. She stood fast, letting him search her.

"We're on a journey and she's helping us."

"You and your journeys." He rolled his eyes and shoved her away. "I can't be in contact with humans. You know that."

"Why?" Nikki interrupted, rubbing her sore chin. "Lack of manners?"

Mace gave her an accusatory look, but the smile toying at his mouth said otherwise.

Icicle eyes narrowed. "I suppose this is just some fun game to you, little girl."

Could he have said anything more stupid? A game, a *fun game*? Her hands slid to her hips. "Absolutely. It's a blast to be chased by demonic dogs and crazed men in SUVs." Nikki let loose every lick of her pent-up anger, and could feel it clash against the impermeable electricity that was Zero.

"Calm down, both of you. It's my fault for bringing Nikki here. Zero has specific instructions to remain away from humans. Not for their sake, for his own. Zero — "

"Tell it like it is, Halfling," he scoffed. "Zero doesn't play well with others. Angels don't want me in their charge. Other Halflings can't stand me."

Mace casually sank his hands into his pockets, a posture Nikki rarely saw him exhibit. He usually remained alert like a predatory cat, ready to bolt or fight at any moment. "It's not like that. Zero has a higher purpose."

"Really?" Nikki's eyes widened innocently. "Even higher than sucking down juice boxes and eating frozen dinners?"

Mace bit his cheeks.

Zero's sneer broke into a smile. "I like her."

"Zero runs the network," Mace said.

"What's that?" Nikki crossed the room and sank into a computer chair. Behind her she could *feel* Zero cringe. It was such a nice computer, top of the line, even. She lightly ran a finger along the edge of the keyboard.

"Don't touch that," he growled.

She batted Bambi eyes and seized the mouse.

"Don't." His hands flew to his head. "Mace, can't you stop her? There are settings and you ..."

When she moved to hit *send*, he slapped the table. "No. Don't do that." He stumbled over his words until finally she spun in the chair, grinning.

"I didn't do anything," she admitted. "I promise."

He heaved a sigh, then grabbed and dragged her from the seat with those shockingly thin fingers. After pushing her away, Zero spun to the computer and stroked the monitor with an open hand.

Mace laughed. "Zero, you really need to get out more."

Feeling satisfied, Nikki crossed her arms and donned a Cheshire grin. "I suppose on the rare occasion, it's like a fun game. Thanks for playing, little *boy.*"

Zero's sneer returned. But this time it was Mace's eyes that surprised her. Softly focused, they seemed to smile. He was ... proud of her. When the understanding surfaced, she realized she wanted, no *needed* him to feel that way. A silent moment of understanding crossed between them.

Breaking the spell, Mace pulled the charred computer from his backpack. "Can you do anything with this?"

Zero smirked. "Looks like you've done enough already."

"We got it from this lab about thirty miles from here."

"Omega Corporation?" Zero took the laptop into loving

160

hands and rested it gently on the table. From four inches above, his eyes scanned the charred mess. He coughed at a puff of dust when he pulled a dingy disk from the wreck and slid it into another system.

"Yes. How'd you know?" Mace asked.

One eye peeked from under strips of silver-blond hair. "Please."

Mace gestured toward the supercomputer. "You've been tracking them?"

"As much as I can."

Mace's eyes widened. "You haven't broken their security code?"

"Their systems are encrypted, of course. But they're layered too. I get close then, *bam*! They shut me out."

"What do they do there? Weapons, nuclear stuff?" Mace asked.

"Look, they're locked into an international network. It's not like I can just flip a switch and ..." Zero's words trailed.

"But Zero, what are they *doing*?" Mace said.

"You want the short answer or the million-dollar answer?"

Mace's jaw clenched. "Any answer at this point will suffice."

"Studying EMP."

"What?" Mace frowned.

"Electromagnetic pulse," Zero said.

"Thanks, I know what it is."

"Good, then you understand the implications."

Nikki interrupted the two. "Excuse me." She waved her hands. "Human present. Could someone please translate?"

A *humph* slipped from Zero's thin lips. "Under the right circumstances, EMP could become the backbone of modern warfare. Nuclear EMP is the worst, but Omega doesn't seem to wade on the nuclear side of the swimming pool."

"So what are they doing?" Mace sank his hands into his hair, the casual demeanor of a few minutes ago gone. "What could they do?"

"Don't know. Nuclear EMP is pretty antiquated for warfare — with its discovery years ago, too many countries placed devices for protection. But non-nuclear EMP has smaller, still horrific effects."

Mace nodded.

"Still lost here," Nikki said.

Mace turned to her. "Electromagnetic pulses are magnetic fields produced by electricity. They have the capability to make every electrical device in range completely useless. Cell phones, vehicles, even the US military."

"Try every military," Zero said.

"Anyway, it's like technology's kryptonite. When an EMP happens, everything dies. Tanks, trucks, computers. Think of an electromagnetic pulse like a giant magnet. The pulse goes out and erases … everything in range."

"So," she said, "it would disable the bad guy's stuff too. Right?"

"Not if they've figured out a way to direct it," Mace said. "If man obtained the power to shut down specific pieces of equipment, technology, or specific computers, there would be no end to the damage."

"Or the power." Zero's words fell with a thud. "An entire nation could be rendered helpless. With no defenses."

"Whoever wielded the power could eventually control the world," Mace inserted.

She dropped. Luckily, most of her weight fell into a chair. As if being a target for termination wasn't enough, now she had the entire world to worry about? "Wait, are you telling me sixty miles from my home, some madmen are creating a device to *take over the world*?"

Zero pointed at her, but directed his question to Mace. "It sounds so sci-fi when she says it. It's not just one facility. I take it you got this computer from the small Omega lab that burned tonight. But, there's another one. Much bigger, right outside of Harrison. Plus, they're global. And EMP isn't the only thing they do."

She blanched. "Can it get any worse?"

"Sure, it could get much worse." Zero peered at the ceiling, rubbing thin, white fingers over his chin. "Actually, no. It really can't get worse."

Mace walked to her. "Nikki, this is what we do. This is why we're sent. It's not to rescue kittens from tree limbs. Every journey has eternal consequences. And sometimes many lives hang in the balance."

Her head felt light, and Mace's words were just fluttery little pieces of dust passing by. Maybe she was about to pass out. With any luck, she'd hit her head and forget everything she'd heard. Did they realize what they were talking about? This was World War Three kind of stuff. *As if the war between heaven and hell wasn't enough ...*

She jetted out of the chair. "I don't want to do this. I can't save the world. You — " She pointed accusingly. "You all have powers, and can" — she flailed her arms — "can break glass without getting cut and can see in the dark. But I'm just a girl. Like Zero said."

His face scrunched. "I never said that."

Mace kept telling her she'd learned enough. Finally, she believed him. It was too much, in fact. Too big of a problem for a human mind, too insurmountable an obstacle, and right now there was way too much concrete and dirt separating her from clean, fresh air. She needed to get out. "Look, I'll, uh, just meet you in the car." Her pace quickened as she headed toward the exit. "You two have fun talking about your war strategies. I'll head on up and listen to the radio until you're done."

As she pulled the door open, Zero's voice stopped her momentum. "Don't you want to know what's on the computer you brought?"

No. Thanks, but no. I just want to leave. But what if the information could help Mace and the others? What if it could stop the bad guys? Such a big part of her wanted this nightmare to end. And yet ...

Yet a tiny part of her wanted to embrace it. Like a moth to flame, Nikki was drawn to the task. With a long, surrendering sigh, she turned. "You've already retrieved the information?"

"What's left of it." His almost colorless eyes scanned her. "Up to you. You can walk out and have Mace take you home and you're free, baby girl."

She chewed her lip, one hand on the door, the other ready to grab the banister and propel herself up. She chanced a look to Mace. *You'll never run from the battle*, he'd told her. But she *wanted* to run. Her feet carried her one step higher. When she glanced at him again, she saw the flash of disappointment. He'd also said he'd see it through to the end.

Zero's voice mocked. "You're right. You're only a human. What could you do? Go on, chicken. Run home."

Nikki jumped off the step, slammed the door, and leveled her gaze on Zero. "No. I might be a chicken. But I don't run."

Both guys smiled. Zero's was a grudging admiration, but she didn't care. And Mace's ... well, she'd have to process that look later.

"What's on the computer, Zero?" Mace asked.

"The hard drive is toast. I'll keep working with it, but don't hold your breath."

"Is that it?"

"I retrieved a few words from the disk. First ones are *Genesis Project*, second's a name. Nick."

Mace frowned. "As in Nicolas?"

"No, the full name is Nicole Youngblood."

Chapter
15

Back at the house, exhausted and really, *really* ready to call it a night, Mace dragged himself from the car, then slammed the door. Before stepping away, he peered in through the driver's window. "Nikki, I just need to brief Will on what we learned from Zero. Give me five minutes. Then I'll get you home." He'd barely taken three steps toward the front door when he heard a slam. He turned to the car, still pinging and popping from the drive.

Little to his surprise, Nikki stood beside the passenger door. But instead of the defiant posture she'd had earlier, she fidgeted, hands clasped together.

Mace's heart did a painful little thump. She looked lost, a tiny bird in need of strong wings able to lift her above the storm.

"I'm coming with you. I have a right to know what's going on." Her eyes turned to liquid. "Mace, my name was in that computer. They knew me. That scientist, *he* knew me." She choked on a sob.

He stepped toward her. "But you're exhausted," he said, wanting to hold her. Knowing he wouldn't. The bad dream had just gotten worse. He'd been fooling himself to think Nikki was just a Seer. Admitting the truth meant admitting the possibility of failure. And failure meant death.

"You're exhausted too," she said.

He couldn't argue. Battle made him weary, and trying to protect her with the clouded judgment he fought made him fatigued. Sure, he could lift her from the storm. He could be her shelter if he could keep his mind in the game and stop toying with romantic ideas that were both dangerous and impossible.

Not impossible. Too costly. Eternity wasn't a gamble he could take, no matter how helpless the bird.

From the moment Raven's gaze dropped on Nikki, he couldn't look away from her. She stood just inside the front door, arms interlocked with Mace's as if she couldn't stand on her own.

But he saw through the veneer. Her eyes were bright and alert. Her hands were open and relaxed, her shoulders down. *Man, she looks good.* Never mind the messy hair pulled from her face and clustered at the back of her neck with — pencils? Never mind the rumpled clothes. Nikki, skin hot from the battle and face smooth, looked more alive now than in any moment before. Even the moment he revealed the true nature of her painting — and in fact, the true nature of Nikki herself — couldn't compare.

Now, if she'd just let go of Mr. Soft and Sweet . . .

"So you're not just the Seer," Will said while checking her hands and arms for marks and burns.

"I'm fine," she assured, though she seemed thrown by all

the attention. Will and Vine had met them at the door when they entered. But Raven had been content to admire her from a distance.

But a wave washed over him, and in a heartbeat he was there too. He stopped at her side and Mace stiffened, arm closing protectively around her. She smelled amazing, like battle and heaven all rolled together. Raven reached behind her head and ever so gently tugged. The pencils fell to the floor while her dark hair cascaded down over her shoulders.

Her eyes closed and opened, too slowly for a blink. She seemed to catch herself and quickly gestured to the mass of boys hovering over her. "This is a bit ..." She forced a sweet smile. "Stifling."

Will shooed them away and everyone found a place to sit while Mace filled them in on what they'd witnessed at the lab and what Zero found on the computer.

Will leaned forward, resting his elbows on his knees. "So, Omega Corporation tests EMP theories? What does that have to do with Nicole Youngblood?" His tight skin pulled into an inquisitive look. "And what is the Genesis Project?"

Raven sighed loudly. "Genesis clearly means the beginning." But his eyes refused to leave Nikki, who sat on the couch beside Mace. Fidgeting hands, twitch in her cheek, eyes that kept roaming the room and landing on Raven ... Oh yeah, she wanted him. She was just trying to act like she didn't.

"And Omega means the end," Vine added.

"So what can we gather?" Will asked.

Raven spread his arms and rubbed a hand back and forth against the soft leather of his chair. "That whoever runs Omega Corporation thinks they're both the beginning and the end?" he said.

168

Will folded giant arms across his chest. "Possibly," he said.

Raven threw his hands into the air. "You got something better?"

"No."

"We aren't ignorant of how the enemy thinks," Raven said.

Mace's eyes narrowed on him. "That's for sure," he spat.

Will pointed at him. "Right you are, Raven." He turned his attention to Nikki. "I'm afraid you may be the target."

"No. I'm *telling* you *Richmond* is the target. I've been saying it all night." Conviction and agitation threaded his words.

"And what are you basing that on?" Will questioned.

"My gut."

Will stood and crossed the room to him. "Your gut?"

Raven straightened, jaw set. "That's right."

"And we're supposed to base an entire operation on your gut?"

Vine swallowed and sank into the couch, out of harm's way. Mace sat motionless.

"Do whatever you want, but my gut says Richmond's the target."

A wide smile spread across Will's face, while looks of shock and surprise bounced around the room. "Excellent," he yelled, posture softening.

Raven flashed a confused frown. *Freak.* His caregiver was a freak.

Vine's body relaxed, but his eyes still flitted from Will to Raven.

Will pulled Raven to his feet and slapped him on the back. "Way to go." He placed a hand on Raven's stomach and rubbed in a circular motion. *Watch it, buddy.* "Right here is the seat of your consciousness. You might even say the *heart* of your *gut*.

Follow your instincts. Trust your gut. For now, we shall guard both Richmond and Nikki." With a smooth, fluid motion, he crossed the room to her. "We don't have all the pieces of the puzzle, Miss Youngblood. But I can promise you this. My boys will protect you. You've no need to fear." He gestured to Vine. "Bloom, bring me the gift before Mace drives her home."

Mace and Nikki rose and moved toward the front door.

Vine disappeared and materialized at the door beside them. "Here you go." He handed a box to Nikki. "It will help you understand."

She pulled the lid from the case and the smell of leather wafted up. A Bible lay inside. Mace took the lid from her as she admired the gold-leaf book. "It's beautiful," she uttered.

Who knew a Bible would make her so mushy?

"There is quite a bit of commentary. I agree with ..." Will stared at the ceiling for a few moments. "Most of it. I think the commentary will help you understand the significance of the days in which you live."

"Thank you. I don't know what to say." Her fingers drifted over the cover.

"You're welcome."

"Is this sort of like a rule book?" She clutched it to her chest.

"More like a new paradigm." His eyes narrowed. "Do you know what a paradigm is?"

"You know, I actually do."

"Be sure and read about Esther," Will said. "You remind me of her."

"Okay." She returned the box's lid and addressed Raven. "Do you really think Dr. Richmond is in danger?"

Again, Raven saw a warrior looking out from behind her eyes. *Much better.*

Will crossed his arms over his chest. "If Omega Corporation is gaining too much momentum, everyone you know could be in danger."

"EMP isn't the only thing they do," Mace inserted.

"What else?" Will asked. The thought visibly troubled him, which only excited Raven. A real battle was coming. The kind of combat he was trained to fight, rather than this, "Go for the good-girl" war he was dealing with.

"We don't know. Zero is trying to gather information. He doesn't feel like Genesis Project has anything to do with their EMP program."

Will's concentration deepened. "On what is he basing his assumptions?"

Mace smiled. "His gut."

"Why'd you bring me here?" Mace's words echoed off the rock ledge above them where they sat on the ground with backs against a cool stone and eyes gazing out at the lake. The sun had disappeared behind the mountain before they reached the area.

This was Nikki's favorite place. Before them, an old fishing pier spiked into the water, a solitary haven for the spiders that fought for rights to the weathered wood corners. Many evenings she'd sat here while the sun dropped and fish jumped to grab the night bugs landing on the smooth lake.

"Shhh." Nikki scooted close enough to clamp her hand over his mouth. Against her fingers, she felt him sigh. But his breathing returned to normal as the soft stillness of Lake Taneycomo closed around them. "When the fog rolls in, everything will disappear into it."

He took her by the wrist and ever so gently removed her hand from his mouth. "Why do you get to talk and I have to stay quiet?"

Her eyes found his just as the first bits of warm wind settled on the dark, cold water. "Because if you talk I might wake up and realize this is just a dream."

"It's not a dream, Nikki."

A blanket of billowy fog rose as the temperature fell. Warm air, cool water, a sea of hazy stillness that crept ever closer to their haven offered a place of security for silly things like admissions. "I brought you here because I wanted to say thank you ... for everything. This has always been a special place to me and I guess I wanted to share it with you. One time, I sat right here and told my dad I'd painted one of the antique swords with my mom's fingernail polish." The rolling fog moved closer, and with it the air chilled by the water. "I was so ashamed. You know what he said?"

Mace shook his head.

"He said that the fog would take it all away."

When she shivered, Mace wrapped an arm around her. "Did it work?"

She nodded then dropped her head to his chest. "Yes."

"Thank you, Nikki."

"For what?"

He swept a hand in front of them. "For this. I'll never forget it." Mace licked his lips and inched closer to her.

Oh.

Oh my. He's going to kiss me. Well, what had she expected bringing a guy somewhere romantic like this? But it had never been romantic before. Just quiet and safe and secure. Nikki swallowed. *Okay. If he's going to kiss me, I'm ready.*

And then his lips were there as the white fog surrounded them and closed them in. Soft against her own, his mouth warmed and Nikki was utterly and completely swept away. But only a moment later, his lips left hers in a rush.

He was barely visible through the fog, but his body crackled with tension. She didn't dare utter a word. Maybe she was really bad at kissing.

Mace rose and pulled her to her feet. "Come on. We better go."

She let herself be dragged along, really, *really* confused about what had just happened.

So much for safe places and fog that takes the shame away. She shouldn't have brought him here. But as they walked up the hill to return to Mace's car, he slipped his hand into hers, thoroughly confusing and equally thrilling.

Another day passed without incident, other than a strange conversation she overheard between her mom and dad. Nikki hadn't meant to eavesdrop, but her folks were acting strange. More so than normal and she couldn't shake the conversation between her parents this morning when they didn't know she was sitting on the stairs listening. She replayed it again and again. "Something's wrong, Dale. It's horribly wrong. I keep having these nightmares that Nikki is taken away—"

"Nikki's fine, honey. You're just worried because she's nearly eighteen, and you know what Vessler—"

"Stop it!" her mother had ordered. "I can't deal with this. He's coming and we have no way to stop him." That's where Nikki tuned out. It was stupid to worry about a conversation she'd only gotten bits of … especially when there were so many other things to concentrate on, like staying alive. *So far so good.* At least she had help with that one.

One of the Halflings graced each and every class she attended. Grateful for their protection, she refrained from complaining about the constancy of a sidekick. Besides, a part of her was almost enjoying the attention. Okay, so having attention from Mace had always been nice. But Raven? Not as much. Except now she was starting to look forward to science and English, where Raven was her guardian. She hated to admit that she anticipated seeing him, but fact was, she did. More and more.

The Lost Boys appeared nonchalant, but their continual assistance caused a flurry of *unwanted* attention from other male students. Josh Nolens — football star and general hottie — had suddenly started talking to her. Gag. She'd been crushing on him for the better part of forever, but now he seemed so ... shallow. One dimensional. Ordinary.

After the last bell, Nikki and Krissy meandered down the long, narrow hall. The scent of fresh sweat accosted them as they passed the gym doors.

"I've hardly seen you the last few days," Krissy said.

"I know. I'm sorry."

Her best friend heaved a drama-laden sigh. "So, have I told you about running into Raven and Vine at the bowling alley?"

The night of the laboratory fire. Krissy *had* told her, but Nikki wouldn't admit it. Her friend loved the story too much, so it was best to act interested when really, Nikki just wanted to get outside to her bike and to a waiting Mace, who would follow her home.

"Okay," Krissy bubbled, hugging her pink, sparkly note-book. Her lips flashed with the same silver flecks that also graced her fingernails, and Nikki wondered how much time she'd spent planning the ensemble.

As Krissy launched into her bowling alley story, Nikki scanned her own T-shirt and jeans. Krissy'd given up on her after the first week of school, leaving new clothes with tags still dangling hanging lonely in Nikki's closet. A stab of regret surprised her. Sparkly notebooks, boys at the bowling alley, the hope of a homecoming date ... Nikki filled her lungs and hefted her own heavy exhale. No shred of normalcy anchored her life. Except Mace. But actually, things had been a little weird there too. They'd be all cozy, almost couple-ish, then he'd shut down. Mace and his infernal boundaries were wearing on her patience. Raven never pushed her away—his reactions were quite the opposite. Nikki scolded herself. *Don't go down that road. There's a nasty drop off at the end.*

Krissy talked on. "Suzy Carmichael is going to ask the young one, Vine—isn't that the coolest name?—to go to homecoming. She swears she's going to do it, but I think she'll wimp out. She's terrified he'll laugh in her face or puke or something. He's only fifteen, but who cares? They're all like a million feet tall and ..." Something at the end of the hall stopped Krissy's forward momentum—a mammoth task, to be sure.

Nikki followed Krissy's gaze. At the end of the hall, Mace lounged against the doorframe. His face came alive when he saw them, eyes dancing and strands of hair fringing his cheekbones.

Krissy's glances split between him and her best friend as the girls lessened the gap. "Well, at least *someone* is dating one of them."

"I'm not dating one of them!" But Nikki's heart betrayed her by jumping into her throat and making her denial resemble a pig's squeal. Normalcy was highly overrated. As were football players. But Halflings …

Krissy held her sparkly hand up. "Stop. Can't lie to a BFF."

"We're just friends," Nikki hissed as they paused in front of Mace.

His gaze settled on Nikki, and Krissy grinned.

"Hey, chicken." He smiled down at her, his light-gray T-shirt disappearing into frayed jeans that hugged his legs oh-so-nicely.

Krissy's brows rode high on her forehead. "Chicken?" she mouthed, leaning closer to Nikki. "That's his pet name for you? It's not very romantic."

Nikki elbowed her in the stomach. "It's apropos."

Krissy held up a finger to Mace. "Excuse us, best friend chat." She dragged Nikki to the corner of the building. "Enough of the secrecy. I want to know what's going on. It seems like one of them is with you all the time. And Mace looks at you like you're the only human on the planet."

Nikki feigned innocence. "You're the one who said we should show them around town, help them acclimate."

"Yes. We." She grabbed her shoulders. "*We*, Nikki."

Nikki barely heard her. She was grinning at Mace and he was grinning back.

Krissy threw her hands up. "You know what, never mind. Keep your dirty little secrets." Her glossy bottom lip tipped out in a pout. "Just tell me one thing?"

"What?"

"When did he nickname you chicken?"

Nikki's grin turned into a full-on smile. "Right after he kissed away my boo-boos."

Krissy's gaping mouth released a sigh and she clenched her notebook tighter.

Nikki returned to Mace and the two locked arms and walked toward the parking lot, into what was surely a beautiful fall afternoon. Around them, classmates loitered at vehicles, and off to the right, the football team ran drills in the field. Not that Nikki bothered to notice. Mace's gaze was only upon her, and she returned the gesture by ignoring everything but him.

Raven watched from the opposite corner of the building. Faded jeans hung low on his hips. His hands sank into the pockets. A graphic T graced his chest. He could feel the weathered, thin material hugging his lean muscles. The dark gray and black graphic featured a knight slaying a dragon. The word *vengeance* spread across the chest in ornate, bone-white, old-English lettering. His eyes trailed to Nikki.

She stopped at her motorcycle and her dark hair flowed in the afternoon's breeze. Tilting her head, strands feathered over one shoulder. Mace said something to her and she laughed, contractions of joy causing her shoulders to bounce.

Raven's heart squeezed. In moments like this he was thankful for his ability to slow motion. A giant oak leaf tumbled toward her, flipping end over end. Its intricacy caught Raven's attention. He followed its path, examining each detail of the veins on either side. They stretched like fingers, once alive, now dead, reaching, straining for life.

Life. Ha. Raven longed for death. Sweet sleep, then resurrection. But he'd likely never taste death, never have the privilege of hearing, "Well done, thy good and faithful servant." Mouth filling with the distaste of his fate, Raven spit on the ground.

His gaze returned to Nikki. She was a light. She was hope. Before heading in her direction, he cast a glance to the ground where he'd spat.

The grass had withered.

Chapter
16

"Y"ou're sure you don't mind, Nikki?" Mace asked. Apprehension seemed to lace his words.

She waved to Raven sauntering across the lot toward them. "No, I'll meet up with you later."

Even from the distance, Raven could see Mace's reluctance about leaving Nikki alone with him. *Smart boy.*

He and Mace exchanged a nod. As soon as Mace climbed into his car, Raven turned to Nikki and raked his eyes over her. "So, lover boy has to dump you for the afternoon?"

"FYI, he's not lover boy, and he's not dumping me. If you don't want to hang, that's fine. I'm a big girl and I can get myself home safely."

A flirtatious smile curved his lips. "Fire sparks in your eyes when you get mad. Did you know that?"

"No." She cocked her hip. "Is that why you keep provoking me?"

"It's sexy."

She blushed.

"Come on." He slid onto the back of her bike and grabbed the extra helmet.

Her face lit, and his heart jolted.

She didn't bother to hide the excitement. "Guys usually don't want to ride on the back. Mace just follows me in his car."

"I'm not Mace. Let's go for a ride, Nikki," he purred. "I promise you won't forget it."

"Seriously?" she said, fingers tightening around her helmet. "Why not?"

Nikki slid onto the bike in front of him and tugged on her helmet. She tossed a look over her shoulder. "You ready?"

Her voice was threaded with anticipation. He slipped his hands onto her back, then took his time sliding them around her midsection. One tug, and he'd pulled her snug against him. "I'm ready for everything you've got."

Nikki gunned the engine and they tore out of the parking lot, barely pausing to wave at Krissy.

Krissy's eyes and mouth rounded even more, the pink-polished, sparkly lips forming a perfect *O*. Raven sent her a half smile. Her bottom dropped onto a car hood. When the vehicle's alarm sounded, she didn't bother to move.

Halflings were hot and Raven knew it. She could tell by the way he moved, worked that half smile, rocked those frayed jeans. *She knew Raven was dangerous, yet she couldn't help the little jolt she got whenever he looked at her. The girl who never notices boys suddenly loves the attention.* But these weren't boys. And Raven's looks hadn't always thrilled her. To be honest, they'd scared her at first. That fear had melted into a grudging appreciation of the unique protection he offered, an innate confidence in his powers that Mace couldn't always carry off — but now it was melting again into some new compound she couldn't name.

"Where to?" she hollered over her shoulder, and realized he was drawing the breath she released. *Why does he insist on doing that?*

"Arkansas."

She slowed, eyes leaving the road. "It's about an hour away."

"Not the way I drive." His hands left her stomach and grasped hers on the handlebars. He squeezed the throttle and the bike jumped forward.

When they squealed around a corner, she couldn't stop the tremor that coursed through her. "Isn't this dangerous?"

"Nikki, even if you were to fly off the bike, I'd catch you before you touched the ground."

"Well, I'd just as soon not put that to the test," she hollered.

Once across the state line, Raven took his hands off hers and she breathed a sigh of relief. The Ozark Mountains that had disappeared behind them led way to higher and rockier mountains separated by long areas of woods. The bike cut a shadow on the road that appeared and disappeared in tandem with the sun's rays. Raven removed his helmet.

She brought the bike to a stop beneath a massive oak tree anchoring a mineral spring. "That was incredible." Her eyes were watery from the wind and she was sure color flushed her cheeks.

"Yeah," he said with a yawn. "I guess."

"Stop it. You were having as much fun as I was. I could feel it."

"You could *feel* it?"

"Yeah." She threw her leg off the bike. "It's really weird, but around you guys I'm so much more in tune with what's happening around me." *And somewhat cautious about how you all make me feel.* It was different, of course, with Mace. With all three she felt alive, strong, powerful. But with Mace, there was a deep river of security. Raven … he caused these fluttery, almost alarming jitters, the kind one would get in a cage with a sleeping lion. That was it: Mace was safety and Raven was danger. *Only a sick, twisted mind would be drawn to both.*

He studied her in that way he had; half curiosity, half strategy, and all question. He draped a hand across one handlebar, then hooked his foot on a chrome foot peg. "Show me what you mean," he said, but there was a strange sound in his voice, something suggesting understanding was only a breath away.

"How should I show you?"

Raven's tongue darted out and licked his lips as he stood. "Close your eyes."

She shrugged, obeyed. *Why argue now?*

He was straddling the bike and she was close. Close enough for him to lean over and kiss her. Is that what he intended to do? When his shadow slowly shifted across her face, she knew it was. Before his lips met hers, her hand flew between them.

"That's pretty good," he said. "Open your eyes." Inches apart, he dropped the kiss onto the palm of her hand.

She stood breathless and confused. What had his little stunt proven?

"Come on." He tossed his leg off the bike and tugged her away from the motorcycle. As he dragged her into the woods, he said, "I want you to show me what you can really do."

Strips of sunlight slashed across the pine-covered ground where they stopped in a clearing. Alive with chatter, the woods closed in around them like a cotton cocoon.

In the distance, a waterfall rushed a continual stream over the rocky mountainside and deposited water and bubbles into a pool below. Rich vegetation glowed green, lush from the fall's constant spray. She really tried to focus on the soothing nest it created, but all she could think of was the kiss she narrowly escaped. *Raven's* kiss. She shouldn't be here. She should be with Mace. But wasn't it Raven who'd seen through her artist's mask? He'd seen her for the fraud she was and liked her anyway. She was no artist, just a good copier. The heart of the painting really had laid in the significance of the broken pot, and in some small way, that did make her an artist, not just an imitator. But she hadn't known until ... Raven saw it.

Mace had looked at the painting and saw possibilities. To him, the gate was an invitation.

Mace was her invitation. He embraced her destiny, saw her as a future warrior, and swore to see her through.

And that made Raven her broken pot. The one who embraced the person she was right now. Odds were, he'd likely stand beside her and die to protect her as well, if she gave him the chance.

Which one understands the real me? She bit the inside of her cheek.

Raven leaned against a pine tree, his words pulling her from her thoughts. "What's Mace been teaching you?"

"What do you mean?" She kicked at a clump of dirt and hoped he hadn't been reading her mind.

"About self preservation? Come on, I know he's not stupid enough to spend all this time with you but not show you how to fight or at least how to defend yourself."

She frowned. She'd spent quite a bit of time with Mace, but the subject had never come up.

He dragged his weight from the tree. "Nikki, these are eternal enemies. Surely he's preparing you."

She shook her head, a bit of panic settling over her. Were she and Mace playing infatuated teenager games when she should be in training for this realm-crossing war?

"Oh, I get it." He stepped closer. "He has to be your knight in shining armor." Raven reached up and tugged on a branch. "Pathetic. Well, don't send a boy to do a man's job. It's time for you to learn." When the branch snapped, it flung bits of bark in all directions. He dusted the mess from his hands and raised his fists.

Fear jumped in her stomach but she slowly slid into a fighting position. "Wha-what are we doing?"

He winked. "Come after me. Or are you scared?"

She pulled two pencils from her jacket pocket and twisted them into her hair. "Am I scared? Are you *kidding*? You're half angel. Of course I'm scared."

"Also half man, which means I have weaknesses." He winked again, and the motion was accompanied by a long, slow perusal of her from head to toe. "So use them against me."

"Stop it," she ordered. Raven was always a little over-the-top with his flirting, but the way his gaze trailed over her and lingered here and there was way too bold, even for him.

"Make me." His eyes passed over her again with painful slowness. "Come on, Nikki, don't prove me right."

"Right about what?" Her fists opened into flat hands, war hands.

"That you're a sissy."

She ran for him, determined to teach him good manners the hard way. Two leaps and they were face-to-face, fighting distance apart. But she stopped, catching herself. This was crazy.

He wanted to fight her? He actually wanted her to attack him? But it was okay, right? Raven wouldn't *hurt* her.

Would he?

He stiffened. "Come on."

Distributing her weight, she rolled onto the ball of her back foot, then threw a front kick to his stomach.

He caught it easily, moving in a flash. While he held her foot, she used his grab as a springboard and kicked toward his face with her other foot. The jumping front kick landed in his other hand. With one smooth sweep, he flipped her up and over. She landed on her stomach with a thud.

"Sorry," he said, and gently used the toe of his boot against her hip to coax her onto her back. But there was a distinct laugh in his voice when he reached to draw her to her feet. "Now it's my turn. You defend."

She felt her blood drain.

"Don't worry, I'll take it easy." He intertwined his fingers and straightened his arms so that every knuckle in his hands popped. When he rushed toward her, she cowered.

"No," he yelled, and skidded to a stop. "If you're afraid to take a hit, I've already beaten you."

She stiffened, slid her front leg into a cat stance, set her jaw, and waited. The punch came at her, but slowed almost to a halt as it approached. Reaching, she grabbed the fist inches from her.

A strange recognition flittered across his face, like the one he'd had when she said she could feel his excitement on the bike. "Good," he said.

"What did I do?" She heaved between breaths, the world around still moving at a sluggish pace.

"You stopped me."

185

"Everything slowed down. Like how everything slows in a wreck."

"Cool, huh?" With a flick of his head, he tossed hair from his eyes.

"Did you do that?" she whispered.

He nodded. "Yeah."

"Can you do that anytime?"

"Pretty much. What you saw is what we always see, Nikki. Everything moves at a slower speed for us. And when we try, we can stretch the immediate atmosphere. Sometimes, humans are aware of it — like in the wrecks you mentioned. Most often, that's where humans become aware of the supernatural at work around them, though they seem to remain clueless as to what it is. Not that I'd expect your brains to get it: we can move so fast, the molecules disappear. It's also where you get the term déjà vu."

"No, I read about that. It has to do with the brain misfiring."

"Really?" Raven said.

She nodded. A flash, and she frowned.

"How about that time?" he asked.

"Whoa." Again, the immediate seconds stretched.

"How about that time?" he repeated.

She shook her head. "Stop it. That's freaky." She reached behind her for something, anything to steady her balance. Everything seemed off, her judgment included. Suddenly she knew coming to Arkansas with Raven had been a grave mistake.

And yet . . .

He was training her. How could she find fault in that? He wanted to give her something Mace had never offered. Self preservation.

"I can relive any moment I've experienced." His eyes dropped to her lips. "Again and again and again."

She swallowed the newly formed lump in her throat. "I suppose that's faster than the speed of light?" she asked, training her thoughts on the lesson. Sensei Coble taught her to always rely on her training.

"Uh, yeah."

"Amazing." She dropped her hands. "There's no way I can win against a supernatural foe."

"Wrong," he corrected. "First, all foes won't be supernatural. You're being hunted, Nikki. And not just by hell's army. Human armies as well. Flesh and blood. Bone and joint. They share your weaknesses, but what they don't have is your advantage."

"What's my advantage?"

"They're never going to expect *you* to hunt *them*."

She had to admit it made sense. If she hadn't been a fighter, she'd have never survived this long. "Hmm. Predator becomes the prey?"

"Exactly." He stepped away from her. "Or you can continue being a damsel in distress and let Mace protect you." He shrugged one shoulder. "But wouldn't you rather be your own hero?"

"Yes," she said, and as quickly as she answered, she formed a plan. When he dropped his hands, she advanced. Faking a spinning crescent kick, she landed a roundhouse kick to his jaw.

His head barely moved from the jolt. "Nice, but not enough power to stop me. Where was your target?"

She pulled a breath and reached to touch his right jaw.

He grabbed her hand. "No. Not here." He slung her hand to the opposite cheek. "*Here*."

"I should have kicked the other side of your face?" she asked.

"No! You should have driven through my jaw. Your target is always six inches past the point of contact." Roughly, he dragged her hand to his chin. "If you're trying to punch me here, where should your target be?"

Before she could answer, he put her hand to the back of his neck. "Here, Nikki." He tapped her fingers against his neckline, hot from the sun's rays and the fight. "Six inches past. Drive through. You get it?"

"I get it."

He threw her hand down. "Now do it."

She punched and connected soundly with his rock-hard stomach. "Wow." The power behind the strike shocked her.

He smiled.

"In self-defense, they teach girls to strike and run." Suddenly, Raven disappeared.

She spun, looking for him.

From her right side, she felt him grab her loose T-shirt, twist, and toss her to the ground. "If you're going to insist on being a victim, please continue to dress like one. It makes my job so much easier." His voice bounded off a tree behind her, and she jumped, turning to it.

"What's wrong with strike and run?" she asked, twirling the hem of her T into a knot, lessening his ability to grab.

"You don't have that luxury anymore. You have to strike and kill because you can't outrun us."

When he appeared before her, she attempted a ridge hand to his temple, but grabbed only air. "And we'll never give up." He threw his fist into a tree beside her and bark rained around her head.

Alarm fought for control of her mind, but she fought back. Raven was *helping* her, not trying to *hurt* her.

"Mace said he didn't think there were Halflings fighting on the enemy's side."

"He's wrong. Poor little naïve Mace. He's dead wrong."

"Glad you're more enlightened," she said when he reappeared at her feet, and for a fleeting moment she gazed right into his soul. What she saw frightened her. When she spoke, the words were distant. "Maybe you don't know which side you're on."

It stopped him cold. Dust settled around them.

This was her chance. She lunged, swept his leg, and threw him to the ground. He landed flat on his back. Nikki dropped to her knees. Hovering above him, she smiled, a hand planted on each side of his head. "Used your weakness."

Raven's midnight-blue eyes changed to something needful. He closed his fingers around her arms and pulled her closer. "I'm a good teacher."

"I'm a better student," she countered. She cast a glance at his strong fingers wrapped tightly above her elbows, which sent waves of syrupy heat into her skin. "You should let me go."

"Your lesson isn't over yet," Raven said. His hair fell away from his face, highlighting the contours of his cheekbones, his strong jaw, his bow-shaped lips. People always looked different when flat on their backs, and it was doubly true now. Everything beautiful about Raven seemed magnified by his vulnerable posture.

She tried to return her focus to the fight. "I ... I can't beat you," she said, and wondered on just how many levels she meant the comment. "It's impossible. You can't be hurt, at least not by me and my bare hands."

"I can, Nikki." His fingers glided down her arm and clasped her wrist with such tenderness, it shocked her. He dragged her hand to the center of his chest and pressed.

Beneath his shirt his heart pounded, synchronized to the beat of her own. Something so sad, so human entered his gaze. A longing she — and she alone — was able to fill. For a brief moment she *wanted* to kiss him, if for no other reason than to stop his pain. Danger flashed like a warning sign in her mind, but there was something so beautiful about his desire to protect her. *No,* she corrected. *About his desire to teach her to protect herself.* Why hadn't Mace done that? Why didn't he want her to be able to defend herself?

As she bent closer, his hand moved to the back of her head. Pulling the pencils from their place sent a wave of hair floating around her. *Another bad habit I'll have to break.* She tucked it back with the hand not planted on Raven's chest. Dark-blue eyes scanned every feature of her face, burning a trail wherever they lingered. His gaze flickered as he whispered to her. "Don't forget, I'm the enemy."

She faltered. This was a lesson. Trust no one, perhaps even herself. Warring with her thoughts, Nikki licked her lips. "Raven," she whispered, tilting closer. "Thanks for teaching me how to destroy you."

"Anytime." His eyes closed, and when they did she grabbed the pencils, clasped one in each hand, yelled, and came down hard to bury them into his chest. She stopped millimeters above his beating heart. A mixture of fear and horror swept her.

He didn't even flinch. Raven lay motionless, eyes still shut.

Trembling, she dropped the pencils. They rolled off him passively. "Raven! You didn't stop me!" She fisted a hand and pounded his chest. "What's wrong with you?"

Slowly, his eyes drifted open while his trademark smirk tilted his cheek.

"You *taught* me to *drive through*!" She pushed angry, shaking hands through her hair. In fact, her whole body was quivering and she knew exactly why. He'd given her the key to his destruction … then trusted her not to use it. "I could have *killed* you." She smacked his chest with an open hand and tried to pull away.

He restrained her, hands closing on her upper arms. When he chuckled, she pounded on his chest again. "I could have killed you! Don't ever do that again."

His chuckle became a laugh.

"Stop it," she said through hot tears.

"I saw you coming," he said, casually. "I knew exactly what you intended to do. Besides, you'd never kill me, Nikki."

She shoved off of him and stood. *Oh, I would. Right now if I could just reach my pencils again.* "What makes you think I wouldn't?"

"You're in love with me."

Something jumped in her stomach. "I am *not* in love with you," she gritted through clenched teeth. "I'm not even sure I like you." She stomped toward the bike, crushing fallen leaves and soft grass as she went. She threw a look over her shoulder as he followed her. "And I certainly don't trust you."

He leaned forward and murmured in her ear. "Trust is for the weak."

She shooed him away like a pesky fly. "And love is for victims." She shoved her helmet onto her head. "And like you said, I don't have that luxury anymore."

Chapter
17

As soon as she pulled into her driveway, warning alarms rang in Nikki's senses like internal sirens. She parked her bike, then pulled her helmet from her head. In less than a heartbeat, she was being mauled by a monster of fur and a wet tongue.

"Bo," she sputtered when his slobber made contact with her lips. "Ew. Stop." She shoved the yellow lab away, but her giggle only enticed him into round two. She grabbed his massive head in a headlock. The dog squirmed, growling and wagging a golden tail.

When she trapped him he pleaded for release with eyes too innocent for a hundred-pound beast.

She melted, mumbled an "Aw," and sank onto the ground. The headlock became a hug. "I know I've been neglecting you, Bo." *Sorry, all my time is consumed with infuriating half-angel boys right now.*

The huge animal sighed and nuzzled deeper into her side.

"Soon as I check in, we'll go for a walk." She scrubbed his ears. "Okay? Just you and me." A walk would be nice. It would give her time to process the whole Raven and Mace thing. *Like it can be worked out in one trip to the park.*

Bo mouthed her arm. "Okay, okay. We'll go to the tennis courts. I'll take your tennis ball."

At the word, his ears perked, head cocking to the side. He barked.

"You're so easy to please. I think I could forget to feed you for a week and you'd forgive my transgression." Transgression? Now that's what her dad would call a three-dollar word. Where'd she get that? Ah, yes, the Bible Will had given her. "Hope I don't start talking in King James." While she and Bo sat in the driveway, a black Camaro pulled in.

Mace stepped from the vehicle and slammed the door hard. "Where were you?"

Annoyance at his tone tightened her lungs. She stood, evening the playing field. "Why didn't you use your *spider sense* to find us?"

He shoved a hand through his hair. "That's not funny, Nikki. This isn't some pastime."

Her hands flew up. "Really? It's not? But it's *sooooo* much fun! Maybe you're just jealous because I wasn't with *you*."

"Hardly," he scoffed.

The words stung.

"You're a job to me."

That hurt even more. *How much of that is true?*

"You're an assignment, and, in case you haven't noticed, one I take seriously."

"Oh, is that right?" A more biting comeback failed to come. Words like *job* and *assignment* kept swirling in her mind.

"Yes, that's right."

"Then why haven't you taught me how to fight?" She closed the distance to him and shoved her finger into his chest. "You are constantly sending me these mixed signals. One minute you look at me like you're going to kiss me and the next, you look like you want to vomit. I don't get you, Mace."

"I'm not sending mixed signals. I just — It's very complicated."

"Well, at least Raven is honest."

Fury washed over him. "Honest?" he spat. "I'm not sure Raven remembers how to be honest. Do yourself a favor and stay as far away from him as you can."

"Why?"

He gripped her arms. Hard enough it hurt. "Because he's bad for you."

"Why? Because he doesn't want me to be a victim? Because he doesn't have to be my personal bodyguard?" She wanted to lash out, strike him, but her arms were pinned. Her hands fisted and the fact they did angered her even more.

Bo growled.

She leveled her gaze. "Or is it because he can be honest about his feelings for me?"

She hated the look on Mace's face. It was both hurt and regret. "You really think he's being honest? He's playing with you, Nikki. Nothing more. You're just another piece of arm candy to him."

Ouch! She unwillingly pulled those hurtful words into her being. "Arm candy?"

"Ask him yourself. Raven admittedly looks for hot girls on every journey. He tends to go for the mean ones."

And ouch again. She shook her head. "You're the one who

runs hot and cold, not him. At least with Raven I know where I stand."

"No, you don't." His tone was filled with as much certainty as her own.

"He's in love with me," she yelled.

Something hot, practically deadly veiled his eyes. His jaw clenched so tightly, she thought it might break into pieces. "No. He. Is. Not." And with that, he threw his hands down.

"How do you know?" she countered, and took a step back, desperate to leave the charged atmosphere that constantly surrounded Mace.

"Because if he was, he'd feel the same way I do."

She sucked in a breath at his admission. *The same way he does? Did he mean, does that mean he loves —*

"And," Mace continued, "he'd be slightly more upset about the situation."

"Why?" Her feet carried her back to him, his words a magnet drawing her in.

"Never mind. It doesn't matter." Now it was Mace's turn to attempt to get away. He stumbled back.

"It matters to me. Why would he be upset?" There was an emotion surging over him she couldn't place, couldn't hope to understand, and it terrified her.

After a long, slow breath, he said, "Because for Halflings, falling in love with a human is the unpardonable sin."

Chapter 18

Her heart stopped and with it, time itself. "What does that mean?"

Mace was shrouded in despair — it almost bled from every pore of his being. "If we fall in love with a human, it guarantees we're doomed for all eternity, because we're furthering the enemy's plan. It voids all our journeys. Everything we've worked to obtain. Everything we've done."

And Nikki knew that meant, very simply, destroying everything Mace was. He was nothing without rules and orders and boundaries.

The world flew off kilter, spinning out of control. She wanted to grab it and stop its rotation. No air, she couldn't get any air. With no oxygen to her brain, she was about to pass out. Everything began to slowly darken. Nikki reached instinctively but grabbed nothing, until strong arms closed around her. The muscles of his chest became a wall of safety. For a moment, she savored his touch, but cold reality blasted her and she shoved away.

Unpardonable sin.

Her feelings for Mace and his for her were that wrong?

"Look," Mace offered, sliding his hands into his pockets. She knew it was so he wouldn't reach out to her again. "You couldn't have known. Don't worry about it."

Indescribable pain tore through her. Her vision blurred with fresh tears. "Why didn't you tell me?" Embarrassment shot like a rocket in the cold, wintery place that was now her heart. "Why didn't you stop me? I made such a fool of myself."

Mace looked away and something — a tear? — slipped down his cheek. He scrubbed at it with a flat hand, but another followed. Nikki watched in agony as her angel, her beautiful invitation, warred with the unfair world that was his prison. He swallowed and choked back a sound so filled with pain, she could barely stand hearing it.

No. No. No. No. No. No. She hated herself right now for causing this.

She'd reduced him to a broken pot. Her words slipped from her lips, hardly a whisper. "I'm … I'm so, so sorry." She turned and fled into the house.

Mace stood outside on her front porch for nearly a half hour, trying, unsuccessfully to think of another way. He started to knock — again — but lowered his hand from the wooden door. She was asleep in the living room with the TV on, its glow throwing a blue haze against the walls of the room. All this he witnessed from the glass pane in the front door. He rested his head against the cool window, and a moment later his hand rummaged across the top of the doorframe. Nothing. The front porch was dotted with plants. He began lifting their pots until he spotted the key.

Once inside the night quiet house, he made his way to her. Mace stood for a moment at the edge of the couch. It was wrong for him to be there, he knew, but what was one more rule to break? He'd already sought Will and asked for reassignment. Will had reluctantly agreed. But he couldn't leave without telling her good-bye.

"Nikki," he whispered.

She roused, but only to turn onto her side and mumble his name. His fingers itched to touch her. Thanks to the extremely remote assignment he requested, it would be the last human touch for him for a long time. Maybe ever. But if the rest of his days were to be spent without human contact, he wanted her touch to be the last upon his flesh.

"Nikki," he whispered again, this time louder. Her brown hair covered part of her face, so he traced a finger along her hairline.

When she moaned, his heart shattered into a million pieces. But he'd readied for this. Every argument she might construct to change his mind, he'd gone over. There'd be no dissuading him from what he had to do.

Her eyes finally fluttered open.

"I have to go, Nikki. My presence on this journey is putting you at greater risk."

She sat up, shaking off the sleep. He plunged into all the reasons, powered through every argument, and all the while she remained silent, listening. Her hair framed sleepy eyes that blinked now and then, but revealed nothing. Her full lips pressed together when she swallowed and he wanted to rub a finger across them and feel the velvet smoothness. She'd drawn her knees up to her chest and hugged them, holding on and refusing to crack. She was light and life and he was about to walk away from the only thing that had ever made him feel real happiness.

When he reached the end of his speech, she said one thing. "You promised to see this through to the end."

It broke him. Mace sank onto the couch. What could he do? He was the one who'd learned everything about Nikki: her ticks, her impulses. He was the one who could protect her the most. She trusted him, or had. And worst of all, she was right. He *did* make a promise.

A fresh war began to rage in his gut. Could he actually leave her? Could he walk away from the girl who, time and time again, had shown her strength by facing whatever horror was thrust upon her? She'd met every challenge with a fierce fighter's drive. She'd been tossed into an unseen world and had taken it on like a champion.

One challenge is thrown at me and what do I do? Try to run away.

Nikki inched closer. "You promised to see this through." She repeated the words gently, knowing, somehow knowing, they eroded the walls of his resolve.

With a sigh, Mace reached out and caressed her cheek. She leaned into his touch.

He tilted her chin up so he could look at her. "Nikki, there are so many things Lost Boys can never have. Our world is different from yours — I'm simply bound here, an outcast on earth and heaven. As a result I never thought I'd feel like I belong somewhere, but you did it for me. For a few untainted moments, I was able to forget. You made me feel human, Nikki. You made me feel alive." On a long exhale, he said, "I'll see it through." Because, really, what choice did he have?

She remained silent for what felt like an eternity. "How do we do this, Mace? How can I be with you, but deny what's happening in my heart?"

He laughed without humor. "Welcome to my world."

"This has happened before? When you were on other journeys?"

He pivoted on the couch and sank his hands into her hair, watching his fingers thread through the strands. "No. Never. This is new territory for me."

She bit her bottom lip. "New territory for me too."

"Wait a minute." His voice filled with sarcasm — which was good, because he couldn't take another moment of the relief engulfing him. He didn't have to say good-bye. "I thought you were falling for Raven."

She shook her head. "Do I look stupid? Girls don't fall for the bad boy."

"No, you just go on long motorcycle rides with them."

She blushed. "Well, we're not perfect. I mean, Raven — like all of you — is really cute and extremely persuasive. I should have discouraged him."

He gripped her arms protectively. "What did he do to you?"

"Nothing. Well, we fought."

"He *fought* you?"

She nodded.

"Raven always did have a way with the ladies."

"His actions aren't what scared me, Mace. It was my own." She pressed her hand to her forehead. "I felt ... wild ... with him. Like I could defy every law and it wouldn't matter. What *was* that?"

"Nikki, Raven offered you the seed of rebellion. It may seem small and seductive, but when it grows, it's a difficult giant to kill. It's the same sin that caused Lucifer to fall."

Her brows rose. "Excuse me?"

"We fight on the side of good, and humility is the only anchor we have to keep from drifting toward the jagged rocks of darkness. Pride is the archenemy of humility, and it's something Raven has plenty of. If we as Halflings — or you as humans — trade humility for pride, it's only a matter of time until we find ourselves fully given to the evil side. In short, Raven sees our future and doesn't like it."

"What is your future, Mace? You labor so hard in this life, then what?"

"Well, if we're not offered mercy, we're doomed to hell with Satan, the demons, the fallen angels, and men who forfeit their contract."

He watched her heart break all over again. *This is an impossible situation.*

"Mace, you don't deserve that!"

"Hell wasn't created for me. And it certainly wasn't created for humans. But it is a reality we can't ignore."

"I'm sorry about everything." She pushed from him. "Maybe you're right. You should go. Far away. Have Will send someone else to protect me. Go somewhere safe."

In one quick movement, he tugged her into his arms, his hands flattening against her back. "I can't love you, Nikki. But that doesn't mean I won't cherish the time I spend with you."

She pulled a breath. "And then one day you'll leave?"

He nodded. "I'll have no choice. When the journey is over ..."

"Tell me one more time — why is it such a sin for you to fall in love with me?"

"Because it's what the enemy wants."

Nikki's eyes dropped. "We're trapped. I won't be your downfall, Mace." She took a hold of his chin so he couldn't look away. "Promise me I won't."

"You won't be," Mace said. *Though you already are.* He drank from her, filling his soul with her essence, her love. Her desire to protect him — even at the risk of her own safety — pulled him ever deeper.

Delicate tears had slipped from her eyes, trickling over her soft skin before dropping onto his. What would it be like to awaken a thousand mornings and feel this? To knit his heart with another, to share every emotion? For all the journeys he'd walked, all the forces he'd observed, none proved stronger than this. The power of pure love.

When her phone rang Saturday afternoon, Nikki jumped. She waved to Mace as he drove away, then flipped her phone open. "What? No, Mom, calm down, I'm right outside." Bo rubbed her leg, reminding her about her unfulfilled promise from yesterday. "Everything is fine. Yes, Mace and I had a great day today." He'd taken her to a new art gallery that just opened in downtown Springfield. *We need to learn how to be friends,* he'd told her. So that's what they were doing. No hugging, no handholding, no long, lazy stares. But it was okay. Better than okay, it was good — and hopefully it was as innocent and pure as she liked to think.

She focused her thoughts back to the call. "I'm going to take Bo to the tennis courts, then I'll be in for dinner." She punched numbers on the garage panel. *Doing good,* she told herself for the thousandth time. Though her exterior remained strong, Mace's words yesterday had nearly demolished her. *Sticks and stones may break my bones, but if you want to destroy me, use words.* Before the garage door opened fully, she ducked inside and retrieved a tennis ball. Bo went nuts.

A small patch of woods separated her backyard from the tennis courts. Since it was no more than a couple of acres, she usually opted to cross through it. But as she stepped into the brush, she hesitated. Chewing her lip, she angled toward the long, winding sidewalk that would lead her down streets and around houses. *No, that will take way too long. It's not like anything's actually in the woods.* As she plunged forward trees shaded her steps, offering a reprieve from the afternoon's heat. September in Missouri meant chilly mornings, warm afternoons, and perfect, cool evenings. Her thoughts strayed to Mace and how things had changed since they first sat on his porch swing taking advantage of the crisp air and discussing another realm, one she now understood as both beautiful and terrible.

Halfway to the courts, she stopped. Icy fingers clamped around her heart and crept up her back, though Bo seemed impervious to the chilling sensation. Something rustled along the leaves. Moments later a soft breeze brought the responsible creature's scent to her. Like death, the vile odor of charred flesh and fur filled her nose. She coughed against it, repulsed as it permeated her lungs.

A rumble vibrated in Bo's throat, confirming that her imagination hadn't gotten the better of her. She took a tentative step back, only to freeze. Panic rushed her. *No,* she resolved. *Don't let fear take over.* Squaring her shoulders, she continued to walk.

Bo took cautious steps beside her, his head turning and nose working to encompass the perimeter. A line of hair stood spiked along his back. She'd had Bo for eight years. In all that time, she'd never witnessed such defensive behavior. His attention sharpened, targeting any movement as they crept through the woods, and his posture demonstrated he was ready to shed his domestication for primal power. He stepped closer to Nikki in an act of protection. She welcomed it.

When the clearing appeared less than a hundred yards in front of them, she released the breath she'd been holding. When the hell hound leapt at her, she quickly inhaled another.

Will towered over Raven. "One thing we don't do is encourage humans to break natural law."

Raven dropped onto the couch. "It's not like she could have gotten hurt." Will had been all up in Mace's business since yesterday, which usually was a fantastic respite from Will's nagging, for a variety of reasons. The problem was Mace had incurred Will's wrath because Mr. Does-Nothing-Wrong was in love with Nikki. Mace's flirtation with his dark side just didn't fit into Raven's plans.

"You understand the principles of our laws, Raven. They're given to protect, and when we *willfully*, rebelliously ignore them, we're removing ourselves from the protection offered to us. And to lead a human down that path …" Frustration stole the rest of Will's words.

Raven sprung from the couch, squaring off with his so-called guardian. "We. Us," he mimicked.

Will took a step back, his face flickering surprise.

"You talk like you're one of us. You're not, Will. You're just a heaven-reject. At least we're doomed because of someone else's actions. You're doomed because of your own." New vitriol filled Raven as Will's face fell. "You were there. You walked the streets, experienced the power, lead the unbeatable army. And look at you now — a babysitter."

Vine, who'd remained quiet through the exchange, stood

and came to rest near Will. "That's enough, Raven. It isn't fair." Vine, candy-munching, human-admiring Vine, with his sure posture and soft words, wanted a part of this? Fine.

Raven turned to his "brother." "Fair? You want to talk about fair? What's fair about this?" He spread his arms and unfurled his wings. "I look like a man, but am built like an angel. I desire heaven, but can't have it. Fine." A tear welled in his eye and he fought to keep it back. "I'll settle for earth. Oh, wait, I can't have that either."

Vine stepped directly in front of Will and met Raven face-to-face. White-blond hair nestled behind his ears and clear blue eyes portraying the deepest of love. "We are a small race. How many Halflings roam? A few hundred? A few thousand maybe?" The gentleness of his words purged the tension even from Raven. "We're the product of rebellion, and rebellion floods our souls. But we can choose to be more. We can bring nobility and honor to our names. We don't have to let our heritage define our future." His hands rose to Raven's shoulders. "I will always stand with you. And if I can offer my life to protect yours, I will, because *that's* what I choose to be. Though I love you too much to let you speak to Will this way."

Why does that kid always have to be so ... right? Raven grabbed Vine, hugged him hard, then stole down the hall toward his room. Over his shoulder, he called. "And if you mention that hug to anyone, I'll kill you."

Before he could open his bedroom door, Will spoke. "Quiet, heaven whispers." Celestial silence filled the house, pressing against Raven's skin, saturating the air with the particles of heaven's atmosphere. When he returned to the living room, Will's already-pale face was ashen. "It's Nicole. You must get to her."

Chapter
19

Friends ... yeah. Mace nodded as he drove home from Nikki's house. While at the art galleries and ice cream shop, and during their conversations, he'd done well. He hadn't focused on the way her eyes liquefied as she stared at the sunset painting of children playing with a dog. He hadn't chuckled at the speck of ice cream left on the end of her nose after she lost her battle with a melting mound of rocky road. He hadn't even tried to kiss away her pain when a thorn pierced her flesh while they were in the rose garden, where she just had to dig into one of the bushes to catch a glimpse of a butterfly. *Oh, yeah, I'm doing great.*

Halfway home, an unsettling sensation stole over him. Whipping into a grocery store parking lot, Mace turned the car around. Tires squealed as he wrestled with his thoughts and the lethal feeling welling inside his gut. "She said she was going inside," he muttered. She should be safe in her house. But wave after wave of uncertainty crashed over him as his right foot lowered to the floorboard.

Careening toward her house, the foreboding only increased. Something was wrong. He sharpened his attention and repeatedly ignored the voice that told him he'd never make it to Nikki in time.

Raven and Vine spread their wings in the living room, leaping out of earth's realm and into the next. Moments later, they materialized at the battle site. As he touched ground, slowing his descent and tucking his wings, Raven knew even the midplane had been too slow.

Two hell hounds encircled Nikki. It looked like she'd been fighting, or at least attempting to keep the hounds at a distance. Her clothes were ripped and a scratch sliced her cheek. A drop of blood slid to her chin.

Raven screamed and leapt atop one of the hounds. Before he could inflict the death the hound deserved, a wraith materialized from the shadows. With twisted fingers, he grabbed Raven by the neck. For a moment, Raven dangled in midair, until he released his wings again, catching the demon off guard.

It tumbled backward, spewing vile words. When it addressed the boys, its voice rose to a painful screech, like bars of raw metal rubbing back and forth. "Ah, sons of God — or should I say runaways. Why do you interfere?" Cold, red eyes shot to Nikki. "She's nothing to you."

"And what is she to you?" Vine said.

Raven shot Vine a look. *Way to go, little brother.*

The demon's focus did not waver from Nikki.

Vine repeated the question.

"She's a promise," it hissed. "A beautiful promise." His eyes flashed to Raven. "Now leave," he commanded, as if desperate to be left alone with Nikki.

Raven laughed. "What? When it's just getting interesting?" He nodded for Vine to move between Nikki and the demon.

As Vine placed a hand on Nikki's shoulder and extended the other toward the wraith, it growled. "I'm in no mood to kill Halflings today," it oozed. "Look." Holding out an arm, the wraith sliced his wrist with a gnarled black fingernail. His eyes widened wildly at the blood, and Raven felt his stomach tighten as its rotting tongue darted out and licked gray, bleeding lips. "The same blood runs in my veins. We need not quarrel." The demon's eyes hardened. "Give me the girl." It reached out, and Raven knew the cold wind of death clamped onto Nikki.

It was as if icy hands closed on her neck, making it a struggle to breathe. Twenty yards away, the demon laughed, his hand still reaching toward her and strengthening the smoky haze encircling her throat.

She attempted a scream as one hell hound jumped Vine while the other attacked Raven.

Terrified eyes flew to both boys, and her pulse skittered as she realized neither would be able to release her in time. Nikki's hands rose to her throat, attempting to dislodge the demon's grip. Straining, she looked up to see Bo leap onto the demon. *This isn't happening . . .*

As if the dog were just an annoying burr, the monster's sharp talons dug into Bo's hide and flung him away.

The unseen fingers then tightened, cutting her air supply and causing her head to pound as blood pooled below the cinched vessels. A black veil closed around Nikki's vision. A tear trickled the length of her cheek — even while asphyxiating, she could feel the cool path it left. She even heard the tear when it dropped to the ground.

"I will not die like this," she gritted, willing herself to calm, to think. With what little consciousness she had, she imagined the fingers at her throat, pictured where the thumb would be — the most vulnerable digit in a choke — and twisted her fingers around the invisible thumb.

And yanked.

The demon screamed and the pressure immediately lifted. Though his face was contorted in agony, he reached for her again. As Nikki braced herself for another bout with its powerful grip, a white flash hit him square in the chest, driving him back.

She fell to the forest floor, gasping as she took in what had happened. Was that Mace with his hands clasped around the demon's throat?

Oxygen filled Nikki's lungs, encouraging consciousness and staving off panic as she lay in a fetal position on the ground. Her hand cupped her throat, which still stung from the remnants of the choke. As the world drifted back into focus, her breath caught. Above and around her, a demon and two hell hounds fought glorious beings so majestic she barely recognized them as her Lost Boys. Raven, Vine, and … yes, Mace. His rage made him even more exquisite. When a hound turned its attention to him and sank its teeth into his back, he seized it with both hands and cast it to the ground.

Perfectly balanced kicks and punches landed again and again while Vine veered his attention to the demon. Their style of fighting was flawless. Each strike hammered its target, powerful as mallets and executed with moves delicate as a ballet.

The boys glistened with sweat, muscles taut with strength and adrenaline as the fight raged on. Despite the demonstration Mace was providing, her eyes were drawn to Vine and the white-blond river of hair that trailed his every move. She'd always viewed him as the tagalong kid-brother type, but now she stared in awe of his ability. Spinning in a perfect arc, his pointed foot connected with the demon's blistered face.

The thing cried out. Vine tossed loose hair behind him and landed another kick, this one to the throat. The demon and the boys fought with precision, as if able to anticipate each other's moves. In unison, like a practiced dance they had performed for ages. And she watched it all in slow motion.

When Raven jumped in to help Vine and Mace with the demon, Nikki was so entranced by the battle before her she failed to notice the hell hound turning his full attention to her. When it was only a few feet away, she scooted back, but there was nowhere to go and she lacked the strength to fight. She didn't have to; yellow fur drifted in front of her and jumped on the hound's back, biting into its throat.

The monstrous being screeched a horrid sound and expelled a puff of foul air that caused Nikki's nose to water. She crept closer to the fray, helpless as the hound snagged Bo with matted front paws and threw him into the dirt. As he struggled, Bo's round, innocent eyes found hers. A moan, something like a whimper but filled with more pain, escaped from her dog, then another.

No, no, no!

With painfully slow movement, the hound ripped into Bo's back with its razor claws. Finally, the dog lay still, moaning as the hound tore his flesh.

A scream gurgled from Nikki's scratchy throat. Her eyes

blurred. Silently, she pleaded with Mace to turn around, to notice what was happening behind him. Bo couldn't last through much more.

Instead Mace held the demon by the shoulders then jumped, planting both feet in the thing's chest. It fell to the ground and disappeared in a puff of vapor.

Nikki blinked.

As Mace landed, he veered his attention behind him. His eyes flashed horror. In seconds that took far too much time, he flew toward Nikki and hovered near Bo and the hound.

Bo yelped once more as the hound sank his teeth yet deeper.

From above the attack, Mace grabbed the hound and jerked it from her dog.

Though her concern remained on Bo, Nikki's mind was working to take in the boy before her. Spread from Mace's shoulders to the small of his back and ten feet to either side were ... "Wings," she muttered. She rubbed her eyes, looked again. Yes, beautiful, creamy gray-white wings flapped up and down gently, causing Mace to float above the chaos. His eyes met hers reluctantly, and she could read the trepidation in his expression. He was afraid. Though he had taken on the hounds and demon with little pause, he feared what she would think of him in his true form. "You're beautiful," she mouthed, but he turned before he saw it.

She pushed to her knees, straining to examine him. But darker-gray wings flapped into her face, and she brushed at them to move. *More wings?* And arms that nestled her, folding her into what she realized was Raven's body. She felt the wind his feathers created as he lifted her off the ground.

Mace grew smaller and smaller below until he finally disappeared in a sea of trees.

When Raven tucked her into the cleft of a high rock, she tried to stand, but faltered. Instead she moved toward the cliff edge on her knees. "Raven, I have to get back to Bo." Looking down to the ground far below, she grabbed for something to hold as the world spun.

Raven's eyes were fire on her, as if still wild from the fight. He spread his wings, chest tightening. "What do you think?"

"Raven, they need help," she pleaded.

He spun from her, scanned the woods below. "It's all over. We're better off up here." His wings rustled loudly as they tucked into his back.

"Are they okay?" she asked. "Is Bo all right?"

He released an angry breath. "They're fine, Nikki." Facing her, he snapped his wings out again. "You didn't answer me. Tell me what you think."

If they're okay ... Dragging her attention from the patch of woods beneath, she reached, but stopped just short of touching. Her gaze flashed him the question.

"Go ahead," he said proudly, and tipped his upper body forward.

Reaching to him, her hand fell to his shoulder. With long, slow movements, she examined the wing. Feathers, and something beneath that felt like bone, but thinner, more pliable. She dug her fingers into the middle of his wing, and he jumped. "Careful," he said with a half smile. "Ticklish."

A tiny laugh escaped her lips. Her other hand moved to examine the strange appendage, her fingers brushing and squeezing at various spots. "Why haven't I seen them before?"

He stepped closer, letting the wings encircle her. "You only saw us in the natural plane. Never in the Spirit. This is what we look like in the supernatural realm."

"Will I always see you like this now?"

"I don't know." He shrank the distance between them yet farther, closing her inside his gray feathers. "Maybe. Is that what you want?"

"I've never seen anything more beautiful."

Raven's eyes closed, and she felt his breath catch.

The sounds of wind increased around them. Raven's eyes flew open, and she thought she heard an angry sigh. His wings spread, allowing her to escape. The wind shoved harder against her, accompanied by a noisy *flap, flap, flap*. She turned to the sound, to see Mace and Vine hovering above the rock. Their outstretched wings lifted and lowered them in seamless waves. Against the fading sun, the sight of the two stole her breath. *It's like a Renaissance painting.* But the awe quickly shifted to panic. Within Mace's arms, Bo lay motionless.

The police arrived at Nikki's house just after Bo died.

"And you think a cougar attacked you?" Officer McMillan asked, seeming to gauge her answer and the honesty that lie within. *I should have said wolves. At least that has a slice of truth.* "When your neighbor called us, they said they heard a young woman screaming. You must have had time to get a good look."

She didn't make eye contact. "I said I don't know what it was, sir. It *screamed* like a cougar."

The heavyset officer turned his attention to Mace, who'd accompanied her and Bo to the house. "Good thing you came along when you did, son. This could have had a terrible outcome."

Nikki turned on the officer. "My dog is dead!" she hollered. Her dad slid a reassuring arm around her.

Officer McMillan lifted the hat from his head. "Yes, well, he's a hero. Saved your life, young lady." Kind eyes seemed determined to apologize for his insensitivity. "We can order a necropsy if you'd like to determine what killed him."

Her dad shot a look to her mom. Nikki watched the exchange, but was too depressed to analyze it further. All she knew was, dead or not, she didn't want doctors slicing and dissecting Bo. "No," she and her dad said simultaneously.

Her dad cleared his throat. "If they determine it's a cougar, what will they do?"

The officer shrugged. "Not much. Unfortunately, one attack this close to the national forest won't constitute a search." He removed his hat. "I'm very sorry for your loss. But your dog died a hero. You can be proud of him."

"Thank you," she tried to say, but the words died in her throat.

As soon as the officer left, her dad wrapped a blanket around Bo's body. Mace hugged her while her parents lifted Bo into the backseat of their car. The entire time, tears slid down Nikki's face.

"What do they want with me?" she asked Mace in a choked sob.

He gently rubbed his hand along her back. "I don't know. But I promise you I won't rest until we find out."

Three weeks and Nikki still mourned the loss of her dog. Coming home to no wagging tail and no excited barks made her world that much more empty. Especially in light of the reality surrounding his death. School had no appeal, and her grades were slipping. Dr. Richmond had cornered her on several occasions, asking if she was all right. She'd lied, of course.

But something in his tone had made her want to confess the depths of her sorrow, to explain the chaos of her life since meeting the Halflings, and to admit her lack of desire to continue this journey.

"I'm worried about you, Nikki," Dr. Richmond said, voice echoing in the quiet stairwell as they hauled another science fair project to the gym.

She forced herself to grin over a clay volcano at him. "Is that why you elected me to stay and help you today?"

He blushed. "Too obvious, huh?" He examined the project. "High school, and we're still making volcanoes for the science fair."

She laughed softly. "It's pretty cool when the vinegar hits the baking soda, and it bubbles out the top."

He stopped. "It is cool, isn't it?" They set the project next to the last and headed back to the science room. "I don't recall seeing your project."

"Oh. Actually, I didn't have time to do one this year."

He held the door for her. "I've never known you to not enter. I always looked forward to your artistic take on science, and I'd thought the fair was very exciting to you."

"Exciting," she echoed, then realized he was judging her words a little too closely. "I have enough excitement in my life right now."

Lifting a lighted circuit board into his hands, he smiled. "You know, most kids think I'm easy to talk to. I've always liked talking to you, Nikki. You remind me of my daughter, Jessica."

She held the door open and followed as he continued to the gym. *Time to get the focus off of me.* "I've met Jessica. I was a freshman when she graduated early as a junior."

"She's now a sophomore at Missouri University."

"Oh, that's nice." She squirmed, trying to access some question about college. Before the school year began, she'd had a thousand of them. Now, nothing came to mind.

"Maybe I could help with what's troubling you."

"No one can help me, Dr. Richmond."

The look in Dr. Richmond's eyes halted both of them. "Nikki, someone can always help. Even when we think it's hopeless."

Good job, Nikki. On top of everything else, now your science teacher thinks you're suicidal. She folded her arms. "I'm being melodramatic. Please." She attempted a laugh. "Don't think I'm going psycho or something. My dog died. I had him for a really long time." *Oh, and by the way, there are creatures straight from the pit of hell trying to kill me. Why? No one really knows. And did I mention they're possibly after you too?*

"I'm very sorry about your pet. I used to have horses, years back when I worked in a laboratory."

"You worked in a lab?" Prickly hairs rose on her neck.

"Yes, I did." A flash of sadness filled his features, and his eyes drifted to the ground. "I don't know what's going on in your life, but when I left Omega Corporation, I thought my life was over."

The words crashed into her mind like bolts of lightning. Her hand gripped his upper arm. "Omega Corporation?" she repeated.

He frowned, his round, watery gaze burrowing into her. "Yes. You know the company?"

"Um." She snatched her hand from him. "I saw on the news that they had a fire."

His lips pressed together. He took a few steps and dropped onto the bleachers. "Some of my friends perished in that blaze." The circuit board project was discarded on the seat beside him.

Her heart pounding like a drum, Nikki sat down at his side. Lemon oil and faint sweat surrounded them but paled to a new scent in the gym. She smelled discovery. *Get him to talk about the place, get him to open up.* "I'm sorry about your friends."

"Thank you, Nikki." He tugged the glasses from his face and wiped the lenses with his shirttail. "I hadn't seen any of them in nearly twenty years. When I left Omega, I thought my life would end. The company didn't want me to leave, but I couldn't stay. They destroyed my reputation as a scientist. Made sure no other laboratory in the free world would want to work with me. But ..." He raised his hands and dropped them with a clop. "I ended up here, and you know, this is my real destiny. This is where I belong. So, I guess I owe them a thank you."

"Why did you have to leave? You said you couldn't stay."

"I didn't agree morally with the steps the laboratory was taking. I have a set of rules I live by — values, you might say — and they were going in a direction I couldn't follow."

"A paradigm?" she said.

"Yes."

"What was the direction?"

His face clouded. "Nikki, there are forces at work around us that desire power at any cost." His fingers threaded together on his lap. "And they'll hurt anything or anyone to get it."

Okay, that sent a jolt of fear through her. *Focus, keep him on track. Get more information.* "You probably had a specialty, right? Don't scientists usually have a specific field of study?"

"Yes, I was a specialist in one field, but my passion was another."

She leaned forward. "What? What two fields?"

"My specialty was electromagnetics. But my passion was genetics."

217

Blood rushed through Nikki's veins at such a rate she thought her heart would stop. "Did Omega Corporation do both?" She tried to soften her intensity, but failed. "Dr. Richmond, did Omega Corporation do both electromagnetics and genetics?"

"Yes. And that's part of what made it so difficult to quit. I had to leave my babies behind. And that's why I understand how you feel about losing your dog."

"What babies?" Hearing *babies* and *genetics* in the same sentence made her queasy. "What do you mean?"

"Horses. I was raising horses, doing genetic testing on them. You grow to love those majestic, beautiful animals."

"What kind of testing? And why horses?" She searched her memory for a connection to equestrian genetics and that of humans.

"As far as why, I wasn't privy to that information. And as far as what kind, I don't feel *you* should be privy. Suffice it to say, to the lab, the horses were lab rats. But to me, they became part of my family." His voice steadied. "So, I think I know how you feel."

She nodded, grinned, nodded again. "Dr. Richmond, would it be okay if I go on home? I need to take care of some things." She stood. "But, I feel a lot better after talking to you. Thanks."

He smiled up at her. "You're welcome."

Mace got out of his car after parking behind her bike, and walked toward the Victorian. It was getting easier to ignore the flutters in her stomach whenever she looked at him. Friends don't cause flutters.

"So tell me why you're so jazzed up about your conversation with Dr. Richmond."

"Let's get inside. I want everyone to hear," she blurted, forcing her fingers through her knotted hair as she forced her stomach to behave. A strong crosswind had wreaked havoc on the strands below her helmet while she rode across town, causing her fingers to snag. "Ouch," she said, and gave up.

Mace laughed and took her helmet from her. But a moment later, he bristled. Head tipped back, he sniffed the air.

"What?" She frowned. "What do you smell?" Then she felt it. *Like electricity dancing across water, like cold fire tickling my skin.* "What *is* that?" she asked as a scent similar to homemade cookies filled her nose.

Mace's eyes flashed excitement. He dropped the helmet into her hands. "Something's happening in the backyard!"

She stared down at her head gear, then watched him scurry into the house. "I guess chivalry is dead," she mumbled wryly and hung the strap on her handlebars.

As she crossed the threshold, the sensation increased. She closed the door, which Mace had left gaping, and traversed the living room. She glanced around. No one. Passing through the kitchen, she realized goose bumps tingled her flesh like a million fireflies kissing her skin. She rubbed her hands over her arms. The feeling, though alarming, brought with it an unusual calm that seemed to curl from the depths of her being and wrap her like a blanket. *At least it's something pleasant for a change.*

When she stepped onto the back patio, her gaze fell on the Lost Boys.

Raven, Vine, and Mace stared, mouths as open as the front door had been, necks craning into the sunlight, and wind whipping their hair.

Nikki stepped fully onto the back deck to see what demanded their attention.

When the objects of their admiration fell into her view, a flash of hot liquid sailed the length of her body.

Hovering above the porch, ten feet from the boys, were three Halfling females.

Chapter 20

Nikki couldn't help but gasp at the girls' unearthly beauty. Brilliant white wings moved effortlessly on the breeze. The one on the far right's feathers seemed to glimmer in the low sun. Varying shades of brown hair cascaded their shoulders, dancing in waves as if orchestrating a dance. And each face was so delicately detailed that Nikki could only stare.

The girl on the right — whose hair was shorter and cut into a trendy bob — flashed a look toward her that sent a shiver down Nikki's spine. Eyes the color of melted gold considered her. Just as quickly as the gaze had started, the female cocked a brow and shifted her attention to Mace. Golden Girl scoured him from head to toe and punctuated the gesture with a tiny smile.

Nikki heard a quick exhale escape her own lips. Her gaze flew to Mace who, seemingly stunned for a moment, swallowed hard. His eyes sparkled with interest and he attempted a smile of his own, but seemed only able to muster half, which tilted one side of his face into a goofy grin. He threw an awkward hand into the air to wave at the Halfling.

The girl with the wings and golden brown hair grinned as if satisfied, then shot another glance to Nikki.

Will stood beside the boys, seemingly less impressed. He directed his comments to the girl on the left, whose form was half obscured by the afternoon sun, making her appear that much more celestial. "So, our journeys intertwine," Will said.

"Yes." She came to rest at his feet, but her hair still danced around her as if floating in water until, mercifully, it stopped. When the other females followed her lead, and halted on the deck, their hair stopped flowing as well. Tucking their wings made them less intimidating, but no less beautiful.

Where Halfling boys were chiseled and lean, Halfling females were shapely. No blond hair and blue eyes. No, everything about them felt soft and warm. The one who had entranced Mace had streaks of blonde sun kisses in her short, curly bob. The girl on the left had hair the color of Nikki's own. The third girl's hair was even darker, silken black and nearly waist length, with long layers that framed and highlighted the most amazing gold eyes she'd ever seen.

When she was small, her mom used to tell her she had golden eyes. Nikki remembered falling asleep at night and wondering how much they might be worth. But her irises paled against the ones now focused on her.

When the Halfling females began introducing themselves, her attention snapped to the present. "I'm Vegan," the one on the left said, holding out a hand to Nikki.

Friendly, the pretty angel girl was actually *friendly. And I know her name from somewhere* ... "Oh, Zero —"

222

"You're the one who's been bringing food to Zero," Mace interrupted.

He shoved his hand in front of Nikki's to grab Vegan's.

Vegan quickly shook his hand then turned her attention back to Nikki. "Nicole Youngblood, it's a pleasure to meet you." And then she bowed at the waist, hands floating out beside her. "If there is any way we can serve you, we offer our help."

Eyes wide, Nikki stammered. "Uh, thanks. Am I your ... mission?"

Vegan took a delicate step closer. "The details of our journey are yet unclear. But we know it is the will of the Throne to protect you."

Vegan pulled an amulet from her throat with graceful fingers. Her skin was flawless as perfect silk and every movement its own song. All three girls wore gold bands on their wrists. "I would like you to take this." Vegan held the necklace to her.

Nikki reached, and the pearly amulet fell into her grasp.

"If you place your lips to it and blow, it will sound an alarm only we" — she gestured to the two beside her — "can hear." Gold eyes shot into her. "We will come to your aid, Nicole. If ever you have need."

"Thank you," Nikki said.

"This is Glimmer," Vegan said as she pointed to the one who'd flirted with Mace. "And this is Winter."

Nikki dropped the necklace into her left hand when Winter reached to shake her right. Clasping her tightly, Nikki threw a quick look to their interlocked fingers. "You're cold," she said before she could stop herself. "I'm sorry." She shook her head. "I didn't mean anything by that."

Winter's face broke into a smile. "It's okay. I am." She shrugged and Nikki warmed. *Icy skin, warm heart.*

Winter stepped back. "I discovered long ago it's best not to question the gifts we've been given, but instead strive to use them."

When Nikki struggled to connect the necklace around her throat, Vegan gestured to Glimmer to help her.

"I think she can do it herself," Glimmer mumbled, crossing her arms and again cocking that perfectly arched brow. Her streaked, light-brown hair bobbed on her shoulder.

"Play nice," Vegan warned.

Glimmer rolled her eyes on the exhale and stepped to Nikki. Reaching around her neck, she nodded toward Mace. "The one in the middle is really cute," she said, just loud enough for Nikki to her.

A slow burn started at Nikki's head, snaked down her torso, and pooled at her feet. Only through complete concentration did she clamp her mouth shut. *Yes, and he seems to be equally intrigued with you.* She swallowed the angry grunt in her throat.

Will cut the silence. "You were saying you know about Omega Corporation?"

Vegan nodded. "Genetics. The worst kind," she said, exhaling deeply. Her face struck a saddening pose, and the flowers in the yard seemed to mourn with her.

"But the lab was destroyed," Vine said.

"Only one. They have many. The one struck by fire was more of an outpost than a full lab. The scientists who perished within rarely used that facility. We have learned they have a main lab about sixty miles from here. Difficult to get to, and most of it is underground."

"Why the fire?" Will asked, brow furrowed.

"To throw off suspicion. And, sadly, to eliminate the scientists they no longer need or want," Vegan said.

"Suspicion of what?"

"INTERPOL received an anonymous tip and started *trying* to monitor their activity," Winter said.

Nikki spoke up. "Why wouldn't they have killed Dr. Richmond?" As soon as she said this, she felt the weight of several stares. "Um, Dr. Richmond just told me that he used to work for Omega Corporation. He quit because he didn't morally agree with the direction of the company. He said he used to have horses."

"Yes," Vegan agreed. "They have been doing genetic testing and alterations on horses for the better part of two decades."

"Horses?" Will asked. "Why?"

Vegan shook her head. "We don't know yet." As she furrowed her brow in thought, gold sparked in the depths of her gaze. "Maybe Richmond has information they need. Maybe he's still tinkering with genetics on his own. If he was close to a breakthrough of some kind, they'd want to let him live, continue his research on his own. After all, they can kill him at will."

Raven stepped forward, hands sliding from his pockets and balling into fists. "Not if I have anything to say about it."

Glimmer's attention drifted to Raven and stayed. *Why does that bother me too?*

"What are genetic alterations?" Nikki asked, forcing the thought of half-horse, half-monkey images from her mind.

"They enhance their performance. The animals are bigger, stronger, more violent. The horses are housed in a facility adjacent to the laboratory. It's covered with camouflage to discourage unwanted eyes. We've seen these animals, they are massive."

Mace grinned. "Like Clydesdales on steroids?"

Glimmer laughed a little too quickly.

Vegan shot a glance at the girl, then nodded. "Exactly."

Winter stepped closer to Nikki. "The fence surrounding the facility is like something you'd find in some maximum-security prison. They don't want those animals escaping."

"Human testing as well?" Will asked.

"We think so, but no Halflings, if that's what you're wondering," Glimmer inserted. "At least as far as we know."

Will crossed the deck and rested his massive hands on the rail. His gaze trailed the yard and forest beyond. "But all the signs point in that direction, don't they?"

Vegan sighed. "Unfortunately, yes. But I don't think they have a Halfling specimen." She linked eyes with Will. "I really don't."

Will cast a glance over his shoulder and smiled at her. "How do you know that? Your gut?"

She nodded.

His grin faded. "No Halflings. Maybe they're just waiting for the right one to come along?"

A shudder ran the length of Nikki's back as she watched the group around her shiver at the possibility. Though they'd been sent to protect *her*, an overwhelming urge to protect *them* welled inside.

When her eyes landed on Glimmer, she saddened. All of the previous jealousy dissipated, replaced by an intense conviction to help these beings. Glimmer — complete with sparkling wings and a golden-brown bob — visibly quaked with fear.

Indignation rose in Nikki. Nothing, *absolutely nothing* should be allowed to strike fear in the hearts of these heavenly beings. And in that instant, surrounded by unearthly creatures and with the sun setting in the west, Nikki knew. Protecting them was what she was born to do.

"Are we still going to homecoming?" Mace asked, leaning closer as they strolled the hall toward her first-hour class.

She stopped. "Why wouldn't we?" Krissy had taken her shopping *again* and made her swear she'd wear the ridiculously shiny homecoming dress they'd found.

"You seemed ... upset yesterday when the females arrived."

She tightened her grip on her science binder when the rush of jealousy resurfaced. "Why? Because you ditched me in the front yard or because you drooled all over yourself when you saw them?" Both really unfair comments between friends. *I should be glad his affections are floating in a different direction.*

He sank his hands into his pockets. "Uh, yeah."

She tipped her shoulder into the air. "Doesn't matter to me," she lied. Under her breath, she mumbled. "It's not like I can compete with that."

"It's not a competition, Nikki."

"Argh! For once could you not have such good hearing?" She grabbed him by the arm and dragged him out the side door. "Look, this is a *good* thing. They're like you." She had to swallow before continuing. "And I'm not. Friends, remember?" The onset of tears tingled her face, but she fought.

"We keep telling ourselves that." Sadness overwhelmed his tone. She wanted to wrap her arms around him and ... "This stinks! It's like a twisted Beauty and the Beast story in reverse, isn't it? And I'm the Beast."

"I've never heard that story."

She pressed her lips together. "Well, you're lucky, because it's a fairy tale. And fairy tales don't really come true." *And dragon slayers don't really exist.*

He reached to touch her hand, but she moved.

"This isn't how I want things to be between us," he said, stepping closer, and his eyes, those drowning pools of green-blue, saddened even more.

She shrank away. "Well, it's how it has to be." She bit her cheek, the memory of yesterday still fresh, like hot lava in her stomach. The females and their perfection, arriving just in time to save her and Mace from themselves. "You'd never seen one before. Did they meet your expectations?"

"They're not as beautiful as you, Nikki," Mace whispered.

Her heart disintegrated, but on the outside, she hardened. "Right, because that's how you acted when you first saw me." Her anger boiled. "Don't patronize me, Mace."

She stormed into the building, leaving him standing alone, but his words drifted to her. Carried by the wind and little more than a whisper, they stopped her blood from flowing.

"No," he said. "When I saw you, I fell in love."

Vessler was here again. She smelled his cologne as soon as she entered her house. *Escape to the powder room,* her mind screamed. Powder room. What a girly name. She'd have opted to call it the half bath or downstairs restroom or even … toilet. She stifled a chuckle. But, no. A first floor half bath was a powder room according to Mary Youngblood. The spare bedroom was the guestroom. And when company visited, they were always served first. That's what she loved about her mom. Sometimes, she wished she was more like her. Maybe if she were more *girly* she'd know how to deal with Mace. If she was more like her mom, maybe she wouldn't be so terrified of the emerald-green homecoming dress hanging in her closet. An image of herself tumbling into the decorated gym flew through Nikki's mind. At least the high-heeled shoes were wedges. Wedges she could wear without tripping over her feet. *Balance, grasshopper.*

Laughter drifted to her as she ran a brush through her gnarled mess. Even though she knew she shouldn't be wasting any more time, Nikki couldn't help but gaze at her own reflection and sigh, reminded of the Halfling females. Her head fell forward and pressed against the mirror. She still wanted to help them. All of them. But they made her feel so ... ugly.

And they could fly. Nikki clamped down on her bottom lip. She'd always wanted to learn to fly. As a child, she'd dreamed of soaring far above the world. Sailing on the breeze, tilting her arms and gliding one direction, then another. Dreams died, she supposed.

Energetic sounds from the kitchen caused her to scowl. *Focus, Nikki. You have bigger things to deal with than pretty, angelic girls and having to wear a stupid dress.* She wondered if, like last time, there'd be that uncomfortable layer of distrust surrounding Damon Vessler and her parents.

As she sat down to dinner, she got her answer. The suspicious concern still drifted back and forth between her parents, but less this time. Of course, her family didn't have guests often, so maybe her folks were just awkward. Maybe anyone would be received in the same manner. Nikki tried to relax. After all, hadn't he said last time he was a humanitarian?

"Your father tells me you like motorcycles."

She nodded.

"Did you notice mine in the garage?" he asked.

She shook her head. "I didn't go through the garage." She questioned her parents with a quick look.

"Mr. Vessler is going to leave his bike here for a few days," her dad said.

Vessler held up a hand. "Please, call me Damon. Mr. Vessler makes me feel old."

"Anyway, I'm going to drive him to the airport this evening, so his bike will be here until he gets back. Nikki, you might be interested in taking a look at his motorcycle. It's rather impressive." He gave her a strained smile. "Why don't the two of you go check it out after dinner?" her dad added.

This keeps getting weirder. Weirder still, though Dad seemed calmer, when Nikki offered to help clean up, her mom said no and encouraged her to go have a look at the bike as well. Vessler — er, Damon — held up a hand to usher her through the house. A gold chain twinkled at his wrist. "After you, my lady."

My lady. She almost laughed out loud.

Once in the garage, she hit the light.

No. *No way.* Gleaming in the corner of the gargantuan room sat a Ducati Monster S4. She stopped cold and blinked to make sure it wasn't a mirage. Sleek lines arced perfectly in an *S* pattern on its side. The front and back tires framed glistening spokes while chrome winked enticingly from the engine. Custom paint adorned the gas tank. The midnight-black swirls with pale, silvery ghost flames spilled onto the front and rear fenders, creating a haunting impression.

His chuckle interrupted her. "Yeah, that was my reaction when I first saw her."

"This is a concept bike," she stammered. "I saw it in a magazine. It's ..." she took a tentative step toward the gleaming mass of metal.

"Amazing? I agree. 990ccs. Made of carbon fiber."

"I read that. It's really light," Nikki said.

"Three hundred forty-five pounds. I bought her from a doctor in Sarasota, Florida, who changed his mind three times before we struck a deal. He didn't want to part with her, but I can be very persuasive." He pressed a warm hand to the small of Nikki's back. "Go on. She's prettier up close."

His words rang true. She was.

They paused a respectable distance from the cycle while Nikki's eyes trailed every inch. A Ducati concept bike in *her* garage. Her hands were sweating.

"She's perfectly balanced." Damon threw a leg over the bike. With both feet planted on either side, he raised the bike from the kickstand with one hand on the handlebars. "See?" He tilted the machine so it touched his inner thigh on one side, then the other. "Makes it easier to control at high speeds."

"High speeds?" she repeated.

He winked. "Let's just say I've had the privilege of seeing what she can do when put to the test."

"It doesn't scare you? I mean, it's not like you have an angel as your copilot or anything." She couldn't resist.

A flicker of recognition seemed to glint in his eyes, but he blinked it away quickly. "Nikki, you learn to trust your instincts if you're going to ride fast. You may not be able to *see* what's up ahead, but that doesn't mean you can't *feel* it."

She understood all too well, especially now that she'd met Halflings. But Damon Vessler seemed desperate to deliver more information than what his words could carry.

Nikki cleared her throat. "People die that way." She bent on her haunches to inspect the paint — and to get out of the trajectory of his gaze. It seemed he was always watching her, inspecting her every move, hanging on her every word.

"Not smart people. Your biggest ally is knowing your boundaries, or your lack thereof."

Then it hit her. He talked like a Halfling. *Could that be why you make me feel so uneasy from a distance yet so calm once I'm near you?* "Everyone doesn't have the same boundaries." She trailed a finger along the front tire.

"True," he agreed. "And often people go their entire lives without testing their ability and pushing themselves to the limit. But not people like us, Nikki. We thrive by living on the edge."

From her squatted position, she tipped her head back to examine his expression. He didn't look like a Halfling, unless they suddenly came with dark eyes, dark hair, and deeply tanned skin.

"You don't have much of a poker face, Nikki."

She blushed. *And why does he act like he knows me? It's irritating.*

"If you have questions about me, just ask." His face held no expression. He'd trained himself that way, she was sure.

She bit her lip. *Just ask.* Okay, simple enough. She opened her mouth, but the words caught. *What am I thinking?* "I do have some questions. First, why haven't I met you until recently if you're such a good friend of my parents? Second, why did you keep coming here? And third, why are you leaving a hundred-thousand-dollar motorcycle in my garage?" *There.*

"You have, in fact, met me. Years ago. I stop in a couple times a year to say hello to your parents, but it's usually during the day when you're at school. Sometimes we meet up at an auction or antique weapons show. In fact, I was with them just a few weeks ago. Around the time school started."

The memory of the lab fire raced into her mind. She had heard his voice ...

Vessler slid a hand to her shoulder. "I'm sorry about Bo. I know it must have been hard for you to lose him."

Confusion changed her focus. "You know about my dog? He died three weeks ago. Why would my parents bring it up to you?"

"I bought Bo for you."

She stood from her squatted position. *"What?"* Time to panic; this was beyond weird.

"It was about eight years ago. I'd visited with your mom and dad most of the morning, and they kept talking about how badly you wanted a puppy. So I said, let's go shopping." He dropped the kickstand and stepped off the bike. "I had a friend who raised Labrador Retrievers. One call and boom. You got Bo."

She frowned, searching her memory. "My parents never told me that. I always thought they bought him at a pet store."

"Well, parents don't tell their kids everything. Here," he said, gesturing to the bike. "Your turn. Sit on her."

She blinked. "Really?"

He shrugged. "You know you're going to after I leave, so might as well start now."

Heat rose to her cheeks, but her smile chased it away.

Charming. That's all she could think of to describe Damon Vessler. She'd discovered that he was a genius who'd graduated college at fifteen with a master's degree in Biology, owned several companies, some kind of mine, and was filthy, stinkin' rich. And somehow, after they returned from the garage, his plans had changed.

Vessler seemed to have a way of gently pushing the conversation until he obtained his desired effect. In the middle of coffee, which Mom had insisted on serving, he'd winked at Nikki, and within minutes her dad was no longer Vessler's ride to the airport.

Yep. That's right. She should call Mace and let him know, but the desire to do so escaped her. Still licking her wounds after the Golden Girls' backyard display, she wasn't in the mood to have Mace tailing her or pressing for information about her new friend. And though Vessler sent off warning bells throughout her system, she couldn't fathom why. He'd been nothing but nice. Her mom and dad seemed fine with him now. Of course, there was that conversation she'd overheard, but she must have heard wrong. Or maybe she'd read too much into it.

No, she wasn't going to call Mace and tell him, that much she'd decided. However, the idea of her angel seeing her with Damon sent an evil thrill down her spine, one guilt quickly swallowed.

"Everything okay, Nikki?" Damon asked.

"Huh?" she said, and realized her forehead was starting to ache from the deep frown.

"You look troubled." She realized they were once again in the garage. She watched as he secured the bike, pulled the key from the ignition, and used his sleeve to shine a spot on the gas tank. But when he pivoted and his eyes blazed to Nikki, she gained his entire focus. "You're far too young and beautiful to get wrinkles. Now, tell me what's troubling you and how I can fix it."

"Fix it?" She laughed. "No way that I can see."

He propped his hands on his hips, gold bracelet blinking. "Everything can be fixed with either time or money."

"Is that what life has taught you?" she said.

"Yes. Unfortunately, time refuses to slow down for me no matter how badly I desire it."

"Why would you want time to slow down? You're about …" Her eyes traced his youthful hair, his trendy clothes. "Twenty-five, right?"

A chuckle jostled his head. "Yeah, uh … pretty close. Now, what's the answer? Time or money?"

"My problem can't be fixed with either," she said.

"Ah, boy trouble."

She exhaled while they crossed the garage. "I like this guy. And he likes me. But this … new girl shows up, and she's all perfect and gorgeous. He promptly forgets about me, which is actually good because we're a terrible match."

Damon paused at the doorway. "I can't imagine anyone in their right mind forgetting about you, Nikki."

Uncomfortable with his words, she clasped her hands together.

"Your answer is simple," he said. "Fight fire with fire."

She frowned. Damon was full of advice, much of it contrary to what she believed. But could he be right?

He held a hand in the air, palm up. "You're already a beautiful girl and you don't even try. Why not hit the salon for a new hairstyle, go shopping for some sexy clothes, don a little makeup. You'd be a knockout."

She scrunched her face. "It's just not *me*."

"And is the current *me* getting what she wants?" He didn't wait for her to answer. "Take me, for instance. I was a skinny, gawky, glasses-wearing geek when I started college at age thirteen. But I looked around and decided I wanted to blend in as much as an adolescent can at college. Know what I did?"

She shook her head.

"I befriended the football team. You may not know this, but some jocks aren't the sharpest tools in the drawer. I tutored them through physics and English literature, and they taught me how to work out. I studied their mannerisms, lifestyles, interactions."

She pointed at him. "And you made the football team the following year?"

He laughed. "At a staggering hundred and twenty pounds? Hardly. Remember, know your boundaries. "

"You don't look like a jock. You look more like a rock star."

"You can be whoever you want, Nikki. That was then, this is now. The beauty of being a human is free will."

The beauty of being a human is free will? Why would he say it that way? As cautious as he seemed with his words — choosing each one with care — why would a statement like that surface? Unless, of course, the idea of both human and non-human beings roaming the earth was so commonplace to him he wouldn't think to guard his words.

When she didn't answer, Damon continued, "You can change your destiny to suit your own needs."

She had to admit, it sounded good. But something wrenched in her gut at this new way of viewing life. It *felt* wrong. Too ego-centric, too self-serving. Wasn't there a name for people like that?

Nikki cleared her head. Damon was trying to help her. How could she find fault in that? Still, a tiny voice inside begged caution, not unlike the voice that warned her about Raven. She was getting good at ignoring its plea.

His face slid into a grin. "I know what will cheer you up." He crossed the garage to the Ducati, studied it a moment, and tossed her the keys.

As she caught them overhead, surprise siphoned the blood from her face.

Damon laughed. "Don't look so scared. Your dad told me you're an expert rider."

"But." Her eyes flew to the keys. "But, this is a hundred-*thousand*-dollar motorcycle."

"No." His smile faded. "This is my possession. It serves me, Nikki. Not the other way around. I didn't purchase this bike to worship it. I appreciate it, but it's nothing more than a piece of equipment designed to bring me joy. And right now, it would bring me a lot of joy to see you ride."

She clutched the keys hard enough it hurt her fingers. Would she argue? No.

Hands on his hips, he seemed to enjoy her lack of composure. "You have an extra helmet?"

Her head bobbed of its own accord. She snagged the helmet from the counter, where tools and old weapons littered the space. "So, we'll go for a quick ride before I take you to the airport?" she asked, fearing and anticipating the answer.

"No, we'll ride the Ducati to the airport, then you can bring her home."

"I had a feeling you'd say that," she mumbled. She placed her leg over the bike with painfully slow motions, then exhaled. "Okay." Her hands shook as she lowered them to the handlebars.

His smile turned up a notch as he stepped to the front of the bike, straddled the front tire, and placed his hands near hers. "You'll never make it out of the garage like that. Didn't your sensei teach you how to control your emotions?"

She nodded. "Sensei Coble says to draw on the well of calm within."

His black gaze flashed to her still-quaking hands. "Looks like you need more practice. Close your eyes, Nikki," he ordered.

She swallowed past the lump and obeyed.

"Now take a deep breath," he whispered. "Tune in to your breathing. Inhale through your nose, exhale through your mouth. Slowly, slowly. Yes, that's it."

It disturbed her how comfortable she felt in the presence of this man she barely knew. He was like hot and cold converging and creating a perfect temperature, and she wondered about his motives. Her eyes flew open to gauge him.

He dropped his hands, a lazy grin of smug delight animating his face. "See? You're calm now."

Outwardly, yes. But warning bells jolted her gut once more. There was something unsettling about his voice, about the satisfaction that drifted from his lips like drops of honey drawing her to an infested hive. She pushed the burdensome chains of propriety aside and focused on the present. *I'm about to ride a Ducati concept bike!*

Raven chewed his lip. This may not rank at the top of his best ideas list, but he had to get some answers. Everything in this journey pointed to Nikki. But his gut, his *heart*, swore Dr. Richmond was the key.

Nikki's name had been in the Omega computer, and she had been continually attacked. Not once had an enemy — human, demon, or Halfling — come after Richmond. Could the fight he'd stopped in science class have been an attempt on Richmond? Possibly. But please. *Camo jacket and a hunting knife? Is that all you've got?*

Raven paused at the front door of the one-story ranch-style house. Flower pots decorated a cozy front porch. A pair of muddy tennis shoes lounged at the foot of a white column anchoring the steps.

Homey. Barf.

He changed his mind and started back down the steps. Will wouldn't approve of him coercing information from a science teacher. Then again, Will didn't approve of a lot of things. Raven returned to the door and knocked.

A fiftyish woman with a smiling face and glasses thick enough to rival Richmond's own goofy goggles answered the door.

If she stared at the sun, she'd burst into flames.

"Hello," she said and pushed the screen door open.

Nice. I could be here to rob you and you just removed every obstacle. Humans were so trusting. "Hi. I'm one of—"

"One of my husband's students," she finished for him. "Come in." She gestured with her free hand while tossing her head back. "Bill, someone's here to see you." Her attention returned to Raven. "It's a good thing you young people stop by periodically or I'd never get him out of the lab."

"The lab?"

"Such as it is. You know scientists, always tinkering." When Dr. Richmond appeared in a doorway adjacent to the living room, she turned toward him. "I'll fix you two some iced tea."

"Raven," Richmond said, crossing the room with his hand out. "Great to see you."

Please. You deal with teenagers all day. Stop with the sappy, gooey niceness. It makes me want to vomit. Raven shook his hand. "It sounds like I'm interrupting you. I can come back later." Actually, he didn't care if he was interrupting or not. But the admission should spark some info about the lab Mrs. Goggles mentioned.

"Not at all. I was just puttering around in my basement laboratory."

"Basement laboratory?" He feigned interest. "That sounds so cool."

"Would you like to see it?"

Sucker. "I would. I'm getting really interested in science since I started your class. You make it come alive, ya know?"

Richmond beamed like he'd just won the Pulitzer. "I do?"

So genuine, Raven almost felt guilty. Almost. "Yeah, so seeing a real lab would be exciting."

After snagging the iced teas from his wife, Richmond flipped the stairwell light with his elbow. "Follow me." He grinned like a goofy kid and practically waltzed his way down the stairs. At the bottom, he handed Raven a tea.

Raven's sharp senses absorbed everything in the lab. Eyes scanned the perimeter: beakers, test tubes, a computer. He sniffed. A bouquet of chemicals dotted the air. Magnesium, copper, even bleach, all blending with the scent of a Bunsen burner flame. And ... lemon? His gaze fell to the iced drink, lemon slice decorating the rim. *Moron.*

"Cool lab." Raven tried to sound convincing. He might as well have said, *Oh boy, this sure is a neat laboratory.* "What do you do in here?"

"Well," Richmond said, abandoning his tea on the counter. Three half-empty glasses would keep it company. "I'm interested in genetics. I've actually been working on splicing some DNA from one type of reptile into another unable to spawn in cool temperatures."

Booooring. "Wow, that's amazing." Raven took a drink. Black Pekoe and brewed in the coffeepot. Yuck. "Snakes, right?"

Richmond's eyes widened with surprise.

"Snakes can only spawn after their temperature heats to a certain level," Raven said.

"Exactly." Excitement laced Richmond's voice.

Doofus, you told us that in class last week. "So, you're interested in snakes?"

"Not snakes specifically. I'm interested in what happens when gene sequences are altered. I believe things, even behaviors, can be manipulated if the right sequences are modified."

They chatted on the better part of an hour. Raven snapped mental photographs of the entire place. Far as he could tell, there was little to learn. Bummer. He'd planned on being the big shot with the key information, and now his hopes were ruined because a squirrely little scientist couldn't muster anything more interesting than snake DNA.

Richmond escorted him toward the door, still yammering about snake genes. When they passed through the hallway, a photo caught Raven's attention.

Richmond pointed. "Oh, that's my daughter."

The pretty, shapely blonde looked nothing like her pudgy, geeky mom and dad. The sand and water in the background suggested a beach somewhere tropical and perfect. She squinted in the sun, but an open-mouthed smile made him smile back. He caught himself. "Excuse me for saying, Dr. Richmond, but your daughter is ridiculously hot."

Richmond sighed, pulled the glasses from his nose, and wiped them on his shirttail — an action Raven decided was more from nervous habit than necessity. "Unfortunately, you're not the first young man to mention that."

A wicked grin laced Raven's face. "Where is she?"

He straightened slightly, eyes round. "You are, however, the first to ask that!"

Raven wiggled his brows.

"Away at college. Missouri University. I worry about her though."

"You should. Probably every guy there is trying to … never mind."

His brow furrowed. "Yes, well. There's that too."

"Huh?" Raven said.

"Jessica is diabetic. She has to give herself insulin shots daily." He heaved a breath. "I worry. So many distractions at school, I'm afraid she'll forget."

"Would that be so bad? I mean, to forget one day?"

Richmond tugged his glasses from his face again. "It would be devastating."

Raven threw a last long look to Jessica Richmond, then headed for the door.

Once outside, he listened as the screen screeched shut. Scientists were weirdos. Freakish and abnormal. Though who was he to talk about abnormal? *Take a look in the mirror, dude.* Pausing, he considered the comfy, cozy porch. Eyes closing, he drew its scent into his lungs. Pie crumbs under the porch swing, the remnants of newspaper and ink, and … horse manure. His eyes flew open. Fertilizer in the plants? No. He sniffed again. His gaze traipsed to the foot of the column anchoring the top step.

The tennis shoes. One shoestring was frayed, dark at the end as if trampled frequently. The soles were spotted with fresh clumps of dirt. Raven bent closer and took another whiff. Richmond wasn't telling all his secrets.

Raven tucked into the trees at the edge of Richmond's house. He snapped his wings open and leapt.

Chapter
21

Wow, what's this?" Nikki asked as her dad unfolded the cloth encasing an ornate sword. Watching her dad's attention to detail as he worked cleaning and polishing bits of history had always been calming for her. When she was little, he'd raise the weapon for her inspection. She'd giggle then give her nod of approval.

Nikki needed calming right now. An invisible force had pressed against her chest for so long, she'd started to think it normal. But that pressure was, in a word, foreboding.

It was an ominous notion or perhaps a promise. Though things seemed bad, rocky, and unstable, the ground on which she stood felt about to break free, proving life could get infinitely worse.

"This, my dear, is our Hawaiian vacation." He caressed the shimmering gold weapon lovingly and hummed some island tune.

"It's amazing. New?" She leaned her weight on the garage counter to get a better look.

"Nah, about five hundred years old." Her dad flipped a switch and a bright work light illuminated the weapon.

She tilted a brow. "New to you?"

"Yes. We found it in an antique store in Arkansas. The shop was going out of business and we purchased a footlocker filled with junk." He angled the sword one way, then the other. "Or so we thought. This and a half-dozen other extremely valuable weapons were inside as well."

Nikki ran a thumb over the blade. "Still sharp. What were weapons like this doing in a footlocker in Arkansas?"

He placed it gently on the counter. "Who knows? Never know what you'll find if you take the time to look."

"And you never know what's right under your nose. Why haven't you ever mentioned Damon?"

He paused and stared at the wall. "I'm sure we have. Known him for years." But he tilted away ever so slightly.

Strike while they're weak. "Why didn't you ever tell me he's the one who bought Bo for me?"

He dropped the sword on the table. "He told you that?" His bifocal glasses left his face as he gave her his full attention. "Princess, Damon has been a close family friend for —"

She raised a hand to stop him. "No, he hasn't. He's been a friend of yours. I never knew he existed until he showed up to loan me a Ducati and informed me he purchased my *dog*."

"He loaned you that bike?"

Her chin jutted forward. "That's right." *How does it feel to be kept out of the loop?*

"Well, I don't want you riding it. It's too fast, too dangerous."

Her jaw set. "It's too late. He made me promise to take it on Saturday to get serviced. I gave my word, Dad. I won't back down." But even as the words left her mouth, she wondered where they came from. This wasn't like her. She turned away from her father before her irrational anger made her say anything else.

Silence born of sorrow reached with tangible limbs. Her relationship with her parents, especially her dad, was one of trust. Unsettled by his lack of explanation, she chanced a look.

He stared helplessly at the ground, and when he spoke, his voice echoed like a hollow cavern. "I'm sorry we hadn't mentioned Damon. He sort of flies in and out of our lives. Twenty years back we were all very close. Best of friends."

She gawked. "Twenty years back? He's only twenty-five!"

His frown deepened, causing his eyes to crinkle. "Is that what he told you?"

"No, I guessed."

"Damon is far from twenty-five. He's nearly forty. And to be perfectly honest, I don't like the interest he's showing in you. Unfortunately, I can't just ban him from the house. Damon's helped us on more than one occasion, and I have to admit I feel a bit obligated." Embarrassment flushed his cheeks. "He's your godfather."

Her eyes widened. "My what?" What little blood still keeping her heart beating quickly drained from her. They owed him. *She* owed him, someone she barely knew? A man whom she was certain on a deep, *deep* level she couldn't trust?

He nodded. "He paid for your motorcycle." Nikki's dad reached for her and clasped her hands. "Honey, our work keeps the bills paid, but usually doesn't leave much at the end of the month. Damon's always been very generous when we needed help."

Nikki ripped her hands from his, now angry. "You should have told me!" Angry and ... sorry for what her parents had needed to do. Her voice cracked. "Why didn't you tell me? I could have been working, helping. Lots of kids my age have jobs." And suddenly, she knew she shouldn't be indebted to anyone. Especially Damon Vessler.

"No, we've wanted you to concentrate on your academics. And then there's your karate."

She paled, thinking of all the tournaments, years of classes, expenses with each new belt rank. Dollar signs flashed in front of her eyes. "All that money."

"Nikki, we're not destitute." His voice sharpened along with his grip on her.

"I've been so selfish my whole life. It never occurred to me that the things I do could be a strain on you guys." Her stomach churned.

"I suppose we didn't mention him because, well, honestly we were embarrassed."

Nikki sighed, determined to restore whatever dignity her father thought he'd lost. She'd always been proud of her dad, but maybe never as much as right now. She took his face in her hands. "You have nothing to be embarrassed about. You are the best father in the world. I love you, Daddy."

Tears spilled onto his sparse lashes and trickled down his cheeks. "No matter what happens, Nikki, I love you too."

He pulled her into an embrace that — coupled with his words — created a dark cloud of uncertainty over her. She tried to tilt back to look at him, but he squeezed tighter, unwilling to let go, even for a moment. Unable to see his face, Nikki did the only thing she could. She clung to him and tried to push the sensation of impending doom from her heart and mind.

"We can put up the windows if you want." Mace escorted her to his black car, freshly washed and shimmering in the street lights illuminating her neighborhood.

"No, it's beautiful out tonight. Let's leave them down."

Mace reached to her cheek and ran his knuckles along her skin. "That's right," he said in almost a whisper. "Nikki likes the wind in her hair."

Well now. The ringing of her phone — Krissy's ringtone — broke the moment. "Excuse me." She fished the phone from her little purse and answered. "Yes, the dress looks fine." She met Mace's gaze and mouthed *sorry.* "Yes, Krissy, I'm wearing the earrings you picked out. Okay, see you at the game." Nikki'd grown more and more comfortable in the tighter jeans and the cute, sometimes sparkly, decorated T-shirts Krissy helped her purchase. After her fight with Raven, proving looser clothes a liability, she'd promised herself to give the outfits a try. To her shock, jeans with a bit of stretchy material actually made it easier to move. But the fitted, green homecoming dress was a whole other matter, one that ushered a new level of unease. Shoulders bare, she squirmed, wishing she'd brought a cover-up. She rolled her eyes at her wedge sandals. *Easy to walk in. Yeah, right.* Adding to her awkwardness, the thing with Mace and the females still loomed above their heads. He could deny it all he wanted, but when she mentioned Glimmer, his eyes got that far away, moony look. Ugh.

Mace rubbed his hands on his pants before opening her door. *Is he actually nervous?*

She glanced inside at the small plastic container on the seat.

"Oh, almost forgot." He reached in. "I bought you a corsage." Dressed in a dark suit, he was absolutely stunning. "I know it's probably cheesy."

247

Tiny flowers surrounded a delicate miniature white rose tied together with a dark-green satin sash. "It's not cheesy." Her eyes narrowed. "How'd you know?"

"Your mom. I asked what color you were wearing, and she told me last week. Nikki—" Her name slid from his lips with a long breath.

Don't, she thought. He wanted to explain about the arrival of the females, about his reaction, all of it. It was just too raw. Too painful. The Golden Girls were ... well, pretty close to perfection, and Nikki was a silly teenage girl. A mixed-up, stuck-in-two-worlds teenage girl with no hope of understanding the epic struggles half angels must face.

At least Raven had steered clear of her lately. What had his reaction to the females been? She hadn't really noticed. And she didn't know why it mattered now. That was the thing—it didn't matter what Raven thought of the females. Just like it didn't matter that Mace loved her.

Homecoming night had a vibe all its own, she discovered. School spirit and teen anticipation. Usually whenever she went to a football game, the marching band and the cheerleaders couldn't get the bleachers full of teenagers barely drifting beyond complacency to summon as much as a feeble yell, if the students bothered to attend the game at all. But not tonight. With every completed pass, the same apathetic kids were on their feet screaming.

Mace and Nikki sat in his car at the edge of the field. With the lights off, they could make out the scoreboard, which showed the opposition trailed by thirteen points. Sounds filtered through the airways to them. "How old are you?" she asked.

He blushed.

Slipping her foot out of the high-heeled death sandal, she said it again. "Mace, how old?"

He frowned. "It's hard to say in human terms. Time doesn't really matter in the midplane."

"What was it like to be a little boy with superhuman powers?"

"I wouldn't know. None of us would. Up until the time we're in our older teens, we seem just like everyone else. Maybe a little more in tune with the other realm, but that's all. Vine is sort of the breakout star of our group. He started realizing power at fourteen. He's only fifteen now, two years younger than me."

"Fifteen human years?"

"Yeah, until we begin journeys, we stay mostly in this realm. After that, when we begin going to the midplane, we sort of lose track of time. We have a permanent home in Europe and a few others throughout the world that other Lost Boys use as well. Once we begin journeys, we spend quite a bit of time in the midplane too, so there's really nowhere we call home."

"Tell me about the midplane."

"It's the part of the spirit realm that's open to us. We aren't allowed to enter heaven, and who'd want to enter hell?"

"But you age?"

"Slowly, yes. I mean, I have knowledge of some pretty ridiculously cool things, but I feel like a teenager. Our personalities fit where we are in human years. Does that make sense?"

"I think so. You're seventeen in human years and you feel like a seventeen-year-old, which is good, because I don't want to hang out with some old man."

"That would be creepy. But our youth is renewed when we spend time in the midplane." He took her hand in his. "Nikki, we have to talk about some things."

She looked up at the scoreboard and swallowed. "No, we don't." Mace was the only thing that kept her from busting apart at each joint. Even her parents, with their admission about Damon Vessler, caused more of the ground to crumble beneath her feet. The last thing she needed was to "talk."

"I've tried to avoid being close to you," he said, words soft and gentle.

No, please, please, please don't say it. He was leaving. What choice did he have? And she was so selfish to want to keep him here, but the thought of losing him, never again hearing his voice, never again seeing that smile that was meant only for her … "You're right," she blurted.

Confusion played across his face.

But somewhere between internally begging him to stay and verbally agreeing he should go, she found strength. Strength that rose from so deep, she'd not known it existed. "You're right," she repeated. If the words brought the power, she needed more. "You can go. We tried to do the friend thing, failed miserably …"

He shook his head and squared his shoulders. "That's not what I was going to say." A look of wonder rested on his face, Nikki wasn't sure what to do.

"Um, okay." *When all else fails, go back to your strength as a brilliant conversationalist.*

He pulled a short, quick breath and gave her hands a light squeeze. "What I'm trying to say is — " He exhaled again.

And she was lost. Lost in his angel breath, lost in his ocean eyes. What was wrong with him right now? *Just say what you have to say!* Even his hands were clammy. Oh, maybe that was her hands creating the cool, slick feeling.

"I've been thinking about us. Nikki, when Halflings fall in love …"

Her heart dropped, and suddenly it all became clear: his nervousness, his energy. This was the "I'm going to let you down easy" speech. Of course. "You don't have to explain." *Please, please don't explain! I can't bear the thought of you and one of those angelic, winged creatures falling in love.* But it made sense, really. Nikki'd caught his attention until the females appeared. Now he knew what he could have, and that made it easier to let go of her. And that was a good thing for him. It was only her heart on the line, but it was his eternal future.

"Nikki, do you think you're going to give me a chance to finish a sentence here? Because it's starting to sound like a pretty one-sided conversation."

She slowly pulled her hands from his grasp. "Mace, you don't need to say it. Somewhere out there is a female Halfling that's a perfect match for you." Oh, those words sounded strong. Even indifferent, but gentle. She should be proud. She could win an Oscar.

His angry breath surprised her. This was where he should be thanking her and relief should be flooding him. Instead, he closed his hands on each side of her face.

Uh-oh. There goes all my award-winning strength. His touch and the sudden intensity and the certainty in his gaze drained the surety from her.

"Nikki, I love you."

Her eyes closed, both trying to reject the words and trying to capture them. Eyes shut, there was only blackness and the sound of Mace's breathing. And his warm, warm hands on her skin. For a fraction of an instant, she pressed into his touch. But only for an instant, because if she loved him, she couldn't let him stay. Seeing the females solidified how much she *didn't* belong with Mace.

"When we're together, I feel alive. And when we're not, I feel dead."

Dead. Yes, that's how she felt right now. Or should feel. What she wanted and what should be were all mixed up in a package marked destruction. In the big scheme of things, feelings didn't really matter. Isn't that what he'd tried to tell her?

"There is no female on this planet, or any other, that can make me feel what you do. Nikki, right or wrong, you're my match."

That was so unfair. Trying to use destiny and providence to justify their emotions. She had to stop the runaway train *right now*.

Nikki had found that, when sparring, there is a moment during a fight when the opponent knows he has the upper hand. Sensei Coble called it the flash-kill moment, because the enemy thinks he's all but won and drops his defenses. It was the second of time when you needed to use every ounce of power against him. Nikki took her chance. "I am your match," she said, and bristled against the long sigh from his lips.

Now the strike. "But you're not mine."

His hands dropped and she watched the color leave his face. And those beautiful eyes seemed to melt before her. Hurt found its way into their depths as his brow quirked and nervous tension rose from him in panicked waves.

She held firm to his gaze, unflinching. If a heart was to break, it should break quickly — anything else would be cruel. But when she could stand the bewildered look no longer, she dropped her eyes and angled to face forward. "I should have told you."

Outside, the scoreboard lit up and cheers filled the air. Another touchdown for the home team. She swallowed the pain.

All the sound that had surrounded them died to deafening quiet as the reality of what she'd just done to him settled into her bones like a disease. After a long time, betrayal and acceptance crackled from Mace. Nikki hoped he wasn't imagining her with Raven. In her peripheral vision, she watched his eyes squeeze shut, trying to block the hurt. The muscle in his jaw worked, and she had to wonder if its job was to keep sorrow from spilling down his face in hot, disloyal tears.

When she reached for the door handle, he grabbed her wrist. She glanced down at his fingers, now trembling as he held her. "Just don't forget why you're here, Nikki."

An urgency was in his voice, masked by his pain. "Separate from me or from … anyone else. You're here to make a choice. Don't lose sight of that."

What? She had made a choice. Then she realized what he meant. There were even greater forces out there pulling her in two directions. Mace's final words to her were a warning for her future. Her soul.

"Don't land on the wrong side of this eternal war."

Her heart hurt. Physically, the pain and its intensity was increasing by the moment. But she couldn't back down now. Mace was still making sacrifices for her protection even though she'd just cut his heart out with a dull knife. *Flash kill. You can't back down during a flash kill.*

"I won't. I made the right choice." With every ounce of will, she stepped out of his car, closed the door, and walked toward the school, away from the football field. The walk became a run. By the time she made it halfway, her face was wet with tears.

He didn't follow her.

Moist air filled her lungs as she disappeared into the shadow of the building and collapsed against its brick wall. Agony tightened around her like a shrinking second skin, stealing her oxygen, choking her lungs. Her core was an empty hole, gaping and unprotected. And Nikki understood what true heartache was. She closed her fist over her chest trying to erase Mace's face and the way it crumbled when she destroyed him. The sounds of the football game echoed to her. Above, a single light illuminated an American flag, which whipped rhythmically each time the breeze kicked up. Thrown by the wind, scrambled by the elements, tattered by the heat of an unforgiving sun … she could relate.

The flag swayed regally, standing strong in the wind assailing it. Perhaps the same material could have ended up as a tablecloth or a dress. But, no, it had a purpose, a destiny to represent a nation of survivors and conquerors. It was a fighter. Like her. And this was a war. She'd do well to remember her place in it.

For a long time, she thought about epic battles and choices and what it meant to truly sacrifice. Her mind trailed to the Catholic church, where Mace told her she needed a sanctuary. The eyes of the Savior had brought calm as she'd gazed into them. He understood sacrifice. If no one else could fathom what she'd just done, certainly Jesus knew.

He knew. Nikki had to wonder what that meant for her. Did she actually believe that he —

Well, she still didn't know for sure. There were too many questions, too many unsolved answers. And yet, at the moment, she couldn't remember one argument she'd used. Not one. But that was only because her heart was broken, she reasoned, thoroughly grounded into powder, making it difficult — no, impossible — to think clearly about things like eternal choices and timeless wars. But until she had time, it was comforting to know someone understood her pain.

"I thought I smelled you." The voice traveled from behind the corner of the building.

Chapter
22

Nikki didn't flinch. "Please, Raven, try to refrain from phrases like that. People wouldn't understand, and it makes me want to do a quick sniff of my underarms."

He scrunched his face. "Gross."

She brushed her hands across her cheeks again, attempting to remove the remnants of her tears. Her skin was cold and too tight from being assaulted by saline.

Raven leaned against the brick. Too close, but rather than move away she allowed his nearness to create a reassuring wall beside her. For a few moments they were still.

Nikki forced the painful conversation with Mace to the back of her mind and turned slightly toward Raven. She smiled wickedly. "You tried to scare me."

"Why would you say that?" His hair and eyes were darker in the night, contrasting with his pale, golden skin.

"I knew you were there before you spoke. I could feel it." She wiggled her fingers toward her stomach. "You had these, like, fluttery sensations inside. You thought you'd make me jump. And that fact thrilled you."

He pressed his shoulder into the wall. "You're getting kind of scary with this *I feel blah, blah, blah* stuff."

"No one asked your opinion about it," she fired back at him, suddenly angry that he was there and she'd launched into a friendly banter with him while deep inside, her soul ached.

"Score." He faked a knife to the heart. "Direct hit."

Her voice eased to warm butter. "There's no real knife there, Raven. Here, let me get you a couple pencils."

"You're killin' me."

The little giggle that escaped surprised her. "I do what I can," she said, and suddenly she *was* glad for Raven's intrusion.

"Good, that's why I came to find you." He blazed a trail over her with his eyes. "Nice dress."

She shrank. "Thanks." Luckily, there were no straps for him to adjust.

"I think Vegan's in trouble. Will you help me?"

Of all the Halfling females, Vegan had offered allegiance to her. "Why me?" And why wasn't he asking one of his kind?

"Mace is useless. I don't know what you said to him, but he tore out of the parking lot like a hell hound dipped in cold water. He said for me to stay with you, and didn't give me a chance to tell him what's going on. Not that I'm complaining about the first part. And I'm not sure where Vine is." He rolled his eyes. "Probably at the bowling alley or the candy store. His two new obsessions."

"I thought Suzy Carmichael was going to ask Vine to homecoming."

"She never did." Raven bumped his shoulder against Nikki's. "Come on, you may get to watch me fight again. It's a good opportunity to learn."

Nikki's hand slid to her throat, where the pearly amulet Vegan had given her graced her collarbone.

"What do you say, Nikki?" he asked.

Her feet were moving before she could answer. "Where's your car?"

"Like I need one." He grabbed her hard, arms encircling her waist and crushing her against him. And then he leapt.

Vegan's mouth bled. As they touched down, Nikki counted four hell hounds surrounding her. *Were these the same as those who'd originally chased me?* A wind song stopped them, that beautiful, soothing, eerie sound like bells ringing underwater. "Raven, the wind song? How does it work?"

He stepped into the middle of the battle, arms out protectively while motioning for Vegan to get behind him. He scowled at Nikki. "What are you talking about?" Then his eyes flashed recognition. "Wait, you mean the Angel Song. It doesn't work, at least not now. We've been here too long. It's only effective when we've just returned to this realm from the midplane."

Vegan nodded a thank you in her direction. Even battered, she was beautiful beyond compare, dressed in a tie-dyed shirt and jeans.

"So what do we do?" Nikki asked when a hell hound lurched closer, causing her to jolt backward.

Raven took a moment to size up the situation. "We fight them."

Instinctively, Nikki slid into a fighting position. Her homecoming dress whooshed against her skin, but her mind reeled. "No, thanks," she said. "I've seen what they can do. Let's just ..." She pointed to the sky repeatedly. "You know, jump."

"We can't, Nikki. We can't leap from battles we've been called into. We finish it. If we run, it just gives the hounds more power and makes them harder to defeat next time."

Okay then. Her fisted hands opened in anticipation as adrenaline caused her heart to pound. She exhaled a puff of air. "Oh, and thanks for picking me up on the way. I'll be sure to return the favor." She slid her feet from her sandals.

His face tilted in a half grin, midnight-blue eyes glistening. "They seem really angry."

She allowed herself a moment to glare at him. "You sound scared. Don't be, I'll protect you."

Vegan wiped the blood from her mouth. "Let's end this."

Quite literally, all hell broke loose. Two hounds jumped at Raven, temporarily pinning him on the ground. He sprang up, eyes scanning.

One of the hounds concentrated his attention on Nikki. The long, oozing scar on the side of his head jogged her memory. *This is the beast who'd killed Bo.* Heart thudding, she leapt before the hound had a chance. Fighting and screaming, she tore into the creature as it had her dog. The world slowed as she ripped, tore, dug into the thing's matted flesh. It shrieked while luscious revenge stole through her. She felt no pain. No wounds marred her skin. Predator became the prey — just like Raven had taught her.

For an eternity she felt bones cracking and breaking beneath her fists. Digging her feet into the ground for a better grip, a stone materialized beneath her knee. She grabbed it with both hands and hammered the beasts head again and again until the skull cracked and broke and rattled with each strike like pebbles in a barrel.

Strong hands fell on her shoulders, pulling her back.

Soothing words drifted from somewhere, but she fought them, enjoying the bitter, beautiful taste of vengeance.

Digging beneath her fingers, Raven's hands stripped hers from the lifeless creature. Fistfuls of blood and fur stunk like death and filled her grasp. He dragged her to her feet, and then his arms were around her, holding her while she cried.

Slowly, he slid his hand from the top of her head down to the middle of her back. And then again. And again as sobs wrenched from her soul. She cried for Bo. She cried for Mace and for the unfair reality of two worlds in a symbiotic relationship allowed to coexist but not allowed to merge.

When the sobs became only tears, she realized his touch. So gentle and so unusual for him. And Nikki had to wonder at the layers that made Raven who he was. The boy who saw the broken pot. The one who looked into her soul and comprehended who she really was. The one who tried to prepare her for her destiny.

He was whispering something against her ear. So soft she couldn't make out the words. She tilted closer to the place where his warm breath met her skin. And what she discovered stunned her. Raven was praying.

Chapter 23

When Nikki raised her head, three hell hounds were dead around them. "The other ran away," Raven said in answer to her unspoken question. The softness of his eyes caused her to pull from his grasp.

Her hands were sticky. As she looked down and forced them open, bits of fur and rotting, half-congealed blood dropped to the ground. Bile rose in her throat. *I'm going to throw up.* She turned away and bent at the waist, but nothing came up.

Raven's hand remained on her back, still moving gently, stroking up and down her spine and coaxing her heart to slow.

Her skin felt both hot and cold, alternating waves crashing over her. She started to wipe the sweat from her face, but saw the bits of hound clinging to her fingers.

Without a word, Raven lifted his shirttail to her face. "Here, let me."

As he swiped her cheeks and forehead, his smell filled her nose. "What happened?" she mumbled.

He threw a nod to the hound. "You killed it." When she tried to turn toward the beasts, he caught her chin. "I've never seen a human take down a hound. There's something special about you, Nikki." His dark eyes sparkled, like there was much more he could say, wanted to say, but refrained from saying. "Guess I have no choice but to admit you're a good student."

Surprise forced a quick puff of air from her lungs. "You're a better teacher."

Vegan crossed the forest to them, smiling with brilliant, glossy lips. "I'm in your debt. Both of you. How'd you know to come?" She turned the question to Raven.

"I just knew," Raven said.

When she frowned, a small smile crept onto his face. "Nah, Zero called me. Apparently, I've been writing things on the network that he disapproves of."

"But the network is safe?" It was both a question and an answer, and accompanied by Vegan's troubled, golden gaze.

"Or so we thought," Raven said.

Her eyes shifted to molten globs of lava.

Raven continued. "In the midst of the argument about my rights as a Halfling to put whatever I want on the network, Zero mentioned you'd brought him food and were planning to stop by the house to give Will some new information. I told him we hadn't seen you." He shrugged. "Zero sent me to search."

Vegan crossed her arms. "*He* sent *you* to search?" Anger, or something like it, crackled around her. "Didn't even bother to check it out for *himself*?" She threw her hands into the air, and Nikki had the sudden feeling she and Vegan would have a lot to talk about later.

Raven laughed. "What could he have done? This is Zero we're talking about. He struggles to get the straw into his drink box."

Vegan slapped him square across the face, and hard.

Raven grinned. "You're welcome, by the way."

"Zero runs the network." Vegan advanced, forcing Raven to step back. "His position is more important than any of us who roll around in the mud with hell hounds."

"Ooh, aah. Good for him. Doesn't mean he's not a wimp," Raven said, rubbing his cheek.

She reached to strike again, but this time Raven caught her hand an inch from his face. That slow, demeaning smile sliced his mouth. "Ohhhh," he purred. "I think someone has a crush."

Nikki backed away from the two. Sparks, *literal* sparks flew around them like firework bursts on the Fourth of July. Vegan and Raven were toe-to-toe and seemed equally matched. But as she watched, Nikki just wanted to go home. She glanced down at her ripped, ruined, stained homecoming dress. "At least I didn't trip and fall in the gym," she said. It was a pitifully small voice, but enough to draw the attention of the two warring Halflings, who gave her a fleeting glance, then returned to their silent battle. *Nice to know where I stand.*

She knelt and scraped her hands against the grass in an attempt to remove the remnants of the hound and to encourage her lungs to fill. *This must be the worst homecoming night in recorded history — watching a childish fight in the middle of a forest, your dress in tatters and covered in things you'd rather not think about.*

Raven puckered as if to kiss Vegan, but sarcasm filled the motion.

"Argh!" Vegan said and pulled from his grasp.

His smile broke into a laugh. "So, what's this all-important information you have?"

She propped her hands on her hips and cocked a brow. "Dr. Richmond's been visiting the horses."

It was homecoming night. The game was probably over by now, and Vine hated admitting Raven was right. Vine wandered the streets downtown until he came across the candy store.

Stupid girls. He'd really thought Suzy Carmichael would bring up a conversation about homecoming so he could ask her to the dance, but she never did. When he found the candy store door locked, he huffed a breath and dropped his weight against the wall.

Fishing for backup gummies in his pocket, he saw Nikki's mom and dad down the street. His wings tingled, causing him to straighten from the wall and follow. They entered a restaurant and Vine slipped silently inside after them. He watched them nervously sit down with the dark haired man from the art gallery — *the one with the dangerous checkbook* — and scoured the place for a way to get closer. But Nikki's parents stayed only a few minutes, then stood and left in a hurry.

So, if this gun-carrying dude knows Nikki's parents, does he know Nikki? If so, why didn't she say she knew him after they tackled the guy at the art show? Vine remembered how quickly it all happened. Nikki probably hadn't gotten a chance to see the guy's face.

When another woman approached the table, Vine paused behind a wall separating the rows of booths and hoped no one would notice him loitering there.

"Are we on task?" His tone was gruff, making Vine dislike him all over again. The gun was there too. He could smell it.

"Yes, Mr. Vessler." Fear drifted in the woman's words.

"Betty, you've been with me for years. Why am I sensing fear in you?" Apparently, Vessler picked up on the woman's attitude as well.

"Apprehension, sir. Not fear." She swallowed. "And it's only because I know how hard you've worked to get here."

"Everything is moving forward. Is the lab being demolished?"

Vine nearly choked on his candy.

"The investigation will likely continue for another few weeks. My hope is that we can clear that land and have it ready to lease again in a matter of months. I'm terribly sorry for what the laboratory's burning has cost you. I know you'd leased it at a very low price for them."

"I have a soft spot for scientists."

"Still, I feel for you," she said, warmth in her tone, though it sounded forced.

"And I appreciate your loyalty. Who knows, maybe another group will lease the land. I'm still open to building-to-suit if necessary."

Vine peeked around the wall in time to see Vessler point at the woman. "You." He spun his fingertip in tiny circles. "Are overdue for a vacation."

The fortyish woman's eyes lit for a moment. "We're much too busy right now."

He lowered his hand. "Ah. Choosing work over vacation. One of your most redeeming qualities, Betty."

"Thank you, sir," she answered flatly.

"When this is all over, I'm giving you the keys to my beach house for a month. Fully staffed, naturally. Would that please you?"

"You're far too kind, Mr. Vessler."

He nodded, looked away from her, and focused his attention on the window and the street beyond. "Yes," he echoed. "Yes, I am."

"Doesn't look like your parents are home. You want me to come in for a while?" Raven asked, touching down in Nikki's backyard.

Her emerald-green dress clung to her, splotched by brownish dried blood. She absently brushed at it. "They were going to meet someone interested in the swords my dad recently purchased."

Raven frowned and seemed to bristle. "At night?"

"It's antiques." She gave him a half smile.

When she did, he stepped closer and placed an arm gently around her shoulders.

She tried not to think about his skin, warm against hers. "Late-night deals are more common than you think. Some dealers have to handle business in the evening if they have shops that are open during the day. I know that's what they were doing—I helped my dad load the weapons into the trunk." She could sense, almost smell his doubt.

"So I'll come in, help you get settled," he said. "You've had a rough night."

True. But her instincts told her to turn down the offer. "I'll be fine, Raven."

He looked unsure. Untrusting. "Well, I'll hang around out here for a while. 'Til your folks get back."

He dropped his arm and turned to face her fully. He was beautiful. They all were: Mace, Vine, Raven. Even Will, though he was a stark contrast, with his linebacker shoulders and thick posture. How could she have three — make that four — supernatural creatures protecting her and still end up in life-or-death fights? "Why do they want me?" she whispered, hoping for an answer she knew he couldn't give.

Midnight-blue eyes trailed her face. Every inch, finally coming to rest on her lips. "I told you. You're special."

"Could I be a little less special?"

He flipped his hair back with one quick motion. When he did, the moonlight flashed in his eyes.

Nikki frowned. "Your eyes seem lighter."

Embarrassment flickered, but he rushed it away with a wink. "Do they? It must be you."

"What?"

"Up until recently, my irises have darkened on each journey."

"What does that mean?" Nikki asked.

He shrugged. "If they darken completely, I'm given over to the other side."

"Raven, no." An ocean of panic rose within her. "That's not … fair."

He laughed, but without humor. "What's fair about any of this?"

"If the journeys are making you turn — "

He spun away from her and she felt herself shiver. "It's never the journey, Nikki. It's the choices we make during. What we decide to do in the places where darkness meets light. Where hate clashes with love."

She'd never pitied the Lost Boys, but right now her heart broke for the creature before her. She took a tentative step toward him and slowly reached up to touch his shoulder.

He flinched before she made contact. "Don't," he ordered.

Inches from him, she stopped. "Raven, let me see your wings again."

He tossed a glance over his shoulder at her. Their eyes locked and held.

"Please, they're so amazing."

With one snap, dark-gray wings flew from side to side with such force her hair lifted from her face. As before, she couldn't help digging her fingers through the cool, soft feathers. Reaching around him, a hand on each side of one wing, she slid the length from his powerful shoulders to the tip of his wing, where velvety feathers pointed sharply toward the ground.

"Raven," she whispered. "I know you hear this a lot, but you're stunning."

His eyes landed on her, glowing like a night creature's in the dark. A moment later his wings snapped shut and he crossed the ten-foot span to where she stood. She was suddenly, painfully aware he intended to kiss her. *Didn't I know that could happen?* He licked his lips and bent close, then closer still, and her mind spun in an attempt to stop him. But the fight had left her.

His lips pressed against hers softly. And *that* surprised her. There'd been such burning intensity in his gaze, in the way he'd marched to her, but the kiss was sweet and soft. Very, very gently, he pulled away, and her eyes opened to find his dark gaze alive and sparkling, and bombarding her with a million unspoken questions.

She blinked, unable to find words. In answer, Raven snapped his wings open again, and she continued to examine them as if the last moments hadn't happened.

Chapter
24

Mace watched Nikki and Raven from his high perch. The distance and wind carried her words away from him, making their conversation impossible to detect, but body language said it all. A fat tear trickled down his cheek. He swiped it with the back of his hand, leaving a stream of cold moisture across his face.

So it was true.

After leaving her in the parking lot, he'd thought maybe she'd been trying to push him away for his own protection, and that hope had fueled him. No way was she saying she'd chosen Raven, that he was her match. Then he watched them kiss while the shadow of clouds against moonlight captured them. Even then, Mace's heart rumbled with hope. She could smack Raven, or turn away and march into her house, or anything.

But no, Nikki rewarded Raven by continuing to caress his gray wings. When she used the wing to push her face toward Raven's again, Mace's heart shattered. She planted a kiss on his cheek, leaned back slowly, and offered a smile beautiful enough to melt stone. Mace's hand fell against his chest in a fist. Pain, physical and powerful, clenched him in a vice.

Never had he hated himself for who and what he was. Never had he coveted another's life. But right now, with the female he loved in the arms of a Halfling he despised, all Mace wanted was to be a normal, regular teenage guy. One with hopes and dreams of college, a job, and Nikki in his arms.

Not that hopes mattered — there was no choice for him. He'd have to soldier on. Dreams were like dust, sifted and strained by the hands of time. Time was one thing he had, though he'd trade it for normalcy in an instant.

Nikki disappeared into the house. The wind shifted, lifting the hair from his forehead.

"I can smell you, brother." Raven said, destroying the silence and interrupting his pain. The twisted grin on the darker Halfling's face sent spikes of anger through Mace's gut.

Mace slid from the tree branch he'd occupied and landed silently on the ground. They crossed the distance to one another, both with hands fisted and ready for the fight.

"I am not your brother," Mace growled.

Raven's lip curled. "No, you're too pure to have my tainted blood running through your veins."

Mace shoved a finger into his chest. "Your blood is what you choose."

"I choose Nikki," Raven countered.

"That *isn't* your choice to make. Raven, you have to stay away from her."

"Why? I'd think you'd be glad." He tsked. "You've worked so hard to keep your heart pure, labored so long to achieve goodness. But you forget your roots. We were born in rebellion. And that rebellion floods our veins. Like a poison, it takes over, eating, devouring. With me it chose the path of anger. With you, it picked the path of forbidden love. Admit it, Mace. You're falling."

Mace shoved him. "*I will not fall.*" Pent-up energy released, he instantly regretted his outburst. It wasn't Raven's fault he'd opened his heart to Nikki. How could he resist her? Life, in its most beautiful form, filled the atmosphere around her. "You — *we* — don't have to fall."

Raven's eyes narrowed. "Don't bother to push me away from the cliff edge you dangle from yourself. Make no mistake, *brother*, eventually we will both fall."

Mace grabbed his shoulders. "No," he screamed, tears blurring his vision once he realized the depths of Raven's resolve. One thing and one thing only kept Halflings trudging forward: Hope.

Suddenly, the battle became *for* his brother rather than *against* his brother.

Without hope, there could be no victory. Raven was giving up, giving in. "Fight it, Raven. Don't let it take you. You're stronger than that, better than that."

He shook his head, eyes focusing on some distant spot far away. The muscle in his jaw went slack. "I'm sick of fighting, Mace. I'm tired of the battle. We win, and what? No accolades, no awards. We lick our wounds and get ready for another journey."

"Reward awaits us at the end."

"So we're told. We have nothing to prove it, no written contract. Even the human's have their covenant. They know their destiny and it's sealed in blood. Ours is hazy, fuzzy. But I *could* have a life right now." He gaze traveled to Nikki's back door. "One where I choose what I do and when."

Mace sighed, surprised by the love he held for this Halfling who hovered between spiritual life and death. "That's the biggest lie of all, Raven. If you turn from the great army, you will be pushed into service for the enemy. Don't you see? The choice has already been made. You must fight — and keep fighting. There's no other path for us."

Several moments ticked by as the forest's nocturnal creatures chattered around them. The sweet scent of honeysuckle drifted on the night's breeze.

Raven's expression melted with his resolve. *I did it, I broke through that hardened shell.* Deep down, Raven had to know there was no going back for Halflings. They simply had nowhere to go back to.

"If I thought Nikki would bring you true happiness, I'd walk away." Mace choked a little on the last words, but they confirmed his honesty.

Raven's eyes searched him, and had to know he spoke the truth.

"But she can't bring happiness to either one of us." Mace's voice was stronger now.

And Raven was melting, practically sinking into the ground at the edge of Nikki's yard. "I can't do this anymore." he whispered, eyes pleading with Mace.

Mace dropped beside him. "We'll do this together, my brother. I'll stand beside you. You have my word. You're not alone."

Mace's arm fell around Raven's shoulder as they both crouched on the ground. They couldn't have her, but at least they had each other.

Voices. She heard voices in the backyard. Somehow, she knew it was Raven and Mace. The policeman lingered at the front door while Nikki crossed the house, floating on feet she could no longer feel. The back door was a million miles away. *Tunnel vision.* She'd heard that in times of shock, the vision narrowed to almost nothing. She pulled the slider open.

And collapsed.

She awakened in the living room with Mace, Raven, and a police officer hovering over her. They emerged from the haze with frowns expressing the deepest of concern. Mace tilted her up, mumbling something about water.

Her head shook back and forth, rejecting the glass he offered. Words, scattered and strange, filtered in and out of her head. *Her parents ... a possible robbery ... bullet holes in the car ... blood. No bodies.*

No bodies?

She'd barely had time to grab a shower and change from her bloody homecoming dress when she'd heard the knock. She'd opened the door to the officer, who removed his hat and asked if he could come in. *This isn't happening.*

Words cemented into place as Mace lifted her shoulders and sat down on the couch beside her. As natural as breathing, she collapsed onto his lap, letting his soothing hand push hair from her face as she processed what the officer had told her at the door.

I'm sorry to inform you of this, Miss Youngblood, but your parents have been involved in an accident.

An accident? Blood, run off the road, bullet holes? That didn't sound like an accident.

We haven't apprehended the perpetrator yet. I wonder if you could answer a few questions for me. Is there someone you could call so you're not alone?

Friend. I have a friend outside.

He'd frowned. *Any family?*

I have no family but my mom and dad.

His expression froze her words. Face melting into bottomless despair, his eyes told her the truth, conveying the finality of the situation. *You don't have them either.*

She remembered stumbling to the back door, hoping Raven was still out there.

And waking on the couch. She sprung up from the sofa. "No. There has to be a mistake. My mom and dad were here just a couple hours ago."

"There's no mistake, Miss Youngblood. We've checked the plates on the vehicle and cross-referenced them to your mother's driver's license. We suspect they were robbed — your mother's wallet had been removed from the purse we located, but there was no cash inside. Also, the trunk had been jimmied."

Her gaze flittered to Mace, then Raven. "My fault," she whispered.

The boys shared a glance that didn't escape the officer's attention. He sharpened. "Why would you say that, Miss Youngblood?"

Raven took a step toward the policeman, drawing his attention. Nikki shot him a grateful smile she was sure he missed. "She told me the antiques her mom and dad were going to sell tonight were so heavy she had to help her dad load them into the trunk."

The officer pulled a notepad from his pocket. "Would these items be worth robbing someone to get?" He directed the question to Raven.

His eyes widened. "Duh, they're *antiques.*"

The officer scowled at him. "Miss Youngblood, do you know who planned to make the purchase?"

She searched her mind for names, though none came. *Bullet holes. Blood.* She shook her head. "No. I don't know. I don't feel well."

Mace rose and grabbed a throw blanket for her shoulders.

"Will you be able to come to the station with me?" the officer asked gently. "I realize what you've been through, but our best chance of locating the perpetrator is within the first few hours after the incident, and any information you can give us about your folks' business may help."

She swallowed, gaze floating to his. "The incident? You're telling me my parents may be dea — dead, and you call it an *incident*?"

Mace wrapped his arm protectively around her. "Sir, I can bring her to the station. But I think she's going to need a little bit of time."

The officer's face softened. "Of course. A half hour?"

Mace nodded.

Raven walked the officer to the door and slammed it hard.

Nikki's eyes scanned Mace's. Fear twisted her stomach.

"It has nothing to do with you, Nikki. Nothing. They were after your mom and dad's valuables."

Wanting to believe him, she slumped against his chest, pressing into his shirt and the firm muscles beneath. After the way she'd left him in the car earlier, she thought she'd never again feel the strength of his arms around her. Never again breathe in Mace's scent of warm skin blended with cotton and a hint of spearmint. He brushed her cheek with his open palm, easing her pain. Safely enveloped in the place created by the circle of his arms, Nikki cried and cried and cried.

275

She heard Damon Vessler storm into the police station with all the fury of a wasp in search of the perfect place to plunge its stinger. He thundered into the office of Captain Bernard Gump, where Nikki waited, still wrapped in the throw. It smelled like her dad, and the realization ushered a fresh wave of tears.

Damon slammed his hand on the desk. "What on earth do you think you're doing, putting a child through this?"

Mace and Raven shared a confused glance after Damon's entrance. She could feel her Lost Boys bristle.

"Standard procedure, sir," the captain commented.

"Procedure?" Damon yelled. "My attorney is on the way, and perhaps you can explain to her how harassment of an innocent teen can be considered procedure!" His muscles drew taut beneath his clothing.

Captain Gump swallowed visibly.

Nikki rose on rubber legs. "Damon," she rasped, voice rough from crying. Her hand slid from the blanket and fell on his shoulder. "I volunteered to come. They don't know who did this." When she wavered, he caught her.

He dragged her to him, arms closing on her. He buried his head in her hair and whispered, "I'm so sorry, Nicole. I won't rest until I get answers." He nuzzled deeper, something she found she didn't mind. "And I promise you I will destroy them." His words sent hot streams of retribution from her head to her heart. "Do you hear me, my lady? I *will* find them and we *will* destroy them."

At the edge of her vision, Mace rose from the chair. Raven held him back with a firm hand and she heard him whisper, "Maybe he can get her out of here."

"Now," Gump interrupted. "We were just asking Miss Youngblood—"

"How long have you been here?" Though Damon's words to her had been soft, this comment carried a nasty bite of authority, more for the officer's benefit than hers, no doubt. Damon was obviously used to giving orders. And not accustomed to being challenged.

She shook her head, helplessly. Time meant nothing. Five minutes, five hours. It was all the same.

"About an hour," Mace said.

Damon pointed to Captain Gump, pinning him to the wall. "Your questions are over. She's told you what she knows. Or does the idea of a lawsuit not concern you?"

"A lawsuit?"

"You're questioning a minor without an adult present."

Captain Gump rose with his hands out in surrender. "She agreed to come. Besides, we have to wait until the social worker arrives. As you mentioned, Miss Youngblood is a minor."

"And I'm her godfather. She will *not* be leaving with any social worker. She's going home with me. Right now. Here's the paperwork to take her with me. If you protest" — he studied the man's nameplate as he dropped the paper onto the desk — "Captain Gump, your department will be thrown into a legal battle you cannot hope to win." Damon reached into his shirt pocket and pulled out a card, which he slammed on top of the paperwork.

Captain Gump's eyes widened as he read. "I'm, uh, sorry for any inconvenience, Mr. Vessler."

Mace took Nikki's shoulder and turned her to face him, eyes filled with questions.

"It's okay," she uttered. "He's been a friend of my family for years. I recently learned that he's my godfather." She leaned closer to Mace. "Besides, if I don't go with him, they're going

277

to send me to a foster home for the next few days. *Strangers*, Mace." Her eyes pleaded. "Complete strangers."

He bent, kissed her forehead. "Nikki, we can work something else out. I can have Will come."

But she was shaking her head. "No, this is better. Don't worry, I'm safe with Damon."

She gauged Mace's reaction to Damon. His gaze left hers long enough to consider the strong, able man beside her. And apparently long enough to decide he didn't like him. She could read his thoughts as easily as if he'd spoken them aloud.

"You sure?" Mace said.

A smile curled Damon's lip. "You go on home, boys. I'm sure your parents are worried. There's an adult in charge now. Everything will be just fine."

But as she left in her father's blanket and under Damon's arm, she heard something so disturbing it was able to cut right through the numbness that had become her chest.

It was Raven's hushed voice. "That's him," he said.

"I know." Mace agreed. "The one from the art gallery."

Chapter
25

When the females arrived, Will asked them all to gather in the living room. Vegan had stopped to pick up Zero, who was pouting in the corner, arms folded over his chest because there were no juice boxes in the house. Vegan reached over to pat him on the shoulder, but Zero cut her an icy silver-blue stare, and she dropped her hand.

For once, Mace considered joining Zero in his funk. He thought his emotions had swung as far as possible in the course of the night, but knowing Nikki was in that house with that man caused a fresh new kind of anger. And fear. Especially after what Vine had told them.

Winter sat down on the edge of the couch, her legs delicately crossed at the ankles. She was so precise, so pristine in her movements that she truly looked like she belonged in another century, especially with her streak of black hair against her light skin. "Does Damon Vessler own Omega Corporation?"

Will tapped his fingers on his leg. "All we know for sure is that he owns the land of the smaller facility. From the conversation Vine heard, he had leased it to the scientists."

"Would be a convenient way to keep your nose clean," Raven said, and turned to face Vegan. "A lot has happened tonight. Do you know why the hell hounds were after you when Nikki and I arrived?"

Mace sliced a hard stare in Raven's direction.

Raven returned the look with a slow smile. "She fought like a champ — you'd have been proud."

Brother or not, Mace wanted to kill Raven for his offhand attitude.

Vegan looked down at her tie-dyed shirt of forest colors and shook her head. "On a whim, I went to the lab to do a little recon. Nothing seemed out of the ordinary, so I entered the midplane to come over here. When I started to leave, however, I felt something wasn't right, so I touched down in the woods a few miles away. That's when the hounds showed up."

Will's chin dropped a degree as he studied Vegan. "Maybe you sensed things were going to go wrong." He pulled a long, deep breath. "Was there anything we could have done to prevent the death of Nikki's parents?"

Silence answered his question and hung heavy in the room. No one knew.

Raven stood. "One thing's for sure."

His voice captured the attention of the other Halflings and Will. "Nikki's in more danger now than she ever was. If Vessler is connected to Omega, we have to get her away from him."

"One problem with that." Mace's heart crumbled as he realized the devastating truth. "We can only help her if she lets us."

Nikki woke in Damon's house in a beautiful room overlooking a freshly planted garden. The scent of new earth met her as she pulled the window open to peer outside. Off in the distance, on a faraway hill, she could see the entrance to her neighborhood. She'd entered it with her mother and father over a thousand times, but now she'd enter it alone.

She needed to be in that house. She needed to put some laundry into the washer and straighten the garage. It always made her dad proud when he'd come home and she'd straightened the garage.

But he wouldn't come home this time. If they were dead, truly dead, they'd never see what she'd done for them, though she would do it anyway. She'd scrub and clean and polish until her fingers were sore and until she couldn't move, then she'd stretch out on their bed and sleep, smelling their pillows and dreaming they were beside her. Yes, that's how Nikki would spend her first day as an orphan.

That's how she would say good-bye.

She dressed in the clothes she'd arrived in, ones she didn't even remember stripping off to sleep. She had no vehicle, so she'd walk. It wasn't far, maybe four streets away. The sun shone mercilessly. Stinging from the glare, her swollen eyes focused at the bottom of the hill. She pushed herself on. Though when she rounded the corner onto her street, nothing seemed right.

There was a semi truck just pulling out of the driveway. *No, a moving truck.* Nikki grasped her hair with her hands. Even as she yelled, "Hey, hey, this is my house!" and ran after him for a few steps, the truck continued on, not even bothering to slow down.

When it was evident he had no intention of listening, she ran toward her front door, and found it ajar. The remnants of

Nikki's heart sank as she pushed her index finger against the door and watched in horror as it opened ... to an empty house.

Nikki stepped inside and the very house seemed to groan with loneliness. She didn't know how long she wandered through the barren rooms. Every piece of furniture, every painting, every bit of clothing had been stripped. The house she'd known since she was a child was a weird empty hole she scarcely recognized. Even the refrigerator had been emptied. Her finger traced the tape outline of her school schedule that had been ripped from the door. She slung a cupboard open, hoping, praying her mother's pans would be inside. But the space was as vacant as a discarded box. She pulled a breath through her nose and could still smell the faint scent of her mom's baking. That was the only remnant of her world.

Nikki meandered upstairs. She braced herself against the doorjamb and stared into her room at the carpet-flattened indentions where her bed had been. Inside her parent's room, the same. Only dust remained to keep her company. She sank onto their floor and pressed her face into the carpet. This room still smelled like them. A lump of raw emotion rode to her throat and expanded until she thought her breathing would fail. She entered their bathroom and caught sight of her reflection in their mirror. And for a moment, she hated herself. For being alive when they weren't, for not protecting them, for being confused for so long. Nikki slammed her fist against the glass and felt it bend, then break beneath her hand. Cracked and splintered sections of her face stared back through the mirror's image. Her eyes fluttered with tears. "I don't believe in bad luck," she uttered. In fact, the shards represented a fairly fitting picture of herself. Broken, jagged, yet somehow still alive.

Dazed, she left the room and traversed the stairs with each

footfall pounding in her head. She wandered outside and did what she knew to do. Walk. One foot in front of the other. Take a step, then again. Nikki paused at the edge of a playground by the wide parking lot that separated her neighborhood from the one where the Lost Boys lived. There, she was caught between heading toward the Victorian or the opposite direction, where her feet would carry her back to Damon. Her body and mind were equally at odds. When she began to step one way, she stopped as if hitting an invisible barrier, and when she began to go the other direction, some different part of her prohibited movement.

So Nikki stood very still and watched the swing where a squirrel had perched. Even from the distance, she could see the small, round nut he protected in his tiny hands.

"Better find somewhere to bury that," she mumbled. "Winter's coming."

The screeching of tires drew her attention away. It was Damon. His car had stopped in the parking lot and he was jogging — no, running — to get to her where she stood at the halfway mark between his home and where the Halflings lived. And that stupid gold bracelet he always wore caught the sun and twinkled happily as if it had a right.

"Nikki, thank goodness you're all right." He grabbed then hugged her.

But her limbs hung loosely at her sides. For once, she didn't feel totally comfortable in his embrace. "Someone emptied my house, Damon. Everything's gone. I ... I wanted to clean it, but—"

He leaned back to look at her. "Clean it? What are you talking about? Nikki, you just lost your parents — the last thing in the world you need to be doing is cleaning."

"It's all gone. Even my clothes. Everything." *If I keep saying it, maybe I'll believe it. Everything* encompassed her karate trophies, artwork, her mom's china, every remnant of her life. Maybe he didn't understand. He didn't look shocked. In fact …

"It's not all gone, sweetheart. I had everything packed up this morning."

She jerked from his grasp. "You what?" *No, I couldn't have heard that right. It would be too cruel, too evil.*

"Nikki." She heard a bit of that authoritative tone he'd used on Captain Gump. It blended nicely with condescension. "A seventeen-year-old girl has no business having to go through her parents' things right after their deaths."

"There's no proof they're dead!" she screamed. Fury blinded her. He was talking again in that soothing tone that made her want to lash out, repeating words like *bullet holes in the car, blood on the seats, robbery.* Why wouldn't he stop? As if she hadn't been hearing those ghost phrases all night. As if she hadn't ran a thousand scenarios in her mind about her parents and the likelihood of escape.

"I know you're upset. But try to understand."

Her voice steeled. "A man I barely know has no business moving my stuff." Anger boiled inside her. Righteous anger. "Who do you think you are? Those were my personal belongings." And he'd stripped them from her. Never, ever had anyone so violated her. "You stole from me."

He moved to her and reached out."I was trying to protect you."

You do not have the right to be within ten feet of where I stand. "You stole everything from me. You stole my good-bye." She realized her voice was rising, and panic and fear and fury were all rising with it. She was very close to showing her weakness.

"Nikki," he continued, now softer toned. "We'll say good-bye together."

And that's when she knew they were there. She turned her head, ever so slightly, to watch as Will touched down across the parking lot, just behind the row of trees.

Damon didn't seem to notice; his focus was intently on her, a display of alarm and uncertainty skating over his features. He knew he'd crossed a line.

Her shoulders twitched, and again she felt the power of the Halflings and Will, her heavenly angel, waiting. Mace and Raven would be there. In her mind's eye she could see them standing on either side of Will. Mace, her invitation. Raven, her broken pot. And she'd already destroyed them both, would keep them waiting forever, because ... because she was poison. It wasn't fair to keep putting Mace and Raven through that. They deserved so much more, yet because of their heritage expected so much less. She was horrid. They'd done nothing but help her and she'd done nothing but hurt them. And being anywhere near them, the pain she created would only intensify. For in her heart, she loved them both. A horrific revelation and a sickening truth she'd have to live with — and the most awful thing she could do to the ones sent to protect her.

Nikki swallowed and took a tentative step toward Damon. Really. It was the only way.

He exhaled a sigh of relief. "That's right, sweetheart."

As she moved, she felt the Halflings tense.

"You're not alone. I'll be your family now."

Nikki stopped while voices echoed in her head. Warnings, encouragements, all from the people who truly had loved her. "I already have a family," she uttered, then with the speed of a racehorse, she spun and bolted. Hard ground battered her feet again and again with each step, though she felt no pain. She zoomed toward Will, whose arms were outstretched and waiting for her.

Behind her, she heard Damon screaming, "No!"

He could scream until the end of the universe: her focus stayed forward, tightly fitted to Will's approving gaze. On one side of him was Raven, whose face came into focus as she neared. On the other side was Mace, whose hand was stretched toward her like—

Like an invitation.

And Nikki ran. She ran so fast the pain in her heart couldn't keep up. She ran toward her future. She ran toward her destiny. And in a few pounding heartbeats, she found herself in Will's arms.

Though Nikki didn't know what would happen to her after this, she knew with vivid certainty she'd found a safe place to land. Will and Mace and Raven and even Vine. The Halfling females who'd pledged allegiance to her, even Zero with his alternating sneers and looks of admiration. Yes, this was definitely a safe place to land.

Now, maybe it was time to learn to fly.

Acknowledgments

Thanks to Jacque Alberta, the most amazing editor on the planet, my publicity team Sara Merritt and Jonathan Michael, the illustrators for "The Making of a Halfling," Lane Shefter Bishop and Vast Entertainment, MobScene — you guys rock — my literary agent, Jennifer Schober, and the team at Spencerhill Associates for seeing the potential in my little orphan angels.

Mentors Tina Wainscott, Joyce Henderson, Melodie Adams, Diane Burch, and Julie Palella.

Critique partner Lynn Gutierrez.

Readers and encouragers Chris and Melinda; Shannon Bartram; Kerry Burch for being the first to read *Halflings* in one sitting; Nicole, Risa, and the rest of my family at SWFRW and TARA; and to all the awesome bloggers who've grabbed the Halflings vision and are running with it.

A special thanks to Youth Over the Edge. You guys know why.

Talk It Up!

Want free books?
First looks at the best new fiction?
Awesome exclusive merchandise?

We want to hear from you!

Give us your opinions on titles, covers, and stories.
Join the Z Street Team.

Visit zstreetteam.zondervan.com/joinnow
to sign up today!

Also—Friend us on Facebook!

www.facebook.com/goodteenreads

- Video Trailers
- Connect with your favorite authors
- Sneak peeks at new releases
- Giveaways
- Fun discussions
- And much more!